T0059047

PRAISE FOR ADRIANA L⎯

"Adriana Locke creates magic with unforgettable romances and captivating characters. She's a go-to author if I want to escape into a great read."

—New York Times bestselling author S.L. Scott

"Adriana Locke writes the most delicious heroes and sassy heroines who bring them to their knees. Her books are funny, raw, and heartfelt. She also has a great smile, but that's beside the point."

—USA Today bestselling author L.J. Shen

"Adriana Locke is the master of small-town contemporary romance. A one-click author for the masses, her perfect blend of wit, sexy banter, and well-developed characters is guaranteed to leave readers satisfied. A book by Adriana is sure to be the romantic escape you're looking for."

—USA Today bestselling author Bethany Lopez

"No one does blue-collar, small-town, 'everyman' (and woman!) romance like Adriana Locke. She masterfully creates truly epic love stories for characters who could be your neighbor, your best friend— you! Each one is more addictive and heart-stoppingly romantic than the last."

—USA Today bestselling author Kennedy Ryan

"Adriana's sharp prose, witty dialogue, and flawless blend of humor and steam meld together to create unputdownable, up-all-night reads!"

—Wall Street Journal bestselling author Winter Renshaw

Like You Love Me

OTHER TITLES BY ADRIANA LOCKE

The Exception Series

The Exception
The Connection: An Exception Novella
The Perception
The Exception Series Box Set

Landry Family Series

Sway
Swing
Switch
Swear
Swink
The Landry Family Series: Part One
The Landry Family Series: Part Two

The Gibson Boys Series

Crank
Craft
Cross (a novella)
Crave
Crazy

Dogwood Lane Series

Tumble
Tangle
Trouble

Stand-Alone Novels

Sacrifice
Wherever It Leads
Written in the Scars
Battle of the Sexes
Lucky Number Eleven

Like You Love Me

Honey Creek, Book One

ADRIANA LOCKE

Montlake

Published by Montlake, Seattle

www.apub.com

Amazon, the Amazon logo, and Montlake are trademarks of Amazon.com, Inc., or its affiliates.

ISBN-13: 9781612180212
ISBN-10: 1612180213

Cover design by Letitia Hasser

Printed in the United States of America

To Georgia:
I learned so much from you in so little time.
As the years go by, so much more of it makes sense.
This book is for you.

CHAPTER ONE
HOLDEN

Y ou're late."
The accusation is tossed my way before the door closes behind me.
The clock on the wall—the one depicting a dalmatian with big, googly eyes and a stethoscope around its neck—proves I technically have one minute to spare.

"Actually, I'm one minute early," I say, pointing at Dr. Dog.

My grandfather's assistant, the one who used to stash Pixy Stix for me in her desk when I'd come to visit every summer, doesn't look convinced. But if I remember one thing about Dottie Haynes, it's that she's a sucker for a smile.

I lower my chin and give her my best cheek-splitting grin. Slowly but surely, it works. The irritation on her face melts away, and a dose of humor takes its place.

"That smile isn't going to get you very far around here, handsome." Her words come out with a laugh.

"Was I being handsome?" I point at myself. "I hate when that happens. I'm sorry."

"I'm sure you are," she teases, coming around the corner of the reception desk. "I can see sorry written all over you."

"All over my handsome face, you mean?"

She swats my shoulder before pulling me into a tight hug. She smells of licorice and vanilla—warm and subtly spicy. It's oddly comforting.

"I'll tell you what," I say as we pull apart. "I promise to try to be as un-handsome as I can while I'm here."

She makes a face as if to say, "You do that." A pair of glasses slips down her nose as she moves to the other side of the counter. "Handsome or not, I'm glad you're here. I can use an extra set of hands." She holds up a finger before lifting a phone from behind her. "Honey Creek Animal Clinic. This is Dottie."

I glance around the waiting area. Pictures of smiling kids wearing shirts emblazoned with the clinic's logo are tacked proudly to the walls. Chairs that my gram reupholstered before she passed away line the room.

It's as simple a place as I remember it to be—void of sundry items for sale, and with no advertisements clinging to open spaces on the windows. As a matter of fact, the only hint that this is a business is an oversize sign behind the counter, which makes it clear that there's a surcharge for farm calls—a whopping ten dollars.

No wonder Pap is still working at his age. You'd have to at these prices.

Dottie places the phone back on the counter.

"Easy flight?" she asks as she makes a quick note on the pad of paper in front of her.

"I sat on the tarmac in Phoenix for over an hour last night. Got in pretty late, so I grabbed a room in Nashville and came over this morning."

"Which is why you are late."

I grin. "I am *not* late. And I would've been even earlier had some antiquated tractor not gone two point six miles per hour for ten miles." The back of my neck tenses again at the thought of that reflective triangle taunting me. "How is that even legal?"

2

"Blue hat or red hat?"

"Huh?"

She laughs. "Did the farmer have a blue hat or a red one?"

I scratch the top of my head. "Blue. I think. Why?"

"That was Bruce. He's the second-largest landowner in Honey County. There isn't a soul that's gonna say a word to him about farming, even if it's a minor inconvenience. His farms keep a lot of this county going."

I ponder this. "What if it was a red hat?"

"Well, that would've been Bob. Bruce's brother. The *largest* landowner in Honey County."

"I need to get some land if it gets you the run of the place," I joke.

Dottie plops her pen on top of the paper in front of her. "So where are you staying while you're here?"

I sigh. "Good question. Pap offered for me to stay at his house, but I don't think I want to sleep on a sofa. I was going to get a room in Nashville, but Bruce and Barry—"

"Bob."

"Whoever they are, they have me reconsidering." I move around the counter and fix myself a cup of coffee. When I look up, Dottie is watching me with a twinkle in her eye. "What?"

"It's just that I haven't seen you in, what? Ten years? You being an adult throws me off a little. I still remember you running around here in that Phoenix Suns hat, trying to get someone to take you fishing."

"Has it been that long?" I ask, although I know it's true.

The last summer I came to Honey Creek was the year I graduated high school. It's a year I won't—*can't*—forget. For so many reasons. It was one of the worst years of my life.

"It has," she says.

Shaking off the memories, I blow out a breath. "Never would've guessed it by looking at you. You just get younger, Dot."

Lines form around the corners of her mouth as she grins. "I was gonna tell you to stop trying to charm me, but I kind of like it."

I chuckle before taking a sip of my coffee. Dottie watches me with a distinct fondness as she passes a mug with the words LOOKIN' LIKE A QUACK, complete with a duck contorted into the letter *k*, back and forth between her hands. A long black braid that's peppered with silvery strands is slung over one of her narrow shoulders.

"So what are we doing today?" I ask.

"Well, we have a few patients on the schedule. It's the first of the month, so we'll have lots of walk-ins too." She glances down at a paper. "What do you want to go by? Dr. McKenzie? Your first name like your pap does? What are we calling you these days?"

"I'm kind of partial to 'handsome,' if you don't mind."

She snorts. "Well, I'm gonna go out on a limb and say your grandfather won't take to everyone calling you that quite as well as you have."

"Probably true. Let's just go with Holden. Dr. Holden, if you want to match Pap and his 'Dr. Fred' thing. Whatever. I'm easy."

"Great," Dottie says, seemingly satisfied at my decision. "Now that's settled, let me give you a quick rundown on some of the patients you'll see today."

I take another look around the waiting area. A double-decker, blue birdcage sits in the corner. It, too, is empty.

"I'm pretty sure I'll be fine," I say. "Animals are animals no matter where you are. That's the beauty of them."

"Maybe they are. But people are not." She smiles smugly and pulls a small white bottle out from beneath the counter. She sets it on top. The contents clatter around inside the plastic. "Grady will be in around a quarter till nine. He'll be with Fancy, his Chihuahua. There will be a story about the dog, probably that he has allergies because Bob's harvesting soybeans out by his house. Inspect the dog, ask Grady about his garden, and then give him these pills for the pooch. In that order."

My brows furrow as I take in her animated features. Surely she knows that none of that makes any damn sense.

"But what if the dog doesn't need the pills?" I ask.

"They're just vitamins."

"*Okay.*" My brain spins, trying to link all this information together in a coherent fashion. "So why do I have to ask him about his garden?"

"What? You don't like gardens?"

She presses her lips together as if she's enjoying watching me try to grasp the information she's tossed my way.

"I don't know," I admit. "Gardens are fine, I guess. I just don't understand why I have to care about Grady's garden."

"You're overcomplicating this. Just ask about the garden and then hand him these," she says, shaking the bottle. "Then go on with your day."

I set my cup down a little harder than necessary. "But *why*? What does growing carrots have to do with if his dog is sick or has allergies or . . . whatever?"

She laughs. "What will it hurt for you to ask him about his garden?"

"It won't *hurt* anything. But what it will do, *mark my words*, is make him think I care. And I do not care about his garden. Or Bruce's soybeans—"

"Bob's."

I narrow my eyes. "Whoever's whatever. The point is that I don't care. I don't even like humans, Dottie. That's why I'm a vet."

Her braid falls off her shoulder as her entire body vibrates with laughter. "You do too. If ya didn't, you wouldn't be a vet, and you sure as heck wouldn't be Fred Harrison's grandson."

My features stay smooth. The only movement is my eyelashes as I try to ward off whatever craziness Dottie is infected with in case it's contagious.

She rolls her eyes and leans against the counter. "Grady's wife died a couple of years ago. He gets lonely. Your grandpa plays along."

"So, Pap's a therapist now? This should be fun."

"What are you talking about? He gives good advice."

I look at her, stone-faced. "When I was seven or eight, I hated math. Couldn't get it. Pap called and I was whining about a homework paper, and he told me to just multiply everything by zero and it would be zero. How could the teacher argue with me getting the right answer?"

Dottie snickers.

"Needless to say, I thought I was big shit. Ended up getting my first F and after-school detention for being, for a lack of a better word, a smart-ass. Then Dad grounded me for a week because I listened to his father-in-law and not to him."

She raises her coffee mug in an attempt to hide her smile. It doesn't work. The tips of her raised lips give her away.

I sigh. "So what else do I need to know? We're clearly operating on a level I wasn't aware of."

"Let's see." She takes a quick sip of her coffee and then sets her mug down. "It's Monday, so Birdie Jones will be in to pay her tab. She runs a small farm and kennel. Your grandpa goes by there and checks on the animals every week. Birdie will come in and pay today. If you're up here when she comes in, just stick it in the fridge."

I blink. Twice. "We put money in the fridge?"

"No, but we put the pies there."

I'm not sure what my face does, but Dottie laughs again.

"We take payment in pie?" I ask.

"And cobbler. Sometimes cake, but not often, which I'm happy about. Don't tell Birdie I told you, but she needs a bit of Crisco in her butter-cream. It's just a little blah. And that's why she lost the blue ribbon three years ago at the Honey Creek Bake-Off, but I'm not telling her that."

I rub a hand down my face.

Dottie cackles.

"Taking payment in pie is . . . It's *ludicrous*," I say because I don't know what else *to* say.

"It's *delicious*. Especially the gooseberry . . ." Her voice trails off.

My brain short-circuits, and I wonder how I ended up here.

Only a month ago I was on the precipice of having everything I'd always wanted. My career was taking off. I was being considered by one of the most prestigious clinics in the world, thanks to my solid track record and work ethic. I was engaged to a girl I'd started dating in college. Everything was lining up.

And now, here I am. Unemployed. Single. And hoping that the universe smiles on me and I can salvage what's left of my life. Somehow.

I remind myself that not all is lost. I still have a shot at Montgomery Farms. I think.

I follow Dottie's gaze to the doorway.

"Well, Sophie Bates," she says. "What brings you by this morning?"

The fog in my head clears as I watch the woman walking toward me.

"Well, if it isn't Holden McKenzie," she says, twisting her gingerbread-colored hair into a messy knot on top of her head.

I lean against the counter and take her in. The apples of her cheeks host a constellation of freckles, and her chin is punctuated by a tiny mole a little to the left of center. She's exactly like I remember her . . . only all grown up.

She sets her sights on me. The corners of her lips curl toward her golden-brown eyes. There, embedded in the veneer of innocence, is the unmistakable glimmer of mischief that has always been her trademark.

"I heard there was trouble in town," she says with a wink. "Had to come and see it with my own eyes."

"What? Are all the mirrors in your house broken?"

She bites the inside of her cheek to keep from smiling. "Fair enough. How have ya been, anyway? It's like you forgot we all existed over here."

"Eh. Been better. Been worse. You?"

"Same."

We exchange a grin like you only can with someone you've connected to on an organic level before the world makes you jaded and changes you. I haven't felt this in a long time.

Seeing her brings back memories of long, carefree days in the sun. Hours lying along the banks of Pine Creek and listening to music. I'm struck with things I thought I'd forgotten, about nights watching movies cast onto the side of the library and wondering what she would do if I ever kissed her.

I never found out.

And now I kind of regret that.

"Did you ever get my gold chain out of Pine Creek?" I ask.

Her brows shoot to the ceiling, too, as she remembers one of the last afternoons we spent together and how I ended up losing more than my chain in the waters of the creek.

At the same time, we both start to laugh.

"You jumped in there willingly," she says.

"No. You dared me."

"That hardly makes anything my fault." She shakes a finger my way as she comes to a stop on the other side of the counter. Her laugh fades, but she's left with an easy smile. "But for your information, we did find it a few years later, buried in a sandbar. You didn't come back, so we pawned it."

"Well, that was nice of you."

"Bought us a couple of bottles of strawberry wine." She looks up at Dottie and sobers her face. "That we were too young to have. I know."

Dottie holds her hands up, shaking her head.

Sophie laughs and leans against the counter. She props her chin on her hand. Her eyes shine.

Sophie was my best friend every summer. As we grew up, so did the chemistry between us. Summer was never quite long enough for the spark to ignite, but I've always wondered what things would've looked like if I didn't live fifteen hundred miles away. I've thought about her through the years. Anytime Pap mentioned her, I'd dig a little to see what the girl who'd held my fascination for a large chunk of my life was up to.

"What are you doing in here today, anyway? Just coming by because you missed me so much?" I tease.

I cock a brow and steel myself against the coy, and adorable, look on her face and thank God I'm now immune to this woman's magical powers. *I think.*

"Actually, I need an antibiotic, *Dr. McKenzie.*" She flutters her long dark eyelashes my way.

"For . . ."

"Strep."

"Strep? Okay. Where is your pet?" I ask.

"Babar is at home. Why?"

Dottie coughs. I glance at her to see her lifting the neckline of her shirt to cover her mouth.

"Well," I say, flipping my attention back to Sophie, "I generally need to see the patient before I can prescribe a medicine."

"Not around here. Dr. Fred just gives me antibiotics and sends me on my way. I mean, there's really no reason to see the same dog repeatedly for the same thing, is there?"

I struggle not to smile.

She narrows her eyes. "You mean that you won't just write me a prescription?"

A laugh topples from my mouth before I can stop it. It triggers a sparkle in her eyes, a fire that switches my laugh to an extended chuckle. She can't be serious.

"You know I'm an animal doctor and not a human doctor, right?" I ask.

"Yes. What's your point?"

"That . . . Are you kidding me?"

Her lips twist into a coy smile. "Are you considering it? Think about the next time I get sick. You could be my savior. You'd be a hero."

"No," I say adamantly. "I don't care how much you beg. I will not break the law for you."

"Easy, Doc. I was joking. But I saw that flicker in your eyes. You were thinking about it," she teases.

"I was not. Not even for you and that pretty little smile you have going on."

She leans back and nods appreciatively. "Ah. Well, thanks. I'll leave on that high note."

"You do that," I say with a laugh.

"Tell Dr. Fred this guy needs a lot of training, Dottie." She jabs her thumb over her shoulder as she heads for the door. "Like *a lot* of training."

"Oh, don't I know it." Dottie tosses me a wink. "See ya later, Sophie."

Sophie presses her back against the door. She pauses and looks at me. The warmth in her eyes, the familiarity, washes over me like a drink of bourbon. It's comfortable and unpretentious and a feeling I totally forgot existed.

"I'm leaving now. Nice to see you, Holden. Hope I don't need those antibiotics anytime soon."

I grin. "I'll say nice words at your funeral and forgo all that pawning-my-possessions stuff."

She fires a playful glare my way before giving Dottie a little wave. With a pop of her hip, the door flies open, and she's gone as quickly as she appeared.

I look over my shoulder to see Dottie smiling at me.

"What?" I ask.

"Nothin'." She tries to smooth her features to hide her grin. "Now, do you have any questions before we open for the day?"

"Nope. I just hope it ends a lot calmer than it's started. I feel like I've been exposed to more bullshit today than I have in my entire life combined."

She laughs. "Oh, handsome. You haven't seen anything yet."

That's what I'm afraid of.

CHAPTER TWO

SOPHIE

What's that smell?" I ask.

I kick the door closed and set the paper bags I'm carrying down on the counter. The kitchen at the Honey House is vacant but looks no worse for wear. There's no smoke, no charred remains of a lunch gone bad despite the odor permeating the air.

The bed-and-breakfast I inherited from my grandmother is quirky. Sometimes I swear I smell Gramma Lois's roast beef in the dead of night, and the hot water in the powder room off the entryway is as emotional as a preteen. But greater than the built-in quirks of the inn are the idiosyncrasies of Olivia Bates, my sister. And she's what I'm putting my money on this time.

"Liv? What's going on?" I look around as I open the window above the sink for some fresh air. "Hello?"

I hear her before I see her. A string of what would be profanities except for her self-censorship precedes her arrival.

"There you are," I say as she rounds the corner. A sputter topples from my lips as I take her in. "What in the world happened to you?"

A blue bandanna is wrapped around her thick auburn hair. Wild splatters of black gunk paint her face, and a large piece of something—possibly cardboard—is stuck to the side of her head just above her ear.

"I couldn't sleep last night," she says, as if that explains it all.

"And . . ."

"And I found myself watching a video about how to clean out a chimney, because that's really been bothering me, you know. Fall is almost here, and the fireplace in the dining area is *such* an attraction. So I tried to clean it to save some money, but . . . well, it wasn't as easy as the cute guy online with the great arms and plaid shirt made it look."

"It never is," I say. "Didn't you learn your lesson after you tried to fix the dishwasher and flooded the kitchen?"

"You want me to quit trying after one failure?"

I raise a brow.

"Okay, more than one," she says, blowing out a breath. A chunk of bangs flutters in the air and then sticks to the black residue at her temple. "I'm not a quitter, Soph. Besides, why should we pad the pockets of men when we are capable of some of this stuff ourselves?"

Her golden eyes shine.

This is the reason that no matter how big of a mess she makes, I can never be mad. Her heart is always in the right place. It's just that sometimes her competence is not.

I pluck a piece of fuzz off her cheek instead of hugging her, which is what I want to do. Despite working her own nine-to-five at Haute Insurance, she helps me almost every day out of the goodness of her heart, because God knows I can't pay her. She always says I can make it up to her when the Honey House is featured on a southern destination show and becomes the hottest ticket in Tennessee. Of course, she also says that if that ever happens, she'll deny she ever called it an insolvent mess and claim she always had faith in the place. But whatever.

Liv adjusts her bandanna. "We might have to call Jobe in for a consult."

"I am *not* calling our brother."

"This was a bigger job than I thought it was going to be," she says, cringing. "A little on-site guidance may not be a bad thing."

"It would be such a cop-out to call a man now after that 'I'm not a quitter' speech."

"I'm not quitting. I didn't say that. I don't quit."

"Sounds an awful lot like quitting to me," I tease.

"Sophie . . ."

The grandfather clock in the foyer chimes. It reminds me that I need to get Mr. and Mrs. Inman, my only guests this week, something whipped up for dinner. My insides twist as I imagine Liv's rant that I shouldn't be making them dinner when it's not included in the rate. She's probably right. I'm just a sucker.

I'm definitely a sucker for Holden McKenzie's smile.

I grin at the thought.

"What?" Liv asks.

"Nothing."

Needing some space and a change of scenery before my older sister starts poking around, I make my way into the hallway that runs down the center of the home. The hardwood floors let me know that she follows me down the corridor, past the staircase, and into the room beside the powder room.

My calendar is open on my desk. Doodles of hearts and flowers cover the white area around the edges. Giant *X*s mark through every day that has already passed. What's *not* there is the countdown running in my head—the countdown to the day next month when I have to come up with almost $5,000 or lose everything that's precious to me.

"I was brainstorming today," Liv says. "And don't even look at me like that. This idea is pure gold."

I sit in my chair. Peering up at her, I try not to roll my eyes. "Your last idea included square dancing."

"Which I still stand behind. It's a lost art that I think, no, *I believe*, people would love to revisit. But we'll come back to that. We need to focus on the fall tourist season right now. We need those northerners staying *here* when they come down to fish or pick persimmons or whatever it is they do."

"We absolutely do need them staying here." I tap a pen against the desk. "I know what will help. I've been thinking about it. We need a gazebo in the back and to repaint the upstairs bedrooms too. I have plans, Liv. Big ones. And I'm getting my feet under me again. I just . . ."

I tap the pen harder and ignore my sister's cocked brow.

Liv knows the Honey House is in financial crisis—mostly because she was here when my ex-husband, Chad, cleaned out more than his half of our savings as he left. She's also aware of the fact that the Honey House needs sprucing up. It needed it before the Sweet Tea, Rockery's newest establishment, opened three towns over. As soon as that fancy-schmancy bed-and-breakfast set up shop, it dipped into my bottom line. But all that beautifying will have to wait until I can save the Honey House from the tax auction next month.

Ugh.

"I just need a fairy godmother," I lament.

"Ew. No. Those are creepy. What you need is a knight in shining armor with five thousand dollars handy."

I laugh. "That's the only way I'd get married again."

Liv takes an embroidered pillow off the chair across from me. After setting it aside, she plops down and grins. "You need to ease up on your anti-maleness."

"I'm not anti-male. I'm just anti-dating." I lean back in my chair and sigh. "I have no need for sweaty palms and compulsory smiles and fake interest in why one of you wore a particular gray sweater. Dating is forced experiences ruined by pressure, expectations, and having to wear real pants in public. Not my jam."

"Well, it's not mine, either, when you put it like that."

"See?"

She rolls her eyes. "So what did you do today?"

Just like that, a surge of energy roars through my veins. It's a crazy mix of currents—a dose of excitement from seeing Holden again, a sprinkle of annoyance at his confidence, and, if I'm being honest, a smidgen of dizziness from his smile.

The little boy I used to play with every summer is now most definitely all grown up.

I wipe my brow with the back of my hand.

"Ooh," Liv singsongs. "What's that look all about?"

"What's what look all about?"

"That smile."

I cross my arms over my chest. "I ran by Dr. Fred's, actually."

Liv leans back, gripping the arms of her chair as she anticipates my next words.

The problem is, I don't know what to say. I haven't had a lot of time to mull it over and boil down my thoughts about Holden. Sure, his angled jaw and brilliant green eyes that remind me of clover in springtime have muscled their way into my brain throughout the afternoon. And maybe the way his shirt clings to his biceps and shoulders did too. *Maybe.*

But if I tell my sister all that, she'll flip out. It'll be taken the wrong way. She'll be trying to marry us off like she did when we were teenagers. There's no doubt she'll be planning our wedding at the nonexistent gazebo in the backyard instead of figuring out how to help me build the wedding prop in the first place.

"I'm going to need you to speak," she prompts, waving a hand through the air. "I need more, Sophie—especially with you sitting there like *that.*"

"There's nothing to tell. Fred's . . . new sidekick is a stickler for rules and"—*hot*—"a little difficult."

"And . . ."

I roll my eyes in case she can somehow see my stomach fluttering. My brain shouts at my mouth to stop there. To cease dialogue. But my lips part, and before I know it, I'm going *there.*

"And he has the straightest, whitest teeth and a smile that probably distracts people, because he kept flashing it my way. But I refused to break. I don't break for a great smile."

Liv moves, her arm hitting a stack of books on the corner of my desk. They hit the chair before dropping to the floor with a boom. She scoots to pick them up.

"Oh my gosh, Sophie. Do I know him?" she asks with a giddiness that inches up the same feeling in me.

"You did. Um, it's Holden. Do you remember him?"

Her head whips to me. "Of course I do."

Liv places the books back on the desk's corner. They aren't squared, and the messiness of it makes me crazy, but I can't worry about that when my brain is misfiring at thoughts of the vet.

Liv smiles as she gets to her feet. "So he's cute?"

"Yes, he's cute," I admit. There's no sense in lying. As soon as she runs into him in town, she'll see for herself and then wonder why I downplayed it. "He's cute . . . but not in an everyday kind of way. He's gone from 'boy next door' to 'man of your dreams.' Does that make sense?"

"So he's hot? That's what you mean?"

I flush. "Well, yeah. I mean, he has the most symmetrical features and a delicious jawline. And his eyelashes are extraordinary. That overpriced tube of crap I put on mine every night to make them grow wouldn't give me ones equal his, even if I used it, and it actually worked, for ten years."

My sister watches me, her eyes dancing with humor. "I can totally envision this. So . . . dark-brown hair?"

"Yes."

"And . . . green eyes? And great shoulders. Like they have that slope from his neck down in a thick, muscled band." She mimics the slope in the air with her hands.

"Wow. You're good at this. Or maybe I'm really good at setting the stage." I think about it. "You know what—it's actually probably me.

All these years of writing marketing material for the Honey House are paying off."

Liv grins. *Hard.* The kind of smile so deep, so mysterious, that my stomach flip-flops.

"What?" I ask.

"It could be all that marketing," she says. "Or it could be that Holden McKenzie is standing right behind you."

"What?"

I shoot to my feet and spin on my heel. The sexy, brown-haired, green-eyed, great-shouldered vet is leaning against the wall.

Crap.

His cheeks are split into a wide, shit-eating smile that inflames me as quickly as it melts me.

Kill. Me. Now.

His smile is deep and wide. "Well, that was the nicest welcome I've ever had."

I want to spit some witty comeback his way. I would, too, if I could unstick the words from my throat.

"Well, here's a nice farewell—goodbye," I say, walking around him in the widest berth I can manage. I head toward the kitchen and mentally kick myself. Repeatedly. Hard.

My face is on fire as my heart pushes blood through my veins at double speed.

I enter the kitchen and head directly to the sink. Gripping the edge, I let the cool air coming in through the open window wash over me.

I'm going to kill Liv for not warning me. *Damn her.*

Holden's voice trails through the house. I'm slightly excited that he's here, though I don't want to be. Those feelings cost me a dose of mortification already.

Come to think of it . . . *damn him too.*

CHAPTER THREE

HOLDEN

S he's still a ball of fire, isn't she?" I don't realize I've asked this out
loud until a voice behind me answers.

"Most of the time."

As a clamor of pots and pans echoes down the hallway, I refocus my
attention on Olivia. She's watching me with amusement . . . and with
a heavy dose of soot covering her face.

"I'm Liv," she says. "In case you don't remember me. But I'm sure
you do, because I'm pretty unforgettable, right?"

"Absolutely." I grin. "You're the wiser Bates sister. And funnier."

Her lips part. "It's nice to see you again. It's been a long time."

"Yes, it has. It's good to see you, too, Liv."

She nods in satisfaction. "So what are you doing here?"

"I was hoping to get a room."

"Well, you'll have to ask Sophie," she says with a smug smile.

"Why? Aren't you running this place?"

"Nope. Sophie is."

I think back to what Dottie said as I left the clinic a little while ago.
Her words are out of my grasp, but I swear she alluded to the fact that
Liv was in charge here.

My stomach rumbles as if to remind me to get on with it.

"Do you know where she went, so I can ask her about staying here?" I ask. "If I have to drive back to Nashville tonight, I want to get started."

Liv winks. "Answer this first: Are you married or otherwise significantly involved with someone on a level of not just friendship?"

"No . . . ," I say carefully, not sure if that's the right or wrong answer but fairly certain there *is* a right or wrong answer.

"Great!" She takes a string of tissues out of a box on Sophie's desk and wipes her face. The soot streaks and smears even more. "Go down the hallway and take the last door on your left to the kitchen. Tell my sister that the soot was getting in my eyes and I had to go home and shower and I sent you back there before I went blind." She pats me on the shoulder with her clean hand as she walks by. "Good luck, Holden."

"Am I actually going to need luck for this?"

"Maybe." She laughs as she slips out the door.

I take a deep breath and blow it out slowly. My stomach rumbles again, reminding me that I haven't eaten since a hurried breakfast at the hotel. Before I can get lost in the hunger, a clatter ricochets down the hallway, and Sophie's voice is blended in with the pings and clanks. I think I hear my name garbled in there, and it makes me grin.

A large chandelier hangs overhead as I step into the foyer. I can imagine the romantic ambiance it creates at night as it glows above the staircase. And as I venture down the hallway, I take in the green-and-white wallpaper adorning the top halves of the walls. White paneling lines the bottoms.

By the time I get to the kitchen doorway, the racket has settled. A quiet comfort fills the bed-and-breakfast. With an anxious flutter in my stomach, I pause.

The room is bathed in sunlight and warmth from the early-evening sun. Wooden beams line the ceiling, and a rack hangs above the island with copper pots and pans dangling overhead. Sophie is standing at the island, a gold apron tied around her waist. Her hair is piled on top of her head as she slices vegetables and pretends not to notice me.

"Hey," I say.

She doesn't startle. "What?"

"Are you mad at me?" I tease.

"Did you bring me an antibiotic?"

"Nope. I did not break the law for you."

She fights a smile. "Then yes, I'm mad at you."

"Well, damn."

She refuses to look up from her work. The knife moves smoothly through the vegetables, although it hits the cutting board with a harder thud than necessary. Still, she stays absorbed with the carrots and onion and pointedly ignores my presence.

"I promise that I won't bat my extraordinary lashes if you look at me," I joke.

Her hand wobbles on the knife. "Have I asked you to leave already? Because if I haven't, I am now."

"You haven't seen me for ten years, and you're kicking me out that fast?"

The knife slams through a pepper. "Yes."

I mosey across the kitchen. She still doesn't focus any direct attention my way. Swiping a piece of carrot, I pop it in my mouth.

That does it. Her eyes flip to mine. The browns melt with the golds, creating a caramellike hue that seems to be lit up from the inside.

"I need a place to stay," I say matter-of-factly.

"I need my dignity back."

"What? Are you talking about that 'He's so amazing' thing back there? Because that was cute."

She groans. "I'm not six. I don't want to be cute."

"Want me to say it was hot? I was trying not to make it awkward."

She looks at me long enough to narrow her eyes. "I want to pretend like it didn't happen."

"Forgot about it already."

She gathers the vegetables into a line down the center of the board. I swipe a couple more carrots. My stomach rumbles again, and I wonder what she'd do if I grabbed the board and ate everything she just prepared.

"So? Room?" I ask.

"I don't know."

"What's there to not know? You're running a business to presumably make money, and I'm offering legal tender for a service you provide."

"Yeah, but the beauty of being a business owner is that I get to make the decisions. There's a sign over the door that says that I reserve the right to refuse service."

I take a slice of pepper as she swipes at my hand. "There is no such sign."

"Well, there should be." She takes the cutting board and sets it by the stove. "What are you doing in town, anyway? Most people can't just up and leave their jobs to come help their grandparents."

My stomach rumbles again, but this time it's not from hunger.

I slide a barstool out from beneath the island and sit across from her. She fires me a disapproving look before turning back toward the stove. A pan of meat simmers away. It smells delicious, and I'm tempted to go poke around and see what I can find to eat, but I don't.

"Well," I say carefully. "Most people can't get dramatically fired from their jobs like me."

She looks at me over her shoulder. "Wanna talk about it?"

"No," I say with a chuckle. "But because I don't want you to think I somehow deserved it, I'll add that the reason behind my termination was because my boss's wife worked in the office and sent an email to her friend about how badly she wanted to bang me. Her husband found it, and I got whacked."

"That's not legal."

"No, it's not," I agree. "But what am I going to do? Fight for a job that just got super weird?"

As if she feels pity for me, Sophie slides a few pieces of sliced pepper my way.

"Besides," I say, popping the pepper into my mouth with a nod of thanks, "everything happens for a reason."

"Do you really believe that?"

"I do. I think."

"What will you do now?"

That's the million-dollar question.

I sit back in my chair and blow out a breath. "I'm not sure. I was in the running to get my dream job before Bang Gate."

She laughs, her cheeks turning a pretty shade of pink. "That sounds like a porno."

"What a dirty mind you have."

She rolls her eyes and turns back to the stove, her body angled so she can keep an eye on me. The aroma from the pan billows through the room as she stirs whatever it is slowly.

"So are you out of contention now?" she asks.

"I'm not sure. I'm worried about it, to be honest." I lean forward and rest my elbows against the counter. "They love stability and look for people that don't hop around from job to job. Which makes sense. And now I'm basically a vagrant with a broken engagement."

Her brows lift. "Broken engagement? Do tell."

She takes a package out of the fridge and plops it into a bowl. I watch her work while I try to figure out what, and how much, to say. It doesn't feel like it matters, and I'd rather talk about her.

"There's not much to tell," I say as she puts the bowl in the microwave. "Jessica and I parted ways after we realized that we'd only been together because it was easier than separating. No drama. No crazy story."

She mulls this around, tucking a stray lock of hair behind her ear while she thinks.

I can't help but appreciate her figure from this angle. Her curves are soft and round, narrowing at the tie from her apron at her waist. Her neck is exposed, thanks to her curls being swept up on top of her head, and I can see the little chocolate milk–like birthmark just below her hairline.

"Can you fix it?" she asks. "The stability problem?"

"Not unless you want to marry me."

She laughs. "Um, the last time I married you, we were seven, and you took the Ring Pop off my left hand and ate it right after the ceremony."

My chest vibrates with my laugh. "I'd forgotten about that."

"Not me. Come to think of it, it's probably part of the reason I have marriage issues."

The microwave buzzes. She removes the bowl and slides it in front of me. An incredible scent wafts up from the ceramic vessel. I peer inside to see miniature sausages with bacon wrapped around them. A shimmer coats the top.

"You're not a healthy eater, are you?" she asks, handing me a fork.

"Not today." I stab one and put it in my mouth. The sweetness of sugar mixes with the smokiness of the bacon and the meatiness of the sausage, blending together on my tongue. "That's amazing."

"I know." She shrugs. "I couldn't watch you sit there and drool while I cooked. I have a thing about people being hungry."

"How about for people needing a room?"

"For how long?"

"I don't know. A few weeks? I have my résumé out in a couple of places. As soon as I hear something, I'm gone." I look up at her with puppy-dog eyes. "Please rent me a room. I'll beg."

A sigh that's laced with both amusement and reservation topples from her lips. "You don't even know how much I charge."

"By the time I factor in gas and my time driving back and forth to Nashville, you could probably double your price and it would still be worth it."

She grins mischievously. "It's eighty-eight a night plus a dose of antibiotics."

"Sophie . . ."

She laughs as she flips off the stove. "*Fine.* I'm teasing. You can have the blue room. Top of the staircase, last door on your left. But keep it down after nine, because the couple in the yellow room go to bed right after the early news."

Her cheeks are a light shade of pink, and I'm not sure if it's from my smile or the heat of the stove. Either way, I pause to appreciate it.

She bites her lip. "The pipes in the bathroom squeak a little. It's on the list of things to replace as soon as I can."

"I can deal with noisy pipes."

"Good." She turns back to the stove. "Dinner isn't included with your room. Just breakfast. It's a bed-and-breakfast. Get it?"

"Oh, so that's what that means," I say, letting my mouth hang open in faux surprise. "I never knew that."

She shakes her head. "I'll whip something up if you want me to, since I'm cooking anyway."

Her back moves in such a way that I'm pretty certain she's laughing. It occurs to me that I haven't had such easy banter with a woman in a very long time. I also can't remember ever feeling this relaxed around a woman. My last interaction with my former fiancée included a migraine and the indifferent return of an engagement ring. Maybe this one is so easy because she keeps me in check, or maybe it's our shared history. Whatever it is, I'm grateful for it right now.

"I'm going to head to the car and grab my bag," I tell her.

"Suit yourself."

I turn away but stop when she calls out to me.

"Holden?"

"Yeah?"

She smiles sheepishly. "The hot water in the shower upstairs is on the right. Not the left. Liv and I installed a new faucet last summer and . . . you know. That stuff gets confusing."

"No worries."

She clears her throat. "I have to go by my brother's and drop off a few things. Then I'm heading to Tank's for a fish sandwich. It's the best part of the week."

"Okay."

"Well, um, if you want to meet me there in a half an hour or something—no pressure. I can bring you something back. Or . . . not. Either way is fine."

My lips twist at her stumbling over her words. "I'd love to meet you."

"Cool. See you there, then." She grins to herself and turns away.

There are dozens of questions on the tip of my tongue—about her and the bed-and-breakfast and Liv and the soot that I can still faintly smell. But instead of asking them, I head outside and get in my rental car.

I sit in the driver's seat and take in the Honey House. It needs a good coat of paint, and one of the shutters is askew. But it's still quaint and looks more or less just like it did when we used to ride our bikes by here as kids.

We had so much fun back then. Hell, I still like being around her now. She's unpretentious and easygoing. Spontaneous, yet grounded. She's a crazy mix of gorgeous and adorable, and to see her as an adult makes me so curious how our friendship would've played out in different circumstances.

"Not unless you want to marry me." My words ring through my mind as Sophie enters the office in front of me. As I watch her look at something on her desk, I'm bothered by the fact that marrying her doesn't seem all that crazy. The words slipped out like an invitation that

I didn't have to think twice about. And I don't think I would've been shocked, or all that weirded out, had she just said, "Yeah, let's do that."

It took me a year to put the words "marry me" into a sentence around Jessica for fear she'd think I was actually asking her. And when I finally did, I vomited right before and carried a nugget of uncertainty in my gut every day after.

I rub a hand down my face. "You're losing your mind, McKenzie," I mutter.

The light goes off in the office. I grab my bag from the back seat and blow out a breath.

"Might as well lose your mind, too, considering you've probably lost everything else," I add as I climb out of the car.

CHAPTER FOUR

SOPHIE

Every face in the restaurant turns to look as Holden and I walk into Tank's. All seven people in various stages of eating and drinking pause to take us in. Debbie, the woman who's waited tables here for the last ten years, lifts her brows as she checks out Holden and his gray sweatpants.

I almost asked him to change out of them. They're utterly and deliciously distracting.

"Hey, everyone," I say loudly. "You all remember Dr. Fred's grandson. This is Holden McKenzie."

And, just like that, they all switch their attention solely to Holden. His hand flies up in a little wave.

"Hi," he says.

"He's helping out Fred for a little bit," I say.

"Well, that's a damn good thing," Bob says from a table in the corner. His red hat hangs on the back of his chair.

I glance at Holden. He's poised to say something else but stops himself. I stifle a laugh at his obvious discomfort at being the center of attention.

Serves him right for making me feel like a dork earlier today.

Various forms of hellos and head nods are sent our way. Birdie Jones smiles at Holden, pressing her red lips together in a shameless pout.

"Well, it is *so* nice to meet you, Holden." Her eyelashes flutter. "I'm Birdie Jones."

"It's nice to finally meet you," he says. "I've heard so much about your pies."

"Oh, well . . ." She waves a hand through the air. "You're just being sweet. They aren't *that* good. Well, maybe my apple pie. And the strawberry rhubarb. And the gooseberry, if I do say so myself."

She sits back in her seat and eyes him like a slab of meat.

A tide of jealousy washes over me as Birdie flirts with Holden right in front of me. Not that I have any right to care who flirts with him . . . or who he flirts back with. Still, the feeling creeps up my spine like a snake.

Before I know what I'm doing, my elbow digs into Holden's side.

"It was nice seeing you, Birdie." I turn toward Holden and drop my voice. "Let's find a seat. *Now.*"

"Gee, we better hurry. Seats around here are going like hotcakes."

I roll my eyes. "Keep it up and I'll sit you by her. She likes younger men."

"I hadn't noticed." His eyes dart over my shoulder. "I've never said this before, but I don't think I can handle her."

"Trust me. You can't."

"I don't like how quickly you answered that," he says, following close behind me as I lead him across the restaurant.

We stop at a table under a window. There are four unmatched wooden chairs—two on each side. I take the one on the far side with a red seat cushion. The fact that Holden's back will be to Birdie is a coincidence.

"I'll have you know," Holden says as he sits, "that I feel slightly compelled to prove to you I can handle her. I don't want to do it, but it feels a bit like a challenge."

"Oh, Doc. Don't even try. She has years on ya, bud. Her level of man-eating exceeds anything you could've experienced in your . . . thirty years of life."

He drops his jaw. "I'm not thirty. Yet."

"You could be fifty and still not be ready for Birdie Jones."

Holden takes a laminated menu from between the napkin dispenser and saltshaker. I'm about to tell him to order the fish—that's why we're here—when my phone dings in my pocket.

I dig it out and see Jobe's name on the screen.

Jobe: You didn't tell me you were going to dinner with the vet.

I roll my eyes as my fingers fly across my screen.

Me: First of all, how do you know that?

Jobe: Debbie. Also, I know everything.

Me: Sure. Just like the name of the girl you slept with last night that you were just telling me about a half an hour ago and couldn't remember her name.

Jobe: I remember important things.

Me: You're a jerk.

Jobe: Probably true. Tell Lover Boy that he and I and Aaron will have to have a beer one night.

I laugh out loud. Shifting in my seat, I type out a response in a matter of seconds.

Me: I'll be sure not to do that.

Jobe: Why not?

Me: Because you and Aaron are troublemakers.

Jobe: Whatever. If you're gonna be all fucked up over this guy, I want to meet him again.

Me: You're way overthinking this. WAY OVERTHINKING THIS.

Jobe: Maybe you're underthinking this. I saw how you're smiling tonight.

Suddenly, the weight of Holden's gaze is heavy on my face. I look up to see him watching me with a quirked brow.

"Sorry," I say, giving my phone a final glance before shoving it into my purse. "My brother is an asshole."

"What's Jobe up to these days, anyway?"

"Driving me crazy."

Holden laughs. Before he can say another word, Debbie appears at our table. She's standing a couple of steps closer to Holden than me and wears a smug grin.

"What can I get you guys?" she asks.

"Fish dinner," I say, giving her a pointed look. "And sweet tea with no lemon, please."

She makes a face to let me know she read my look loud and clear.

"What about you?" she asks Holden.

"Same as Sophie."

Debbie scribbles the orders down. "Anything else?"

"I think we're good," I say.

Still, Debbie lingers. She rests a hand on the edge of the table and looks at me. "I'm just going to say it: he's a much better catch than Chad. You did good, girl."

"Oh no," I say, waving my hands in front of me. "It's not like that. *At all.*"

"*Oh.* Okay." Debbie's voice raises a few octaves, but it's clear she thinks I'm full of crap. Her knuckles rap against the tabletop. "I'll be back with your drinks in a second."

Holden watches her leave. When she's out of earshot, he leans toward me. "So?"

"So, what?"

"So who is Chad?"

I slide back in my seat. The vinyl squeaks as I move.

"If you don't want to tell me, that's cool," he teases. "I can totally find out at work tomorrow. Or I could just head over to the Lemon Aid and put out some feelers."

I cross my arms over my chest. "The Lemon Aid is closed, smarty-pants."

"Um, I was just in there today. They're still in business. Good try, though."

"I mean for the day. It closes at six."

"It closes at six? What kind of . . . Never mind." He shakes his head. "Back to Chad."

I sigh. "You're so nosy."

"'Nosy' has such negative connotations."

"I know. That's how I meant it."

Holden narrows his eyes playfully, making me laugh.

I search his face as I war with my emotions.

Chad is not a topic I like to talk about. It's a subject that's filled with a lot of frustration and grief and anger and sadness. But as I consider trying to brush the topic away, it feels like I'm being pulled back by the kindness in Holden's eyes.

"Chad was my husband," I say finally.

Holden bristles. His pupils go wide as he leans away from me. A softness washes over his face. "I'm sorry," he says quietly.

"Your condolences aren't necessary." I frown as I watch his reaction. "Divorce happens all the time."

He slumps against the table. "Why didn't you just say that?"

"I did."

"No, you said you were married to him. I thought he was dead and was feeling really guilty for teasing you about it."

I laugh. "He would be, but Jobe hasn't found him yet."

Holden relaxes against the back of his chair. There's relief in his face, and I appreciate it.

"This Chad guy sounds like a real champ," he says.

"I'm the moron that married him."

I pick at the edge of the table to keep from meeting his eyes.

Chad was not my best work. Not my best choice, or the greatest guy I've ever dated, nor am I proud that I went through with the whole thing. But I did it and I can't change it. I need to figure out how to accept all that.

"I'm sure you had great intentions," Holden says.

"I did. Want to know how deep *his* intentions ran?" I strum my fingers against the tabletop as I look up at him. "He left me by sticking a note to the kitchen table with a dollop of strawberry jelly."

I blow out a breath and regret word-vomiting all that. It was too deep. Too raw and real. Opening up to Holden is too easy, and I probably just ruined the mood.

He watches me for a few seconds before grinning. "He didn't even use grape? Rude."

I smile, relieved that he didn't dig deeper. "Right? He didn't even use grape on his sandwiches."

"Big red flag right there," he says, pointing a finger my way.

"You know, Gramma always said not to marry a man that cuts the crusts off his peanut butter and jelly sandwiches."

"And why is that?"

"Because that's an indication that someone doesn't like boundaries. Guess I should've listened to her. He even cut the crusts off his grilled cheese."

He gasps, his jaw falling to the table in mock horror. "That's serial-killer shit right there."

"Hey, I don't know what he's been doing the last couple of years of his life." I take a napkin from the dispenser. "You might be right."

"So why *did* you marry him? You didn't get serial-killer vibes from the start?"

It's a question I've asked myself a million times, because down deep, I knew it wasn't right for me. I just ignored my gut and did it anyway.

I look at Holden and frown. "I tried to fill an overwhelming loneliness after Gramma died with something that I convinced myself was love. It wasn't and I knew better. And that almost cost me everything." The heaviness of the conversation forces my eyes to the table. "Chad ruined me financially. I almost lost the Honey House because of him. What a trade that would've been—the place I love most for the guy that loved me the least."

"I just want to say that I'm really sorry about your gramma. She was always so sweet."

My heart fills with a fondness for both Holden and his kind words about my grandmother. He didn't know her very well—we'd only stop in on our bike rides for lemonade here and there—but to know that he remembers her makes my heart swell.

Holden stretches his legs out in front of him. The side of his calf bumps mine, and we both pull away quickly. As our eyes meet, Debbie appears out of thin air.

She sets a drink down in front of each of us. "Need anything else?"

"We're good," Holden says. "Thank you."

"Great. I'll be back with your food shortly." She disappears into the kitchen again.

I watch Holden unwrap his straw. He's so different from Chad. He asks questions about my life instead of just talking about himself. And even more shocking, he seems like he really wants the answers. When he laughs, it's *with* me and not *at* me. But I don't know why I'm surprised. It's exactly how I remember him to be.

"What about you?" I ask, unwrapping my straw too.

"What about me?"

"What did you mean earlier when you said it was just easier to stay with your fiancée than to split up?"

He snatches the shaker up in his hand. "I'm not husband material."

"Um, gonna need more than that."

A sigh escapes his lips as he seems to come to terms with the fact that he'll have to answer me for real. "I met Jessica in college. She's a great person, and she'll make someone a hell of a wife."

"Why not you?" I ask carefully.

Debbie places a plate in front of each of us. She doesn't speak this time. Holden's nod is enough to let her know that we don't need anything else.

I pop a fry in my mouth and wait for Holden to answer. He looks at me and realizes I'm expecting a response. He takes a deep breath.

"Jessica wanted this oversize, fluffy, off-white-colored couch," he says, fumbling for words. "I wanted a black leather sofa with stainless legs. By the time we were ready to leave the store, we walked out of there with a brown corduroy piece that was so stiff that you couldn't even really sit on it."

I sit quietly and slice my fish. I have no idea what a couch has to do with why he's not husband material, as he called it. But the look on his face makes me wonder if he really knows either.

"I hated that thing," he says. "And I hated the lamp in the entryway with its little beads wrapped around the shade, because I wanted to go bead-less like any man I know would and she wanted the thing to be dripping with them. So we compromised. And that was the day I realized that we were compromising our lives so much that I didn't even recognize mine. Or hers. Instead of taking my golden retriever life and mixing it with her poodle life and getting a goldendoodle, we'd turned into a mutt."

He shrugs as if to say, "There you go. It's that easy."

Except I know it's not that easy. It never is.

"Yeah, I call bullshit," I say, pointing a fry his way. A dollop of ketchup falls off the end and splatters on the table. "Total bullshit, actually."

He takes a napkin and wipes up the ketchup. There's something about the situation that amuses me to no end.

"Thanks for your input." He wads the ketchup-smeared napkin into a ball and tosses it to the side. "You might be right, though."

"About what part?"

He sits back in his chair and folds his arms over his chest. "That whole thing I just spit at you about the couches might be bullshit."

I drop the fry in my hand and sit back too. My arms cross over my chest, mirroring his posture. "Then what's the truth?"

"I don't know. I just . . . I probably always knew that Jessica and I weren't right. But she wanted to get married, and the look in her eye on every holiday wore on me."

"Sounds like you have some layers to peel back there."

"You mean in therapy? Probably."

I smile at him. My insides warm as he returns it.

A comfortable silence descends upon us. While he takes out his phone and busies himself with a text, I consider what he just said. I realize that we aren't that different. I, too, have layers to peel back, and they aren't that dissimilar from his. Not really. Not when you boil it down.

He sits up and lifts a fry in the air. "If I can get the job at Montgomery Farms, that will help."

"Why?"

He ponders this before answering. Shifting his weight in his seat, he sighs. "Because it will be something I did on my own that my father can't criticize. At all."

"Why would he criticize you? You're successful from what I can tell."

He gives me a slight grin. "He thinks I'm an idiot for going into veterinary medicine to start with. He equates it to some small-town, small-mind thing because of Pap and that I should've been a heart surgeon like him—something worthy of a McKenzie."

I furrow a brow. "Being a vet is a really honorable thing."

He shrugs. "He hates that I was fired. Didn't even listen as to why. He also thinks I'm an idiot for breaking off my engagement, and he loathes the fact that I'm here and not working in some half-assed clinic in Phoenix just so I'm employed."

"Well, being employed *is* kind of a good thing," I tease.

"True. But I want to make an actual step to something better. Not simply scurry around from one job to another. If I can just get this job in Florida, he won't be able to say a word about it. It's the most prestigious company in the country, maybe the world."

I take a bite of my sandwich. "When will you know if you get it?"

"Soon, I hope."

"What would you do?"

His eyes light up, a twinkle shining in the depths of his irises. "I'd be working at a rescue center near Orlando. My mom and I went there when I was a little kid, and we both fell in love with it. I told her then that I'd work there someday." He smiles at the memory. "They do wildlife studies and rehabilitation. Their community outreach is first class."

I watch him come alive. It's clear this means something to him. He looks how I feel when I think of the Honey House.

My heart tugs as I watch him mull over his plight. I know if Montgomery Farms would just talk to him, they'd hire him. He's passionate and intelligent. He's kind and funny. They'd be crazy not to snap him right up.

"I really hope you get the job, Holden." I take a bite of my fry. "Do you think you have a good chance?"

He shrugs. "They're super picky about who they hire and have this insane vetting process—pun intended—to get accepted," he says with a grin. "But if you get hired, they literally pay for you to have all of these extra qualifications and opportunities, so I get why they are really choosy. The wait is just nerve-racking, you know? Especially since I might not have a great reference from my last job and now have a new living arrangement."

"I'm sure it'll be okay," I offer.

"Will it, though? Or will they look at me and be like, 'Hey, this guy was doing great but lost his job and fiancée in the course of a month. He's probably going through something that we don't want to be a part of.'"

"Well . . . that does sound bad when you put it like that."

We both laugh, the sound of our voices mixing together over our fish.

"I'll give you a reference," I joke. "I'm a great personal-reference giver. I gave one to Debbie's sister, Donna, and she got a job at the bank. Probably because of me."

"Oh, I'm *sure* it was because of you. Absolutely."

"Whatever. It probably was. I come across as genuine and a really salt-of-the-earth kind of person," I say, popping a fry into my mouth. "Besides, we've basically been engaged since you asked me to marry you with a giant candy ring."

He laughs. "I might need you to be my fiancée for a while longer. To convince Montgomery I'm a good guy and that he should hire me."

"I'd have him eating out of the palm of my hand." I wink. "You'd probably be vice president of the company before it was over."

Holden takes a bite of his sandwich and watches me over the top of it. There's something about the way he looks at me with a twinkle in his eye that makes me squirm.

In a good way.

I think.

CHAPTER FIVE

HOLDEN

Well, there he is."

I wonder if it's a thing in Tennessee to greet people before they even get in the door. Yesterday, it was Dottie. Today, it's Joe—the man who apparently changes the floor mats.

"It's nice to meet you," Joe says.

He heads toward where I'm standing in the middle of the reception area. His white mustache curls slightly toward his eyes, and I wonder if it's to draw attention to the insane almost-purple color of his irises. He extends a hand and we shake.

"You look so much like your grandfather that I would've known you anywhere," he says.

"I've heard that before. I've also heard that I have his acute ability to tell bad jokes."

He grins. "Let's hope not. We went golfing a few weeks ago. He told the dumbest joke about knees."

"Kid-neys?"

"That one." He points at me. "I guess you've heard it too."

"I think everyone he's met in the last year has heard it."

He releases my hand but places his on my shoulder. His smile grows wider. "I also heard you were getting cozy with Sophie Bates last night at Tank's."

"I . . . What?" I look over my shoulder at Dottie. She just shrugs. "I'm staying at her bed-and-breakfast, and we went to Tank's for a bite to eat."

Joe laughs. "Small-town chatter. Better get used to it. Either way, I'm glad you and Sophie hit it off. She's a dandy. And Dottie said that aside from being late yesterday, you guys hit it off too. She also mentioned that you love Birdie's apple pie as much as I do."

My head drops to the side as I take in Dottie's smug grin. "Is that true, Dottie?"

She holds her hands out to the side. The look on her face proves she knows she's been caught in a fib and doesn't know what to do about it.

I raise a brow and turn back to Joe. "I was on time yesterday, Joe. I was here all day, and I assure you that I haven't tried Birdie's apple pie yet . . . even though she did deliver one yesterday."

He gasps.

Dottie gasps in mock horrification.

"Dottie Mae," Joe says. "Are you holding out on me?"

"You little shit," she says with a laugh. She smacks my shoulder as I walk behind her. She shakes her head. "Lord help me. I'm going to head into the back and start sorting deliveries before I fire you both."

We laugh as she marches through the archway into the supply room. She throws her hands in the air, mumbling to herself about not trusting insolent men.

"Tell your grandfather I said hello," Joe says.

"Will do," I tell him.

Joe leaves with a floor mat stuck under an arm.

With him gone and Dottie still in the back, the building is eerily quiet. I slip off my jacket and hang it on the hook by the window. Then I grab a seat on one of the wooden stools behind the desk.

I've just reached for the schedule when I notice a small stain on the edge of my shirt. Lifting the hem, I see that it's gravy from breakfast.

Chuckling, I drop the fabric.

I had a suspicion that Sophie was a good cook from watching her in the kitchen last night. But I had no idea she could whip up a meal like she did this morning. From-scratch sausage gravy, biscuits that seemed like they were handmade this morning, and eggs so fluffy that they were like pillows awaited me when I woke up. I could totally get used to that.

I could totally get used to other things too—things like having her in my life again. I've had women in my life in various roles, but none I've enjoyed being around quite like her. She was my first best friend. When we toilet-papered Dottie's house, she was my partner in crime.

Just thinking about it makes me laugh.

Glancing down, I see the schedule is open. An oversize green sticky note is slapped in the center. I don't know how I missed it yesterday.

Holden,

If I haven't called by now, I'm reeling in king mackerel the size of my body and the phone service in the Gulf stinks. Hope Dottie is treating you well. If she gets out of hand, bring her a doughnut in the morning. It's a trick that's worked for years.

Love,

Pap

Beneath that, there's a circle with a different set of handwriting inside.

I can read this, you know.—Dottie

I grin and stick the note in my pocket. I'm about to take another drink of my coffee when the door to the clinic bursts open.

A boy, probably around sixteen or so, comes in. His eyes are wide, panic clearly set in, as he carries a ferret to me.

"Where is Dr. Fred?" he asks.

I get off my stool. "He's not in today. Can I help you?"

"Are you a vet?"

"Yes." I round the corner of the desk and do a quick visual exam of the ferret. It appears fine as it squirms around in its yellow harness. "I'm Dr. Holden. I'm filling in for Dr. Fred for a while. Is something wrong with your buddy here?"

He strokes the ferret's head. "This is Fidget. She's been pooping blood all morning. And, um, I don't know what to do."

His voice trembles. His hands shake as he holds Fidget out to me.

I take his pet. Her eyes are clear, her fur soft and shiny. There's no weird discharge from her nose or ears or around her mouth.

"Tell you what," I say. "Let's go into an exam room and have a look at her."

He forces a swallow. "Okay."

Dottie comes around the corner. "Hey, Patrick."

"Hi, Miss Dottie."

"Is Fidget okay?" she asks.

"I . . ." Patrick looks up at me. "I don't know."

"We're going to have a look at her." I smile at Patrick. "But she seems pretty playful. Has she been active?"

He follows me into one of the exam rooms and closes the door behind us.

"She's been acting fine," he says. "I mean, I lost her for about an hour last night. She got out of my room and escaped. She's a freaking Houdini."

"Where did you find her?"

"In the bathroom."

I roll the ferret over in my hands and check her tummy. And then I look at her backside.

"Is this the blood?" I point to some red residue near her bottom.

"Yes."

I press my hand on her belly to feel around. She thinks I'm playing and nibbles at my hand.

"What did you do when you found her?" I ask him.

"Well, I figured she wanted a bath. She loves water. So we did that and then"—he thinks back—"I took her back to my room while I went down for dinner. Then I took a snack up and watched a movie and let her run loose in my room until I went to bed."

"What did you snack on?"

"Cinnamon gummy bears."

"Sugar-free?" I ask.

He wrinkles his nose. "No. Do they even make them sugar-free?"

"They do. And it's important because xylitol is an additive to sugar-free foods that's very toxic to animals, including ferrets." I take a swab out of a container and capture some of the residue. "Is there any chance she's gotten into any cleaning products? Any other food items? Anything she shouldn't have been besides the candy?"

He shakes his head. "No. She's in her cage unless I'm with her. And Mom doesn't let me have food in my room. I had to sneak the gummy bears in there."

"That's good." I hand Fidget back to Patrick. "Hold on to her for me and I'll be right back."

He nods as I take the swab and leave the room.

The lab my grandfather has set up is across the hall. It takes only a few minutes to confirm my suspicions.

I wash my hands before I return to the exam room. Patrick is talking softly to Fidget when I enter.

"It seems to me that your friend here likes the same snacks as you do," I say.

"Huh?"

I smile softly. "Go home. Give her another bath. And next time you have gummy bears, keep them out of her reach." I put my hand on Fidget's head and give it a gentle shake. "She's a fan too."

"Really? Oh, that's great," Patrick says, bringing the pet up to his chin and nuzzling it. "She's gonna be fine, then?"

"She'll be fine. She might have a bit of a sore tummy, though, because cinnamon is pretty strong. Keep an eye on her, but I think she's going to be good as new."

He looks at me like I just hit a game-winning home run. I think he's trying to decide whether he should hug me or not.

"Thanks, Doctor. Seriously, you just saved my life."

"I don't know about that, but you're welcome." I open the door. "Now go see Dottie before you leave, okay?"

"Got it." His grin splits his cheeks as he heads to the counter.

I wash my hands in the sink next to the exam table. I'm drying them off when my phone buzzes in my pocket. I take a peek into the lobby. It's empty.

"Hello?" I say.

"Is this Dr. McKenzie?"

"Yes, it is."

"Hello, Holden. This is Timothy Montgomery from Montgomery Farms."

I close the door. My heartbeat quickens as I switch the phone to my other hand. My palms sweat, and I make a concerted effort not to drop the phone.

"Hi, Dr. Montgomery. How are you?"

"I'm good. Thank you. I'm calling because you've applied for the rehabilitation position at our facility in Orlando. Is that right?"

"It is." My voice cracks more than it should, and I wince at the sound of it. "I'm honored to be considered."

Papers shuffle in the background.

"Well, I'm honored to let you know that you've made it to the final two candidates," he says.

My jaw pops open. I run a hand through my hair at the realization that it's a possibility that this whole damn thing might just actually happen.

Holy shit.

"That's . . . amazing," I say. "I'm . . . Wow. Thank you."

"You're welcome. I founded this organization forty years ago, as you may already know. It's incredibly personal to me. My passion project, if you will. Just a little backstory . . . I was working for a high-profile horse-racing farm fresh out of college. I was disenchanted with the way these glorious animals were treated once their moneymaking days were over. So I partnered with a few investors and created Montgomery Farms."

I knew that. I've read everything there is about the company over the last fifteen years. My mother used to buy me animal magazines, and there were always articles about Montgomery Farms. I remember one in particular about finding your passion. A small segment was from Dr. Montgomery himself and how he'd found his working with retired racehorses. He wrote so passionately, so from the heart, so much like what I felt inside myself, that I knew I'd do anything to work for that company someday.

"It's a world-renowned organization, sir."

"Thank you. As I said, it's very, very close to my heart. It's a family to me and not just a business. It's incredibly important that everyone on the payroll fit into the vision of a close-knit community, working together to support the animals we're caring for, as well as each other. This is very much a team effort."

I force a swallow. "That makes perfect sense."

Papers move around again. The sound causes my anxiety to spike. I plead silently with myself not to say anything stupid.

"One thing I appreciate about you, Holden, besides your impressive answers to the essays on the application, is the fact that you're a family man."

My shoulders fall.

This is where my life bites me in the ass.

I clear my throat. "Of course I am."

My brain starts stringing together potential sentences that aren't off-putting. People separate all the time. Surely he understands things like that.

"My wife and I have been married for forty-five years this coming May. It's that kind of commitment I'm looking for in an employee," he says.

And maybe he doesn't understand things like that.

Oh. Shit.

"Definitely," I say. "I—"

"So many young people in today's world don't understand the concept of commitment. Seeing something out to the end. Standing behind your word and working things out, rolling with the punches. People nowadays quit as soon as things get hard."

My throat closes. It's probably a defense mechanism, but one I'm grateful for at the moment. At least it prevents me from burying myself deeper.

"I love that you're starting a family. It says so much about you. I shouldn't say this, but it gives you an edge," he says. "Are you married yet? You filled this out a while ago."

I close my eyes. "No. No, I'm not. Not yet."

"My wife is wanting to redo our vows next year. I know what it's like to have a bride wanting a perfect day." He chuckles. "When is the big day, if you don't mind my asking?"

"Soon."

As soon as the word is out of my mouth, I cringe. The day isn't soon. It's not happening. *The answer is never.* But I can't say that, because if I do, I've lost my edge and I'll end up back in Phoenix, working for someone else and listening to my father tell me how I've disappointed him yet again.

I can't do that.

I won't.

I'll rent a boat and sail off into the Pacific first.

"That's great," he says. "That's very good news. I'd like to see the final candidates at work. Get an idea of how you prepare for each day, solve problems, operate under pressure. Also, to see how well we collaborate. That sort of thing. Do you think that's possible?"

I glance around the clinic and wish for the first time since coming here that I were back at my old job.

"Well, actually, I'm in Tennessee right now," I say. "My grandfather needed a helping hand at his clinic for a while."

"Oh. Point in your favor. I love the spirit of that." His chair squeaks. "Could I come there? Would that be a problem? I think the second candidate is in Kentucky, so I could make a week out of it and have an answer sooner than I anticipated."

"I think that would be fine."

"I'll get back to you with a day once I talk with my secretary and my wife. I'm going to shoot for midweek next week." He sighs in satisfaction. "Thanks for taking my call, Dr. McKenzie. We'll talk soon."

"Thank you for calling."

"Goodbye."

I end the call and then bury my head in my hands.

Montgomery Farms wants me.

They want *me*.

The me, at least, from a month ago.

The bottom of my stomach falls to the floor.

I am so screwed.

CHAPTER SIX

SOPHIE

I am so screwed.

The moon lights up the kitchen in an eerie glow. Gramma always loved the moon. She said your problems always seem worst at night and the moon is your light, your reminder that the sun will come back up and things will be better.

I turn the bottle around in my hands and look at the label. The corner of the sticker describing the type of wine is starting to lift on its own. With nothing better to do—except for the things I've done all day with little or no success—I pick at it. I pry it off slowly, an inch at a time, and relish in the satisfaction of watching it release from the glass.

The motion is soothing. It gives me a channel to focus on something that isn't overdue statements and impending taxes . . . and the sense of imminent failure if I don't figure something out.

My thoughts trace back through the day—from calling the treasurer's office to confirm that they'd denied my appeal to the hours I spent combing through the basement. I searched through nearly everything down there in the hope of finding something I could sell to help make ends meet. There was nothing worth anything substantial. The only good thing about today was the Ingrams' sweet smiles as they checked out this morning.

The label breaks free as a whole piece, and I slap it onto the counter.

"How mad would you be, Gramma, if I got a loan?" I say out loud. "Like, really, really mad? Or kind of mad? Because I remember how you were so against getting loans and how hard you and Grandpa worked to pay this thing off. But I don't know what else to do."

I take the wineglass I got out earlier and pour myself a drink. Then I pour it down my throat. The tartness of the alcohol reminds me of the time I tried to drink apple cider vinegar to lose weight. I'm not sure what's worse.

What's worse than both of those experiences would be going to the bank for money to help me out of this mess. It's the easy answer. It's the obvious solution. But every time I start to seriously consider it, a heaviness sneaks up on me. Not only would I be going against Gramma's wishes, but I'd also have to face the ladies at the bank. They'd know why I need a loan, and that's humiliating. I can hear the gossip now. "Poor Sophie Bates, needing money after Chad robbed her blind."

Nah. Not doing that.

The glass clinks against the countertop at the same time the front door creaks. My head snaps to the clock. My stomach tightens as I hear Holden's voice call out my name.

"Sophie?"

The sound echoes around the Honey House. The spicy scent of the kitchen, a man's deep voice, and the warmth of the wine in my belly combine to make me a little light-headed.

I pour another drink. "I'm in the kitchen."

Before I get the last syllable out, he rounds the corner. His forehead is crinkled, his lips pressed together. The lines grow deeper as he takes me in.

"You look like you've had a hell of a day," he says.

"You know what? If you wanna judge me, just head on out of here."
I bring the glass to my lips. "Leave me with my wine."

"Judge you? Let's commiserate. Got another glass?"

I point at the cabinet by the refrigerator. "Over there. Bad day for
you, too, I take it."

"You could say that." He glances over his shoulder as he pulls a glass
out of the cupboard. "Do you have anything other than wine?"

"You don't like wine?"

"Not particularly."

"Well, me either." I take a sip and flinch. "This stuff is particularly
awful. It's what I think drinking starter fluid would taste like."

He straddles the stool next to me and sits at the island. The leath-
ery scent of his cologne licks at my skin, and I pull my arm away for
good measure. He must notice, because his brows pull together, but he
doesn't point it out.

"If you don't like it, why are you drinking it?" he asks.

"Because it's all I have."

"Good answer."

He takes the bottle and fills up his glass. He holds it in the air and
inspects it like I used to do when we were kids and I'd steal Liv's drink.
I'd hold it up like that to check for bits of food and backwash floating
around.

"It's clean," I point out.

He sets it back down. "I was just thinking about how this is the
exact color of the cinnamon bear goo that a ferret shit out today."

Gagging, I lean away from him. He means it as a joke, but somehow it triggers the flames from the wine, and I start choking for real.

My cheeks heat from both the lack of air and the heat in his gaze as
he watches me gasp. For half a second, I consider that he might think I
need CPR. That makes me choke harder. I lean farther away to discour-
age him from patting my back or otherwise making contact, because

that will only lift me to the next level of choking. I don't even know what that might be. Death, maybe.

"Are you okay?" he asks.

"Fine," I say, holding a hand against my chest as the air begins to stream more evenly into my lungs. "Sorry. That visual was just disgusting."

He sips the wine, looking halfway proud of himself for grossing me out.

"Is that what you do all day?" I ask, gathering myself.

"What?"

"I don't know. Inspect ferret poop?"

"I'll do whatever duty calls me to do, and today it was making sure a teenage boy's pet ferret wasn't bleeding from its ass." He holds the glass in front of him and swirls the liquid around. "The boy—Patrick, I think his name was—thinks I'm a rock star now, though. So there's that."

"Now I get it. You love your job because people think you're brilliant and it feeds your ego."

He raises his glass to me before taking a drink. I shake my head and try not to watch the way his Adam's apple bobs in his throat.

The refrigerator hums softly, but other than that, the house is quiet. Whether it's from the moonlight coming in through the windows or the wine hitting my veins, I don't know, but a warmth settles over me. It's a slight haze that I welcome with open arms.

"What's all that?" Holden nods to the stuffed file folder next to me.

I eye it like it's my mortal enemy. "A bunch of stuff I have to deal with."

"Like . . ."

"Like it's none ya."

"Huh?"

"It's none ya business."

He rolls his eyes. "So clever."

"Yeah, well, I'm a woman of many talents."

My gaze drops to the folder again. The longer I look at it, the tighter the back of my neck becomes. The irritation builds and builds until I'm reaching over and pulling the pile in front of me.

"Wanna know what this is? Here. I'll show ya." I reach in and take out the tax bills. I slide them in between us. "This is the thing that's going to put me out of business. It's due by next month, or I'm kaput."

He takes a look at it and whistles between his teeth.

"Right? Thanks, Chad, you fucker."

Holden picks up the sheet of paper. "Shit, Sophie. Is that for just one year?"

"It's spring and fall for this year and last. And maybe the fall from the year before that. I don't even know anymore."

"This is due soon."

"No shit. I thought I'd be able to recoup some of it through bookings, but a place opened in Rockery—the Sweet Tea. What kind of a name, even, is that for a bed-and-breakfast?" I scoff. "Anyway, they're pulling just enough of my business to let me not quite get ahead."

He doesn't laugh or smile or even almost crack a grin. I don't blame him. It's pretty mind-blowing that someone can get themselves into this kind of situation.

Peering out the window and ignoring Holden's gaze on the side of my face, I chastise myself for getting into this mess. In my defense, it's like it happened overnight. One minute, I'm conquering the world. Have a savings account with a decent little padding. The next minute, I'm in a hole a mile deep.

What the hell happened?

I squeeze my eyes shut.

Chad happened. Chad happened, and I haven't found my footing. He found me at a time when I was reeling from the loss of Gramma and leaving Florida and feeling so . . . *alone.* As I was wondering what my future looked like and was secretly scared about the possibilities, he waltzed into town and held me tight and said everything I needed to hear.

I took the bait. He reeled me in and left me and my savings account gutted.

Damn it. And damn me.

I look at Holden, ready to change the subject. "What happened to you today, anyway? Dottie give you a hard time?"

He pulls his eyes away from me. "Not any more than any other time I've been around her." He downs the rest of his wine.

"Want a refill?"

"Sure. Tastes like expired mouthwash, but what the hell."

We sit quietly again, both lost in our thoughts. I take a few opportunities to sneak a glance at him, because even if I'm having a bad day, he's still cute. And in my house. And I have to take what little pleasures life offers me.

"I heard about that job I was telling you about," he says.

"The one in Florida that I hoped would provide me with a spot I could use for vacations? Please don't tell me you blew it. I was counting on that."

He grins. "You have so much faith in me."

I sigh. "You blew it, didn't you?"

"No. Not yet, anyway."

"Good. What did they say, then? That they love you and think you're a wizard and you start tomorrow?" I sigh. "That's it, isn't it? You're leaving, and you're sad that you have to go." I pat him on the shoulder. "You'll be okay. I know I'm hard to leave."

A fit of laughter topples out of my lips. It's the wine, I know, but I can't stop it. A few seconds later and he's chuckling right along with me.

"How much of this have you drunk?" Holden asks.

"Not much. I'm a lightweight. I never drink."

"I remember you putting down quite a few beers back in the day," he teases.

I cover my face with my hands. "Don't go there."

"What? Don't remind you how you assured me that you drank all the time and got so shit-faced that I had to carry you into your friend's house?"

"Yeah. Don't remind me of that." I peek through my fingers. "Not my best moment."

He stretches his long legs out in front of him. "Well, I'm not living mine right now. Get this: I'm one of two final candidates for the job I want, and I actually have an edge."

"That's great!"

He grimaces. "Yeah, except that my edge comes from the fact that I'm getting married."

"You are?"

I try to recall that bit of information but come up empty. Surely, he would've mentioned a small detail like marriage.

"No. I'm not getting married," he scoffs.

"But then how are you . . . *Oh* . . ." My face falls. I can feel the heat in my cheeks. "I see. Big problem."

"Yeah. Big problem, indeed."

"Maybe you could just tell them it didn't work out with . . . what's-her-name."

He props an elbow on the edge of the table and rests his chin in his hand. "I could. But I'd likely lose not just the edge but the opportunity altogether."

"I think you're being a little dramatic, Doc."

I make a face and take another long sip of my wine. The more I drink of it, the better it tastes. And the better Holden looks, if it's possible that he could look better than he did in those stupid sweatpants the other night.

He snorts. "I wish. They said married people demonstrate an ability to commit and see problems through. I can only imagine what they'd think if I tell them I ended an engagement and a job."

He has a solid point, but I decide not to tell him that. It's not going to help much. Instead, I try to spin it around.

"Maybe you're looking at this all wrong," I say, pointing at him. My finger bounces in the air, so I put it back on the countertop. "Isn't it possible that they'll see you as a good decision-maker who knows when to pull the plug? That's a good quality to have. Very useful."

His head twists in his palm so he can see me. "Are you always a glass-half-full kind of person?"

"Only when it's other people. Totally a half-empty kind of girl when it's my own life."

He laughs and sits up. There's still a crinkle of worry at the corners of his eyes. I wish I could say something to make him feel better, but I can't think of anything more than I've already tossed out there.

"If this doesn't work out, I'm going to be screwed. I'm going to have to go home, get a random-ass job that's just treading water. And . . . I can just see it now," he says with a sigh.

"See what?"

His face twists in disgust. "Dad letting me know what a failure I am and having to listen to that bullshit." He runs a hand down his face. "Shit."

"Okay, so if that happens, is it really a bad thing? I mean, maybe you'll find something great. Maybe it'll be a new open door."

He flashes me a look. "Maybe, Miss Glass-Half-Full. But then it's starting from the bottom somewhere else and spending the next ten years working my way up for nothing, really. I'll look up and be forty and have nothing to show for it but paychecks. It would be a complete setback." He pours what's left of the wine into his glass. "Montgomery Farms would be a huge step in the right direction. My work would be relevant. Game-changing, even. Their work contributes to studies and new methods of animal care. I just . . . I have to get it."

I hop off my stool and head to the cupboard. The wine is sloshing around in my stomach, and I need to find something to snack on.

I grab a box of crackers and carry them to the island. "But let me play devil's advocate here and say you don't get it. What will happen? You'll go back to Phoenix?"

"I guess. I have an apartment there still."

"Okay. So that's a plus. Right? And you could find a position close to where you want to live, maybe by your friends. Could be cool."

He holds on to the edge of the island and tips his weight so the stool is balanced on the back legs. "But I really don't want to do that. I have this . . . itch to go somewhere new. Somewhere I can really . . . figure it out, you know?"

"Yeah. I wanted to do that once too."

"What happened?"

My heart sinks into my stomach. Regret and sadness creep over me like a poison filling a valley.

"Life, I guess," I say.

I look up at Holden. There's a softness in his eyes that makes my throat tighten. Nervously, I remove a couple of crackers and offer the box to him. He takes it from me.

"I . . ." I've never really talked about this to anyone. Not even my brother and sister, although they could piece it all together if they tried hard enough. Maybe they have. I don't know. But the idea of saying it out loud to Holden—a man whom I won't have to see for much longer—feels freeing.

I take a deep breath.

"I'd always said I wanted to run this place," I tell him. "From the time that I was a little girl, I wanted to be like my gramma. But I got older and felt stifled here."

Holden nods slowly. He sets the stool back down on all four legs.

"I applied to Florida State and got accepted. I think Gramma thought it was a phase or something. She sat me down a couple of weeks before I was supposed to leave and said she'd sign this place over to me the next day. She said she was getting old and that she wanted

55

to see me take over. That it would give her peace." I look at the floor. "I left anyway."

He reaches out and touches the top of my hand. His palm is warm and soft, and he takes it away too quickly.

"I got there and hated it," I say around the lump in my throat. "But I was too proud to call home and tell Gramma that. And . . . she died before I could."

"Shit." He stands, and I think he might reach for me. I hold my breath. "I'm sorry, Sophie."

I exhale. "It's fine."

It's not fine. It won't ever be fine. I left her. I made a bad decision after a terrible decision, mostly out of pride. I was so freaking stupid, and the regret I feel about that gnaws at me every day.

"You know what you need?" Holden asks.

"Yes," I say quickly. "A knight in shining armor with five grand. Do you know what *you* need?"

He opens his mouth but snaps it shut. Slowly, his eyes widen to the size of dinner plates. A smile that doesn't instill confidence in me spreads across his cheeks too. "Actually, I do. I need . . . a *wife*."

CHAPTER SEVEN

HOLDEN

Sophie holds my gaze for a long second. "Well, good luck with that."

"Yeah . . ."

My throat goes dry as my mind begins to take itself seriously. *Too seriously.* So seriously, in fact, that it starts to run certain scenarios in which we both could come out with what we need with nothing but a . . . wedding.

It occurs to me that this idea has been percolating in the back of my mind for a few days. Here and there, little blips of imagery would filter through my brain about what life might be like, being married to Sophie. I thought it was just a giant what-if game, like brains are known to play.

But maybe it's not that. Maybe it was trying to tell me something. To marry her.

I shake my head in the hope that the movement will jolt some sense into me. But when I stop, the same visions are running through my head.

She turns toward the sink and raises the window. Cool air blasts into the room. I wonder if it's really that chilled or if my body temperature is just abnormally high as I think about . . . *marrying Sophie Bates.*

I gulp.

"That air feels good, doesn't it?" she says.

Her back is to me. Her shoulders are rigid. I wonder if she's thinking what I'm thinking, because there's a definite stress in my back that's making me stand tall too.

Shit.

I clear my throat. "Sophie?"

"Yeah?"

"I have a crazy idea."

She takes a deep breath. "Why does the sound of that terrify me in a very real way?"

"Well . . ." I plant my hands on the counter as I watch for any kind of tell as to what she's thinking. "I think I might have found a way to solve both of our problems."

She spins around and grabs the edge of the sink behind her. Her jaw is set. "You are out of your freaking mind if you're thinking what I think you're thinking."

I hold a hand in front of me. "It could work. Think about it."

The longer I think about it, the more I think it could. *It would.* And the deeper my belief in the possibilities of this admittedly crazy idea, the more energy flows through my veins.

I walk toward her slowly. Each step I take causes her chest to rise and fall quicker. Mine too.

"Look, I know this sounds insane," I say carefully. "But think about it."

"Think about what, exactly?"

"You need a knight in shining armor and five grand, right?"

She nods, narrowing her eyes.

"And I need a wife."

Something about the way this comes out snaps her out of her haze. She comes alive with a laugh.

"You. Are. Out. Of. Your. Damn. Mind." She squares her shoulders to mine. The sweetness of the wine on her breath, mixed with the disbelief on her face, makes me grin. "This isn't funny."

"No, it's not."

"You do realize you're insinuating that *I* could be *your* wife, right?"

"I do."

"You're nuts, and you're even nuts-er if you think *you* are my knight in shining armor."

She marches to the counter behind me. After swiping up my glass and the empty wine bottle, she stomps across the kitchen. Looking me straight in the eye, she tosses the bottle into the trash.

"Did you stop at the bar on your way home?" she asks.

"This town has a bar?"

"Good point. Did you do drugs, then?" She places the glass in the sink. "Because there's something seriously wrong with you, Doc."

I shouldn't laugh. I know it. There's really nothing funny about this . . . except watching her be so defiant. Fuck it if she isn't pretty when she's fired up.

She narrows her gaze at my outburst.

I stick my tongue in my cheek. "You know, Jessica was much nicer about it when I asked her to marry me."

"Because she probably liked you."

"Oh, like you don't like me."

She snorts in disgust, but it's not real. We both know it. "I suppose in Jessica's defense you probably never repossessed her engagement ring and ate it in front of her before."

I laugh again. "If I knew how much that was going to haunt me, I would've let you keep it."

"As you should've."

The air between us moves as if it has absorbed some of the energy blasting between us. Because there *is* energy—something comfortably electric between Sophie and me that I can't deny.

And that's why this marriage of convenience could be the ticket.

"That's why this could work, Sophie."

"Why? Because you owe me a ring?"

I ignore her attempt at deflection. "No. Because we get along. We have a history and friendship and a certain built-in trust level."

She places a hand on her hip and blinks as if she's bored.

"And we both . . . like my grandpa?" It's the first thing that pops in my head. "And we enjoy spending time together."

"We do?"

"Yes, we do. You know it. We have fun together."

She rolls her eyes. "You're not totally terrible to be around, but I don't know that I'd go all out and say you are *fun*."

"Yes, I am. You smile the whole time we're together. Or most of the time," I say when she opens her mouth to argue. "See? It's the perfect, or as perfect as we're going to find, setup. I'm not going to have my feelings hurt if you yell at me for leaving my socks on the bathroom floor."

"Ha! I'm not doing your laundry."

"Good, because I have a system and I quite like it."

This seems to calm her down. She crosses her arms over her chest, but the panic in her eyes fades. I'm afraid to say anything else and ruin the progress I think I just made.

The more I think about this, the more perfect this crazy idea becomes. It would be a symbiotic relationship, a mutually beneficial situation in which we would both come out smiling on the other side. That never happens.

But it could.

If Sophie will marry me.

Holy shit.

"I bet you at least got down on one knee when you asked Jessica to marry you," she teases.

I grin. "I did, and I'm more than happy to do that right now if it'll help."

"It won't. It would just tempt me to kick you, and we don't need that."

I laugh.

We stand in the middle of the kitchen and watch one another, feeling each other out. The longer it goes with neither of us speaking, the more it feels like we're waiting on the other to break the ice.

Finally, after a couple of minutes, she sighs. "You aren't really serious, are you?" she asks.

Am I?

I do a quick evaluation of the situation. She can help me get the job, and I can help her find some relief. Neither of us would take it seriously, so there's no harm there. And she's pretty great to look at, which doesn't hurt either.

"Yes," I say with conviction, my mind made up. "I am."

She looks at the ceiling. "I don't even want to get married right now—especially to you."

"And why not me?"

Her brows furrow, but she releases them. The gesture seems like she's letting go of more than that.

"Why not you?" she asks. "Because if I get married again, I want the fairy tale. I want the *real* knight in shining armor. I want . . . I want a man that wants to live the life I live and be happy in it. And that might be stupid—it probably is. But I want it."

There's not a lot I can say to that. She's right to want those things, and she's also right that I'm not any of them.

But that isn't what this is.

"Please be reminded that you needed a two-part solution. You wanted a knight and five grand. They don't necessarily come together. So if I can provide half the equation, it will free you up to focus on the other half."

She puts a hand on her hip. "That does help your case." She holds my gaze for a long moment before beginning to pace through the kitchen.

I don't know whether to give her a few minutes to let this sink in or to keep showing her how perfect this whole thing can be. Because the more I think about it, the more I'm sold that this is the answer to everything.

This is the reason for me coming to Honey Creek.

The universe put me here.

It all makes sense now.

Sophie stops midpace and spins around to face me. "Why can't you just find a girl somewhere and have her pretend to be your fiancée? Don't you have a friend or an ex that you're on good terms with that will do this for you? It seems so much easier."

"You are my friend."

"Eh . . ."

I sigh. "Fine. Montgomery is coming next week, and I don't have that kind of time to find a woman here and ask her to pretend to be my fiancée. That's not something you can just go into the Lemon Aid and throw out there."

"Oh, but you can ask me to be your pretend fiancée?"

"No. I asked you to be my wife."

She glares at me. It's softened with a hidden smile, and that's encouraging enough to continue with my proposition.

"And pretending to be engaged won't work here. Montgomery is coming *here*. Everyone will know that we just got engaged. All it takes is for someone to say something about it, and he won't trust me. He'll know something is up. He thinks I'm on the verge of actually getting married."

Her shoulders fall as she watches me with what I think—hope—is possibility.

"I can't believe I'm asking you this," I tell her. "If someone had told me a few days ago that I'd be asking a woman to marry me, I'd have laughed in their face."

"So why are you, then?"

I ponder that for a moment.

"Because we both have problems, and we can solve them if we work together. We've always been good teammates. Remember when we convinced the pool in town to stay open late on the Fourth of July so we could host a pool party?"

She grins. "I forgot about that."

"And when we got that old guy to pay us, like, twenty-five bucks to mow his grass—"

"So we could buy snow cones," she says, finishing my story with a laugh.

"Exactly. This is like that. Just a more . . . adult version of working together to get what we want."

She paces a slow circle, rubbing her temples with her fingers. I hold my breath and watch her totally overthink this whole thing. Finally, she stops moving.

"What do we tell people around here *if* I agree to this ridiculousness?" She blows out a breath and then quickly takes in another to power her through her thought. "Everyone knows that I've been here and you've been there and those two places are separated by hundreds or thousands of miles. I don't know. A long damn way."

I scratch my head. I hadn't thought of that.

Shit.

"Besides the fact that Debbie emailed me, asking if we were a thing," she almost growls.

I jab a finger in her direction. "And Joe, the floor mat guy, had heard we were *cozy*." I look at her stone-faced. "He actually said we were cozy."

Sophie makes a face. On a normal day, in a normal conversation, I'd pause and ask what that's all about. Is it out of the realm of possibility she'd get cozy with me? But this is not a normal day, so I stay focused on the task at hand.

"How does everyone know we weren't keeping in contact all these years?" I ask. "As far as they know, we've been talking and emailing and our love rekindled when I came to town—assuming we were in love. Maybe we even saw each other while you were in Florida. Right? I mean, is it completely illogical that we had a fling when you were in college?"

"With you? Kind of."

Something about the way she says it prickles me in the wrong way.

"Don't lie," I say. "You know something would've happened between us if I lived here."

"I don't know that."

"Yes, you do. How many times did we almost kiss?"

"Well, it never happened," she says, tucking a strand of hair behind her ear as she looks away.

I clear my throat to refocus. "But it could've. And it's completely plausible that I came to visit you, or vice versa, at some point, and we had something. Felt it wasn't right and let it go. Think about it."

She grabs a towel and begins to wipe off the counter. Her motions are rougher than necessary. I have half a notion to take it out of her hands so she'll focus on what I'm saying, but I don't because I think that will incense her.

Instead, I watch her work this out. She bites her bottom lip and polishes the counter until the rag squeaks as it crosses the laminate. The longer she takes to say something, the more my stomach begins to twist.

"This is insane," she says finally. "Do you know that?"

"Yes. I'm very aware."

Her head falls to the side. "What would I get out of pretending to be your wife again?"

"You'd actually *be* my wife," I point out carefully.

She tosses the towel down. "Why? Remind me."

"I can't risk any weaknesses in this plan. It has to be rock solid and real. I'm trying to prove to Montgomery that I'm the best, sturdiest, most committed guy for the job, and I can't do that if anything looks suspicious. And," I add, "if he finds out that I'm now unemployed, this could be my saving grace."

"I hate that it makes sense."

"And even more important to you is that you'll get out of your tax bind scot-free, and you'll be able to get on my health insurance plan. Legal antibiotics," I say with a wink.

"I was joking about the antibiotics. You know that."

I take a few steps so that we're closer. Her eyes are wary as she tilts her head back and looks up at me.

"If you don't like this, if you have any reservations at all, we're done here," I tell her. "No pressure. Just say the word and I'll drop it, and you'll never hear about it again."

Her lip pops free. "How long would we have to keep up the charade? Because I don't want to be married to you forever. I might find The One."

"I don't know."

"Ballpark it, Doc."

I think fast. "At least until I get the job. Once I'm settled in, we could get divorced or have it annulled."

"So six weeks, maybe?"

"Probably. Not long. I'll go to Orlando, and we'll say you're staying here to try to sell the business. After a few weeks, we can say it won't sell or you can't part with it—whatever you want to say. Then we'll just tell everyone that we decided to part amicably."

"Yeah. I'm not moving from here. This is my home. Period."

"I wouldn't expect you to leave."

"Well, you kind of expect me to marry you, it seems, so how do I know where the line is?"

I laugh. "Fair point."

She walks toward the refrigerator and piles her hair on top of her head. An elastic appears from out of thin air, and she winds it around the ball before turning to face me.

Her features are smoother. The glossiness in her eyes from the wine has waned. She takes a deep breath.

"You know, I find it hilarious that you wouldn't give me a prescription because it was ethically wrong, but you'd propose a marriage of convenience."

"Unlawful dispensing of medication is a major offense. Marrying a woman that willingly agrees to the union is not."

"Whatever."

She steps away and walks around the island.

Goose bumps break out across my skin. Outside, the full moon holds court over the stars. A breeze from the open window flutters the edges of the curtains.

I run a hand down my face. A nervous energy tears through me, and I have to dig deep to override the instinct to start rushing through things. It's a trick I learned in veterinary school—how to focus on what's in front of you and take things a step at a time.

She takes in a long, whooshing breath. "So you would cover half of the property taxes?"

"I would cover them all."

Her head shakes back and forth. "No. I feel weird about that. But if you could pitch in for half, I could scrounge up the other half, and that really would change a lot of things for me." She clears her throat. "It'd save the Honey House, and that's all I really care about."

"That's no problem," I say. "I actually insist on paying them all. It only seems fair."

She considers this. "Okay. Thank you. But should I feel bad about this? I mean, is this a form of prostitution?"

I know she's being serious, and I know, too, that I should take this seriously. But . . . I'm me. So I smirk.

"Are you planning on sleeping with me?" I ask.

"No!"

"Then I don't see how it's prostitution." I step behind the island to adjust myself. The thought of her naked, no matter how brief of a moment it was, is enough to make me hard. "Being dead serious, is it really any different from having a second job? You don't have to do anything other than pretend like you love me for a couple of weeks."

"Well, when you put it like that . . ."

My voice stays remarkably calm despite how anxious I feel inside. "Anything else?"

Her shoulders relax as she sorts through her thoughts. She puts a finger across her lips as she studies me.

"Fine." She drops her hand and straightens her shoulders. "This is crazy and feels like it shouldn't make sense, but it does. And I've done enough things in my life that felt like they made sense but didn't. Plus, your powers of persuasion are on point. And it's not lost on me that I lost money in my first marriage and am gaining it this time. So . . . yes. I'll marry you."

My insides twist into a tight knot before releasing with what feels like a spray of confetti. I watch her for any hint that she's kidding or reconsidering.

But there's nothing. Just a look of resolution on her pretty face.

"We go in the morning, before I back out," she says.

"If you're afraid of backing out, we aren't doing this."

"We are doing this. No take-backs on the proverbial Ring Pops this time." She forces a swallow. "I have a friend in Dogwood Lane named Haley. She loves this kind of stuff. I know she'll help me get it all together."

Holy. Shit.

"Tomorrow?" I ask.

Her hand goes to her hip. "Do you want to do this or not, Doc?"

"Tomorrow sounds great." I flash her a big smile. "We can go tonight if you want to."

"Tomorrow morning. Do you work?"

"I can get out of there by noon."

"Perfect. Let's be on the road by twelve thirty."

She starts to turn away but stops. Her hand is shoved my way. It dangles in the air, all dainty and sweet, and I try to hide my smile as I take her palm in mine.

Her skin is warm and soft. I fight the urge to shiver.

Our eyes hold each other, as if they are making a deal of their own. It's an agreement I don't want to think about. Not right now with her hand in mine and a hefty dose of adrenaline pouring through my body.

She draws away, breaking contact. Her mouth opens in an exaggerated yawn. She stretches her arms over her head, and I have to force myself not to look at the strip of skin that appears between the hem of her shirt and the waistband of her jeans.

"I'm going to bed," she says. "Today has been crazy, to put it mildly."

"All right. I'm . . . going to, too, I guess . . ."

"There's food in the fridge if you're hungry."

I stick my bottom lip out. "I suck at cooking."

She points a finger my way as she heads for the doorway. "Nope. Not getting conned into cooking for you. And," she says before rounding the corner, "I also won't cook for you when we get married."

Her feet stop moving so abruptly that she almost falls forward into the wall. She turns and looks at me.

"I just said *when we get married*," she says in amazement. "What the heck? What happened in here tonight? How much wine did I drink?"

Before I can answer, she shakes her head and disappears into the darkness.

I sit on a stool at the counter. The silence is almost deafening. I tap a finger against the laminate as I look around the kitchen. Strangely, I think I'd feel comfortable enough to get up and make myself something to eat if I really wanted to.

Images of getting up in the morning and coming down for breakfast shoot through my mind. It's not a bad thought. Not at all.

But then again, if it all works out the way it's supposed to, I won't be here long enough to get used to it.

I sigh.

Stay focused, McKenzie. Because this might work if you don't screw it up.

I head toward the doorway and catch the sweet scent of her perfume lingering in the air. I smile.

"Good luck to me."

CHAPTER EIGHT

SOPHIE

The floorboards above me creak. Footsteps shuffle around like they have on and off all night. There's a satisfaction in knowing that Holden can't sleep either. If I thought he was sleeping like a baby after that out-of-nowhere marriage proposal earlier, I'd probably go upstairs and bang around until he woke up.

The clock on my bedside table glows the time in a bright green. Another minute passes as I watch, and I wonder how many I've seen it tick by since I came to bed hours ago. It's been a lot. Many. I've likely watched every one since I laid my head on the pillow, because how is someone supposed to sleep after they've just agreed to marriage in such an off-the-wall way?

Did that really even happen?

The late-night fog in my brain has me considering that I misread the entire situation. That there was no way a man I just got reacquainted with asked me *to be his wife*. That doesn't happen. Not in real life. Not in *my* real life. And definitely not by a man who looks like Holden McKenzie.

But it did. It really must have happened. There's no other way to explain the butterflies in my stomach. Wine wouldn't even cause this kind of craziness.

I roll over onto my side.

"It's the only way not to lose the bed-and-breakfast without getting a loan," I say into the night. "And it'll save me eighty-six million dollars in interest and a whole lot of dignity."

I chew on my bottom lip as I consider my situation. It's not that big of a deal, really. It's not like Holden would be taking my marriage virginity. And there's no way to get hurt emotionally because I know from the onset that he doesn't even really want to be married to me . . . unlike Chad, who convinced me he did.

I toss to my other side and look out the window. Liv's house is dark. I wish a light would come on so I could justify going over there and talking to her.

As I snuggle down into my pillows again and try to get comfortable, I listen for Holden. It just takes a couple of minutes until the footsteps start pattering across the ceiling again. The bed above me squeaks. I curl up in my blankets and try to stop listening for every single sound.

I close my eyes.

Pull my pillow over my head.

Tuck my feet inside the blankets so they are definitely not hanging over the edge and putting themselves at risk for being grabbed by a nonexistent monster.

I lie still. Focus on my breathing. Yet I still jump when an owl hoots outside my window.

"This is ridiculous," I hiss, ripping the covers off me.

Slipping my feet into a pair of sneakers, I glance at the clock again. Two past two in the morning.

"Good thing I've woken Liv up this early . . . late . . . whatever before," I mumble.

I grab a robe off the bedpost and tie it loosely around me. Then I creep quietly into the hall. The kitchen is dark as I pass it. Only the light above the stove is on.

My steps fall softly as I make my way to the door and step outside.

The night air welcomes me with a cold kiss. I pull my robe tighter and hurry my way down the walkway and across the road. I scurry up Liv's driveway and the porch stairs.

The key is cool and damp as I pluck it off the window ledge and stick it in the door lock.

The entryway smells like cinnamon and apples as I step inside. A light glows faintly in the kitchen at the other end of the house. Everything is still and quiet. I sneak through the living room, careful not to trip over the vacuum she's left in the middle of the floor for the last month, and find my way to her bedroom door.

"Liv?" I whisper as I peek inside her room. "You awake?"

She rustles in the darkness. "What? Sophie?" Her voice is heavy with sleep as she gets her bearings.

"You up?"

"No, I'm not up. It's . . . two in the morning?" Panic clears the sleep from her tone. "Are you okay? Is Jobe all right?"

I pad across the carpet and find the edge of her bed. "We're fine. I just want to talk."

"Now?"

I slip off my shoes and climb in beside her. I nestle down in the blankets.

Liv rolls over to face me. The night-light from a wax burner on her dresser provides enough illumination for me to see the outline of her face.

"I couldn't sleep," I tell her.

"Well, thanks for waking me up too."

"No problem."

She grins. "What's keeping you up?"

Taking a deep breath in the hope that it'll calm my internal systems a little bit and let me communicate things clearly, I try to come up with the best way to deliver this information.

"Soph?"

"It's been a weird night."

"Weird like how?"

"Well . . ." I pull the blankets tight against my chest. "I'm getting married tomorrow."

She blinks. "That *is* weird."

"Told you."

She pulls the covers away from her face as if doing so will help her see me, and this situation, more clearly. "You aren't serious."

"I'm as serious as a heart attack. I think." I touch my bottom lip with my finger. "No, I am. I'm getting married."

"Sophie." She lifts her head off the pillow. "What's going on?"

Forcing a swallow, I wonder if I should just say Holden's name or describe my recollection of the night. The latter would be more fun, but I think she might start shaking me if I take too long to get to the good part.

But as I prepare to say his name, an energy shoots through my body. I squirm under the blankets.

"I'm going to kill you if you don't start talking," she warns.

"Okay. Fine." I take a deep, shaky breath. "To make a very long and complicated story short, Holden and I are getting married. Tomorrow. In Dogwood Lane."

"What?" she yelps.

She sits up and scrambles to find the light. I lie perfectly still and await her interrogation.

The lamp switches on and I squint. My sister hovers over me, her eyes narrowed, too, as she tries to figure out whether I'm just screwing with her.

"Will you lie back down?" I ask. "You're letting cool air into the bed, and I'm already cold."

"Shut up. What do you mean you're marrying Holden?"

I shrug. "I mean he asked me to be his wife, and I said yes."

She rubs her eyes with the back of her hands. "I feel like I just missed a chunk of your life. This doesn't make any sense." She drops her hands. "Have I been in a coma or something?"

I can't help but laugh. "It's really not as complicated as you're thinking it is. He needs a wife to get a job, and I'm available and willing. Easy peasy lemon squeezy."

The words sound so matter-of-fact. It's so cut-and-dried, so impersonal, when I say it out loud. Like he just asked me to house-sit or something.

"I . . . He wants to marry you for a job?" She rubs her eyes. "What do you get out of it?"

"Well . . ."

"Besides the benefits of having a man like that in your bed."

I press against the mattress and sit up. "The idea of having Holden in my bed has no room in this conversation. Or any conversation. We're talking about marriage as a business proposition. Because that's what this would be. A business transaction. Not a romantic interlude. He's made that clear. *I've* made that crystal clear."

I think.

Liv completely and utterly ignores everything I just said. She takes in a deep breath, wide awake now, and giggles.

"You little minx," she squeals. "I knew there was fire between you, but—"

"No. Stop it. It's not like that."

Her smile slips. "Then what's it like? Because if I'm marrying anyone, I better get to sleep with him."

I pull my robe away from my neck. "I'm not sleeping with him."

"But you will, right?"

"No."

"That's a shame."

"That's smart," I insist. "You aren't supposed to mix business and pleasure."

She grins wickedly. "I bet that man would be a whole lot of pleasure."

Images of him in his gray sweatpants come back to haunt me. My stomach tightens as I recall how his ass filled out the back and how his thighs looked tight and muscled as he walked into Tank's.

"Not the point," I say, plucking my brain out of that thirst trap. "The point is that we're getting married because it'll help us both out of a bind. He doesn't want me as a wife-wife, which is fine, because I don't want him as a husband-husband either."

She settles back against the headboard. "Okay. Fine. Again—what do you get out of it?"

"He's paying the property taxes."

After squirming around, I sit up and lean against the leather-wrapped headboard beside her. She gives me a moment of peace and doesn't poke.

"Should we just say screw this and go make brownie batter and eat it with a spoon?" she asks.

"Nah. I'm not hungry."

"I figured."

I look at her. She reminds me of my mother with her pointed nose and the mole on the underside of her chin. "I need you to tell me this is okay. Be my big sister and boss me around. Force your opinion on me."

She presses her lips together. "First, answer this: You know Jobe and I would help you, right? We could get the money. And we'd be happy to."

I force a swallow. "I know. But I'm not putting you guys in debt because of my choices. I'm a big girl. The Honey House is my baby. It's my responsibility, and you both help out so much already."

She lets her head fall to the side until it touches mine. "The Honey House might be in your name, but you know it's like home to Jobe and me, too, Soph. We want to help."

"I know. But I want to make this happen on my own. It's important to me. And there's a part of me that feels like having Holden help me out kind of takes that away from me a little bit, but another part says it's the same thing, really, as getting a loan. Which I really don't want to do, because Gramma would roll over in her grave." I pause. "And Candace at the bank is the last thing I want to face since she told everyone Chad left me to start with."

"Yeah. Good point."

We sit, heads touching, for a long time. I watch the shadows from the wax burner dance on the walls and listen to Liv's breathing.

"You know, you should probably use a mouthwash when you get married. Your breath stinks in the middle of the night," I tease.

She huffs and lifts her head off mine. "You are such a brat. I should just breathe all over you for waking me up." She knocks my shoulder with hers before settling back against the headboard. "You know that I'll back you in whatever you do. You're a smart girl, and if this is what you think works for you, then you do it balls-out."

I wrinkle my nose at the expression but let it go. "Even though my track record proves I pick terrible men?"

She laughs. "Yeah. Because we all get one screwup, and Chad was yours."

"I'm not sure this could be a screwup. I mean, there's not a lot that can go wrong."

Maybe this—*maybe Holden*—is the answer to my prayers. Maybe Gramma is somewhere, laughing her butt off right now.

"Like you said, what do you have to lose?" she asks. "It's not like you haven't been married before. And it's not like it's a marriage *for real*. You can think of it like . . . a very long, serious, expensive date."

"That's one way to look at it."

She twists around to face me. "I mean it, Soph. You've been so stressed out lately. Chad kind of stole your spark a little. I say you marry

Holden and have fun and play it up and enjoy it. Maybe you'll discover the little pizzazz that you used to have."

"I had pizzazz?"

"A little." She winks. "So yeah, find your pizzazz and have some fun. If nothing else, it'll be a damned good story for your grandkids someday."

"I will not tell my grandkids this," I say with a laugh. "Are you crazy?"

"I'm not the one marrying a man. Tomorrow."

"Yeah." I blow out a breath. "Do you think I need to tell Jobe?"

"For sure."

"How do you think he'll take it?"

She shrugs. "Let's find out."

I pull my phone from my robe's pocket and pull up my brother's texts. Sitting on the edge of the bed, I begin to type.

Hey, Jobe.

Almost immediately, the three little bubbles dance on the screen to let me know he's texting.

Jobe: It's late.

Me: I have some news.

Jobe: ?

Me: I'm getting married tomorrow.

I cringe as I wait for his answer. My stomach flip-flops. Liv places her hand on my shoulder while we watch the screen.

Jobe: How much did I drink tonight?

Me: Ha.

Jobe: Let me guess. The vet.

Me: Good guess.

Liv laughs. "Well, he seems less surprised than me."

Jobe: You happy?

Me: Yes.

Jobe: Then go for it.

Liv and I look at each other. Her brow is arched toward the ceiling. She looks as confused at Jobe's reply as I feel.

I don't know what I was expecting from my brother, but going all in wasn't it.

My fingers fly across the screen.

Me: That's it? No warning or threats or outbursts?

Jobe: You know what? I trust your judgment.

Me: Since when?

"Someone must have his phone tonight," Liv says with a laugh.

Jobe: I believe and live by the idea that someone gets to make their own choices and either reap the rewards or suffer the consequences. Just know I've got your back if it doesn't work out.

Me: You aren't giving me the warm fuzzies over here, brother.

Jobe: Nope. That's why you're at Liv's. You are at Liv's, aren't you?

I look at my sister. We laugh.

Me: Yes.

Jobe: Good. Do your thing. Just take into consideration that I will be less patient to castrate him than I have been in the past with men you and Livvie date. Make sure he's clear on that too.

Me: Noted.

Jobe: Good. Then I'm going to go back to what I was doing. Love you.

Me: Love you.

I blow out a breath and look at my sister. She's watching me with a dose of curiosity. Walking around the foot of the bed, she pulls me into a hug. I rest my cheek against her shoulder as we embrace.

"I know it sounds weird to be excited for you, but I am," she says as she lets me go. "The world works in mysterious ways. If you aren't willing to take some shots in the dark, you may never hit your target. And Jobe seems okay with it. The threats were his brotherly duty."

"You're so wise in the middle of the night," I tease.

"That I am. Now get out of here, or get in bed and be quiet, because I'm tired."

I head to the door. "I'm going home. Love ya, Liv."

"Love you, Sophie McKenzie."

"Shut up," I say as the light goes off.

I make my way back through her house feeling a little lighter than when I came in earlier. I step outside and lock the door behind me. After I hide the key, I turn to face the Honey House.

My home.

The place where my fiancé is probably sleeping.

I think back to the night I left Liv's after Chad moved out. In a way, I felt . . . relief. Just in a completely different way.

"It's time to live a little," I say softly. "It's time to do myself a favor for once."

With a smile, I head back across the street.

CHAPTER NINE

HOLDEN

That will be seventeen eighty-two." The cashier looks at me expectantly. The red apron covering her body matches the tobacco sign hanging behind her and almost disguises the pizza stain on her chest. "Would you like to donate a dollar to help with research for Phelan-McDermid Syndrome?"

"Absolutely."

I hand her a twenty, and she doles out my change. Not bothering with my wallet, I stuff the bill and coins into my pocket and take the plastic bag from the counter.

The door whines as I push it open. I step outside, and my eyes immediately flick to the rental car.

My lips tug toward the sky.

Sophie is sitting in the passenger's seat. One leg is bent and her elbow rests on top of it. She gazes out the windshield toward the row of evergreen trees on the edge of the gas station parking lot. She looks calm and collected as she waits for me to return—like she has not a care in the world.

Not at all like we're on our way to get married.

I wait for my stomach to flip, to sour—for my chest to tighten as my brain flashes a red light and screeches, "Abort!"

But none of that happens. Each step I take toward my newly minted fiancée feels like the same ones I took yesterday and every day before that.

Normal.

Routine.

Familiar.

It's from all the summers together as kids. I'm comfortable with her. That's all it is.

I blow out a breath. The sound whooshes from my body, but I still don't feel jittery. And *that* absolutely worries me.

Shouldn't I be a little anxious about this?

I thought she'd tell me this morning that she'd changed her mind, that the wine got to her last night. Instead, she let me know that Haley was expecting us by four o'clock, so I needed to be out of the office by noon, sharp.

My brain is fuzzy as I walk back to the car. Part of it is from the pace of everything. The other part is from the lack of sleep last night.

Sophie turns her head as I climb in next to her.

"Took you long enough. I thought you just had to pee?" she asks.

"There was a line."

"There's like two people in there." She eyes the bag. "What the heck is all that?"

I toss the bag onto the dashboard. The mountain of chocolate bars and hard candies rustle together.

It took far too long to make my selections. I don't know what Sophie likes, and for some reason unbeknownst to me, it felt absolutely critical that I get something she'd enjoy. The longer I looked, the more pressure piled onto my shoulders and the more desperate I was to get it right.

So I did what any reasonable person would: I bought one of almost everything. Except the orange slices and peach rings. Nobody ever likes those.

My face flushes as Sophie tugs the bag onto her lap. Before she can say a word, I start the car and pull onto the highway.

"Holy crap. Did you leave anything for anyone else?" she asks with a laugh.

"If you have negative opinions about junk food on road trips, then you can keep them—and your hands—to yourself."

She narrows her eyes playfully. "I didn't say I have negative opinions about it. I was just sort of passive-aggressively implying that you might have a problem."

I narrow my eyes back. "We aren't married yet. I don't have to justify anything to you."

She holds the bag in the air. The candy nests at the bottom, stretching the plastic into an egg shape.

"This must weigh ten pounds," she says.

I roll my eyes, trying not to notice how cute her nose looks all wrinkled up.

"I didn't know what you liked, okay? So I got a lot of options."

"Aw," she says, the bag hitting her lap again with a thud. She places a hand on her heart. "You got all this for me? Without me asking? Why, Doc. How sweet."

I glance at her out of the corner of my eye. Her cheeks are pink from holding back a laugh as she dramatizes my thoughtfulness.

"It was a goodwill gesture," I tell her. "Keep making fun of me, and you'll get an apple on the way home."

Her hand falls on top of the bag. "No one eats apples on road trips."

"Except you if you keep making fun of me."

"I'm not making fun of you . . ." Her voice falls away as she peers into the bag. She pulls out a candy bar. "Especially since you got me a PayDay."

"That one's for me," I say, swiping it out of her hand.

"Hey!"

She stares at me in disbelief for a long second. Her eyes sparkle at my actions, and before I know it, she reaches for the candy.

I switch it quickly into my left hand and hold it near the window.

"Gotta be quicker than that," I tease.

"Or more forceful, maybe."

She places the bag on the floor. Her seatbelt is unbuckled. She plants one of her hands on the middle console, her legs drawing up toward her body in the seat.

I squeeze the candy. The plastic wrap crinkles in my hand.

Sophie starts toward me. I lean away, keeping the loot as far away from her as possible and ignoring the zap of energy from her shoulder bumping mine. Our eyes meet each other's just as she's about to reach for the candy, and we come to the same quiet realization: she'll have to literally climb onto my lap to get the PayDay.

My brain starts the "Abort!" procedure I was waiting for earlier, and I know I should keep my mouth shut.

But I can't help it. Because I'm a man.

"How bad do you want it?" I ask, lifting a brow.

There's a hint of defiance in her eyes that causes my breath to stall in my chest. I have to force myself to look away from her and at the road so we don't crash. Still, I can feel her beside me, contemplating her options.

Finally, she slinks back into her seat. "Damn you."

Relief and disappointment wash over me in equal doses. I force a long, hard swallow and reach for the window switch.

The cool air fills the car as the glass is lowered. I twist my face to it in the hope that it will calm the heated blood roaring through my veins and bring some sense of rationality back to my brain.

Get a grip, McKenzie. Don't make it weird.

I toss the candy bar on her lap. "Here. You can have it."

"Really?" She eyes the PayDay suspiciously. "No. Forget that I said that. I don't want you to rethink it."

She swipes up the bar and begins to tear the wrapper. Her cheeks are flushed as she refuses to make eye contact with me.

"You might make a decent fake husband after all," she says.

I snort. "You do realize this is going to be a real marriage, right?"

"Yeah. But you'll just be my real *legal* husband. Still my fake *real* husband."

"I like how you differentiate that, crazy lady."

"It's all about the justification." She chomps off the end of the candy bar and shrugs. The color in her face begins to even back out. "So did you really want this PayDay? Or were you just screwing with me?"

"It's actually my favorite. For real," I tell her, rolling the window back up.

"Mine too. That's weird."

"I lived on them in vet school. Figured they couldn't be that terrible for me since they're loaded with peanuts."

She furrows her brows like I'm out of my mind. "Keep telling yourself that. I just accept that I've trained my body to operate on sugar and caffeine."

Shadows dance through the car as we go around a long, meandering bend. Sophie breaks the PayDay in half and hands me one chunk.

"Here," she says as I take it. "I have a thing about people being hungry."

"You're so sweet."

"Ugh . . ." She laughs softly to herself as she shoves the wrapper back in the bag. "Don't tell anyone."

She rests an arm on the console and gazes out the window.

I watch her out of the corner of my eye, sneaking in longer glances here and there. The light-yellow shirt that looks like silk brings out the gold in her eyes. A pair of belted black pants flaunts the dip of her waist and showcases the curve of her hips.

I didn't give much thought as to what she, or I, would wear for our nuptials. There wasn't time. But when I saw her with her hair flowing down her back in loose waves, like she woke up like that in the morning, I was stunned. She'd put time and energy into looking pretty—*very fucking pretty*—for this, and all I had with me was a pair of khakis and a polo shirt.

Not only that, but how do I tell her she looks gorgeous? Do I even tell her that to start with? If it were a date, I absolutely would, but it's not. It's a real-but-sham marriage, and I'm not sure what the protocol is for something of this . . . magnitude.

Shit.

I look at her again.

"I would've worn something nicer if I had more lead time for this," I say. "I only brought stuff for work and screwing off."

She whips her head my way. Her brows tug together, framing surprised yet assessing eyes.

"What are you talking about?" she asks. "You look great."

I sigh. "I feel underdressed next to you, and I don't want you to think I didn't try."

Her laugh flows through my ears. "Are you just fishing for compliments?"

"What? No."

"You are, aren't you?" She settles back in her seat again. "But since you gave me the PayDay, I'll play along. You look *great*, Holden. Very handsome."

"No—stop," I say with a laugh. "I was just saying I wanted you to know that I did my best under the circumstances . . . especially since you look beautiful."

She looks at me and tries to hide her smile. But the way her eyes light up makes my day, even without a full-blown grin.

"Well, thank you," she says. Her head falls back against the headrest. "I don't think this outfit compares with the dress I wore the last time I got married. But the veil and all that crap didn't help then, so maybe just winging it will help this go-round."

There's something about her vulnerability that has me wanting to move my hand three inches to the right and touch hers. I want to reassure her that her first marriage didn't fail because of her—*there's no damn way*—and to promise her that ours will be as easy, and quick, as she hopes.

As *we* hope.

"Why are you bad husband material?" she asks.

The question catches me off guard. "Huh?"

"At Tank's the other night, you said you weren't husband material. Why not? Really. No bullshit."

I regrip the steering wheel.

The conversation from what feels both like just yesterday and ten years ago trickles through my mind. I did say that. I know what I meant too. I just don't know how to explain it to her.

I blow out a breath and let my mind try to sort it out. As we drive over a small creek, the car bouncing around on the rough concrete, I start.

"You know what it is?" I ask.

"No, or I wouldn't have asked."

"Smart-ass," I say, taking in her animated face beside me. "It's that . . . I don't want people to need me. I mean, I could say it all sorts of different ways and try to make it sound less . . . asshole-ish, but that's what it is in a nutshell. I know it sounds like bullshit, but people relying on you equates to disappointment to me."

The way she twists her entire body my way lets me know that she's not about to just let this go.

Unfortunately.

"I don't really believe you," she says.

"Well, I don't know what to tell you."

"That can't be true, Holden. You're a vet. By choice. It's a very need-driven career." She crosses her arms over her chest. "Don't you think your clients need you?"

Adriana Locke

"Yes, my clients need me. But they're animals, not humans. I'm okay with that."

"So you just don't want *humans* to need you," she states, waiting on my confirmation.

I nod.

"What happened to make you so . . ."

"Honest?" I offer.

"Not exactly the word I was going for." She takes the bag off the floor and sorts through the candy again. "I was going to say scared, but whatever."

"I'm not scared," I protest. "That's not what I'm saying."

She opens a package of Nerds and pops a handful in her mouth. "Well, that's what I heard."

"You heard wrong."

She swallows and then proceeds to fill her mouth with candy again. It's only after a few minutes that I realize she's waiting me out. Waiting for a reaction.

"I've had a lot of people need me. It's a lot of pressure," I say quietly.

The Nerds are forgotten. She holds them in her hand, but her attention is squarely on me. I can feel her stare on the side of my cheek, and it makes me shift in my seat.

I don't know why I'm telling her this. It's really none of her business and not something I like to delve into. As I'm about to tell her as much, it occurs to me that we are in this car together because we have some level of trust in each other. She's doing me a hellacious favor, and I need to honor that.

And be open.

"I was the only child growing up. My father's only son," I say as if that explains everything. "There was so much pressure to do everything his way and to do it well. Pitching in Little League. Wide receiver on the football team. He made me learn how to play piano, and I hated those damn lessons. Honor roll."

86

I clear my throat. If I had a shirt with the top button fastened, I'd loosen it. My chest is constricted as I think about how to further explain myself to Sophie.

"I'd come home from Honey Creek at the end of summer," I say, "and he'd try to erase anything I might've picked up from here. He wouldn't bad-mouth Pap or Tennessee, specifically. He'd just make it clear what he thought of the place and that I was above it somehow."

"That's shitty."

I nod. "I grew up feeling like his expectations and somehow . . . his successes in life were on my shoulders. Like if I didn't live up to what he wanted me to be and check off all those boxes, then we'd both fail. Then I would be this huge disappointment, and that was the hardest thing. Seeing that in his eyes."

Sophie sighs. "You know, it's usually the girl with daddy issues."

When I look at her, she's smiling softly. It makes the tension in the back of my neck relax. There's no judgment on her face or smugness, like I've seen in women before when you show them your vulnerabilities or truth.

Not that I've ever told a woman before that I more or less have daddy issues, but still.

"Oh, but I also have mommy issues. My mother"—I blow out a breath before just spilling all the words into the air between us—"she died of a crazy-aggressive form of bone cancer between my junior and senior year."

The words come out more strangled than I'd like. Even after all these years, I still can't talk about her passing in normal conversation. The fact that I just tried to proves how weird this whole situation really is.

"I'm so sorry, Holden. I remember Pap telling me that, and I cried for you. It broke my heart that I couldn't be there with you."

Sophie's hand covers mine on the console. The weight of her palm resting on the top of my hand brings me more comfort than any hug I've ever gotten, any story ever shared, any well-wish from someone over this event in my life.

It's as if she truly is sorry for me. Not because she knew my mother or because anyone losing their mother is an awful thing. Maybe it's because she lost her mother too. I don't know. But the warmth that spreads through my body is a relief.

I ease up on the accelerator and look down at her flesh sitting on mine. Her hand is so small, and I wonder how it can feel so heavy.

She pulls it away too soon.

"So there's that," I say, raising my voice a little. I give her a tentative smile. "You still want to marry me with all my issues?"

She winks. "Yup. Only 'cause it's fake and you're paying off my debts."

I can't help but laugh. "I'm glad you're so shallow."

"I'm not shallow. I'm a realist." She tucks one leg up underneath her. "If I were marrying you out of love or some other crazy thing, I might want to make sure you were mentally stable and ready to actually be a husband. But what do I care? You can be a lunatic with issues out the ass, and it doesn't matter to me."

"Good point. Good point."

A small incline brings my attention back to the road. We pass one sign for a lower speed limit, and another welcomes us to Dogwood Lane. A spark of excitement inches its way through me.

"We're here," Sophie says.

"I don't know where to go."

"Oh, um, just take this road, and it'll be on the left. You can't miss it. It's the only flower shop in town."

Sure enough, we pass a little restaurant with a couple of girls doing cartwheels on the front porch, a building that says it's a salon, and a few other nondescript places before coming upon Buds and Branches.

I park the car a few spots down from the main entrance and cut the engine.

My heartbeat picks up as I look across my shoulder at Sophie. She fiddles with the hem of her shirt and doesn't meet my gaze.

"You okay?" I ask.

"Me? Yeah. I'm great." She finally lifts her eyes to mine. "You okay?"

"Never been better."

She laughs. "This is your last moment of freedom. Have anything you want to do or say before you're tied with a ball and chain?"

I study her as she laughs at her own joke. There's nothing about her that's remotely like a ball and chain. And despite the fact that I'm going to marry her in a few minutes, I'm less nervous about that than I was at the thought of marrying Jessica at some point in the future.

A man walks in front of my car. He's wearing a sleeve of colorful tattoos and a toolbelt around his waist. A black backward hat sits on top of his head. He looks in the car and gives us a little wave before disappearing into the florist shop. I notice Sophie watching him until he disappears.

I bite my bottom lip. "We didn't address one thing."

"What's that?"

"I won't be sleeping with other women during our marriage. I think that's obvious, but I want to make sure that's clear."

"Good."

I force a swallow and shift in my seat. "I would appreciate it if you wouldn't sleep with other men either."

A slow, wide smile splits her cheeks. "That wasn't in our agreement."

"I—"

"But that's fine. It's been a long damn time since I've had sex, and my guess is that won't change for a while either."

My lips twist as a hundred questions spark through my brain. Why isn't she having sex? Is she on some kind of spiritual journey? Has she not had the time? Does she have self-esteem issues?

"Besides," she says, "if we are really playing this marriage off as real, I can't be screwing around with someone else. I'd have the whole town talking before I got home, and our cover would be blown. As long as we're married, I'm celibate."

I look away to keep her from seeing how relieved I am. It shouldn't matter, and I'm not even sure I had the right to ask her that, really. But I did and it's done now.

"I have a quick question myself," she says, the smile slipping. "What do we do about the whole 'kiss your bride' thing?"

My throat goes dry as I try to deflect all attention away from the way my cock just sprang to life.

"I don't know," I admit. "I guess we kiss."

She blows out a breath. "I've been thinking about this."

I've been trying not to.

"If we don't pull it off just right, Haley will know something's up," she says. "But is it necessary? Or is there a way around it? Or do we just use it to break the ice?"

I shrug. "I'm not sure. We have to really sell people on this, you know?"

"Right."

She mulls this over. I don't offer any additional thoughts, because I want her to be comfortable, and if she comes up with something on her own, she's more likely to be okay with it.

"We have to sell this to Jobe too," she says, picking at her hem again. "He's cool with this and all, but if he thinks I married you for money, he'd probably kill both of us. Mostly you. We'll end up being a *Dateline* special."

"Great," I mumble.

I exhale long and loud as I try to figure out how to handle this. It's trickier than I imagined, considering she's the first woman I've been attracted to whom I can't sleep with.

Because I can't.

I cannot sleep with her.

Touching her, kissing her, feeling her—all that will overly complicate this.

Finally, Sophie sits up.

"I think we just try to be adults and be as normal as possible," she says. "I mean, it shouldn't be hard. It's not like we can't keep our hands off each other."

She follows this with a tight laugh.

And no eye contact.

The car suddenly seems close and stuffy. I pull at the collar of my shirt, wishing I had a bit of fresh air and some bourbon.

"We're like brother and sister," she says. *She lies.* "If we have to kiss, we keep it modest and clean, and we'll be fine. Right?"

"Right," I agree roughly.

She looks up at the front entrance to the flower shop. The tattooed guy walks out. He stops on the stoop and looks our way before heading to a truck across the street.

"Haley is waiting on us," Sophie says. "You ready?"

I remove the keys from the ignition and climb out of the car. By the time I get to the front, she is standing on the sidewalk and waiting for me.

My palms start to sweat as I approach her. "Let's do this."

She looks up through her eyelashes before looking down again. I want to tip her chin toward me and promise her this will be okay. But before I can, she starts off in the direction of the shop.

"Hey," I call after her.

She slows her pace. "What?"

I step in front of her and wrap my hand around the door handle. Glancing down at her, I grin. "Nice justification that we're like brother and sister. You're so full of shit."

"Hey!" she exclaims.

But I cut her off by opening the door.

A squeal from inside the flower shop breezes our way, and Sophie's torn about where to put her attention. I make the decision for her.

I toss her a wink and step inside.

CHAPTER TEN

SOPHIE

Holden holds the door open for me. His lips are twisted into a full-blown smirk as he watches my reaction to his last sentence.

If I could look away from his stupidly gorgeous green eyes and kissable lips—the bottom one with a slight line running down the center, making it look poutier than it even is—I totally would. That's what I need to do. I know that. I just . . . can't.

And not just because he's devilishly handsome, standing there and waiting on me to come inside and *marry him*.

No. What's truly intoxicating is the bubble that's captured the two of us. It descended around us at some point between the car and the doorway, bringing us closer together with our shenanigans. It's like it's him and me against the world.

And I kind of like it. No, I like it a lot. More than I've liked anything in a long time.

"Bastard," I whisper as my feet finally move.

His chuckle reverberates across my skin as I walk by him.

"Sophie!" Haley shouts.

I look up to see her heading across the room with her arms wide open.

She's as pretty as ever with her long, black hair and glossy lips. As soon as she reaches me, she pulls me into a warm hug.

"How are you?" she asks as she pulls back. Glancing over my shoulder, she grins. "Looks like you're doing pretty dang good from here."

I swipe at her shoulder. "Stop. Don't embarrass me."

"I'd never think of doing such a thing."

Before I can get my wits about me, a hand lies on my shoulder. I don't have to look at it to know it's Holden's.

The gesture catches me off guard, and I think I jump. Haley doesn't seem to notice as her eyes are set on him. I watch her light up as she takes him in like the tall drink of water that he is.

"Hello. I'm Holden." He's so close to me that I can feel his words bounce off my back. "You must be Haley."

"I am. It's so nice to meet you."

I step to the side to give my brain some space to find its equilibrium. There are too many stimuli swirling to keep a level head.

Walking over to the counter for some fresh, Holden-free air, I take in Haley's business. It's beyond gorgeous in a palette of pinks and grays and yellows. The large center section of the building is a flower shop. To the right is a small, cozy bookstore that neatly incorporates sitting spaces for lounging. A coffee bar is flawlessly woven into the decor and brings both spaces together.

It's typical Haley—a hodgepodge of directions that somehow come together beautifully.

"How did you two meet?" she asks.

I turn on my heel, my heart racing, to see Holden running a hand through his hair.

"We were great friends growing up," he says easily. "I'd come to Honey Creek every summer and spend every minute I could get with her."

So far, so good.

"We always had a connection . . ." He drops his hand and his eyes find mine. There's a hint of a smile on his lips. "I ended up back there for a few weeks to help out my grandfather, and we just . . . clicked again."

"Yeah. Just like that," I add.

Haley flashes me a wide smile. "I *love* love. And second chances are the most romantic of them all."

"That's us," I say, probably an octave too high. "A second-chance love story."

"One for the ages," Holden says, holding back a laugh.

He walks up beside me and pulls me into his side. I'm swallowed up in his firm, yet gentle touch.

"We used to hold hands while we built sandcastles at the park. Do you remember that, sugar?" he asks.

I look up at him. He's grinning like the cat that caught the canary.

Haley laughs. "Your love is too cute. Okay, I have the judge already here in the prep room. He brought a marriage license for you, just in case. I'm going to see if he's ready, and then we can get started. Sound good?"

"Sounds super," I tell her.

As soon as she's out of earshot, I shove away from Holden. "'Sugar'?" I ask, unable to hold back a shot of laughter. "No pet names."

"You just look like a sugar. I can't help it."

"You're going to look like a man without a wife if you keep it up."

"I—"

"Are you two ready?" Haley's voice rings through the flower shop, cutting off our debate.

Holden faces me so that Haley can't see his face. The playfulness in his eyes fades as I stare into them.

I hold my breath as my ears fill with the sound of blood pouring through them.

"You ready?" he asks me softly.

I take in the emotions on the surface of his gaze. There's kindness and concern, friendship and respect. If I told him I wasn't ready and didn't want to do this, there's no doubt that he would tell Haley we changed our minds. He'd walk me to his car, and we'd eat candy and laugh on the way home about how we almost signed a marriage certificate.

But as I stand here surrounded by the smell of coffee and roses, knowing that a judge is a few feet away, it feels . . . like the right answer. This is the first time I've breathed easy in months.

Simply put, this is how I keep the Honey House. And if keeping everything that means anything to me requires putting my trust in a man whom I have more faith won't screw me over than I did the guy I married the first time, then I'll do it.

I'm game.

"Ready if you are," I say to him.

A slow smile spreads across his face. "Let's go."

We turn toward Haley.

"Lead the way," Holden says.

Haley's face lights up as she waves for us to follow her. I fall in line behind Holden as we slip around the bar and through a doorway outfitted with dangling lights.

Once inside the small room, I gasp.

Roses in the faintest pink and lavender form a small arch above a doorway leading deeper into the building. Topiaries are arranged in displays on either side. Along the wall sits a long workbench decorated with ivy and a rope of soft white lights pinned to its edge.

A man in a black suit stands next to the far end of the bench. His hair is combed over a balding spot on top. He greets me with a warm, grandfatherly smile.

"Haley," I say, her name coming out in a gush. "You didn't have to do all of this."

"Uh, yes, I did. You are getting married, Soph. Every bride needs flowers—especially ones getting married in a flower shop," she says.

My will softens right along with my shoulders. "It's beautiful. Thank you, friend."

"Of course." She beams. "Now, this is Mr. Cates. Mr. Cates, this is the bride and groom."

Holden shakes his hand. "Thank you for coming, sir. I'm Holden McKenzie."

"It's my pleasure. Truly. I spend most of my days making people angry. It's not often I get to take part in something so special," Mr. Cates says.

"We're happy to have you here," Holden says. He turns to me. "This is my beautiful bride, Sophie."

I want to roll my eyes or otherwise tease Holden, but now isn't the time.

"Thank you for coming, Your Honor," I say.

"Please. You can call me Mr. Cates, or George would even be fine." He digs into a folder on the bench and pulls out a piece of paper. "If you could show me your identification and sign this paper, we can make things legal."

The room is eerily quiet as we retrieve the items. Mr. Cates has Haley make a copy of our licenses as we sign our names to a black-and-white piece of paper. My signature isn't as smooth as it usually is, and I kind of hate the way it loops around on the end. I also don't love the way I'm obsessing over things like my signature so I don't concentrate on what's happening otherwise.

"That will do it," Mr. Cates says as he takes the photocopies from Haley and gives us back our identification. As we put them away, he places the marriage license and copies back in the folder. "Do you want to walk in to music? Or are we just going to stand in front of the lovely little arch over there?"

Holden looks at me.

"Oh, um, I don't need to walk in," I say, feeling my cheeks pinken. "We can just stand up there and get this over with."

Mr. Cates's face wrinkles as if he doesn't understand.

"I just can't wait to be his wife," I say as enthusiastically as I can. "Can't wait. *So* excited."

Holden's snort is stifled, but not enough for me to miss it. I turn to face Haley, but as I do, I whisper to him under my breath. "Stop it," I say without moving my lips.

He begins to laugh but covers it with a cough.

"All right. Well, let's head over to the flowers, then, and get started," Mr. Cates says.

Haley thrusts a bouquet of roses the same color as the ones on the arch into my hands. "I know. I didn't have to do this either, but I did it, so here."

My hand shakes a bit as I take the flowers from my friend. "You are truly the best."

"Yeah, yeah, yeah."

I inhale a deep, rose-scented breath before turning around. When I do, my gaze lands on Holden. He's standing at the arch with Mr. Cates. A quiet conversation takes place between the two of them. Holden listens with rapt attention as the judge moves his hands through the air to drive home his point.

"I can't believe Liv let you come without her," Haley says as she brushes a piece of lint off my shirt. "She's not my sister, but I would kill Neely if she married Dane without me."

Suddenly, a pang of emotion floods through me as I wish I had let my sister come. It might not be a real wedding, but it feels wrong without her here. My stomach tosses with unease as I wish she were standing beside me.

"Are you ready?" Mr. Cates's question seems to fill the room.

Everyone looks at me. I force a swallow.

"I am." I turn to face Haley once more. "Thank you again. For everything."

She shakes her head. "No worries. Now go. Marry your man."

My smile is weak as I turn toward Holden. His brows furrow as I get closer, and his eyes search mine.

I know what he's thinking—that I want to bail. And I know what he'll do—call this off.

"Mr. Cates—" Holden begins, but I interject before he can go any further.

"Ready to make me yours?" I ask.

His head turns slowly. A puzzled yet amused look is painted on his handsome face. "Absolutely."

I stand shoulder to shoulder with Holden and face Mr. Cates. His tanned face is lined with years of experience, and that somehow helps to settle me down.

The judge starts off by giving a little speech about happiness and how it's defined. I try to focus on what he's saying but find my attention drifting to the man beside me.

Holden stands tall, shoulders back, and concentrates on the words being spoken. His face is completely sober, as if he's taking this with all due seriousness. The only hint that he's a little antsy is the way his chest rises and falls more quickly than usual.

I gaze up at him, taking in the hard line of his jaw. It's sturdy and durable, and something tells me that this is the kind of man he is altogether. Dependable. Studious. Determined. The kind of man who makes me proud to stand beside him, even if the entire thing is a facade.

He looks down out of the corner of his eye. His lips twitch as he reaches for my hand.

I hold my breath as I place mine into his, which is huge in comparison, easily covering my palm with his own. It's muscled and strong, but also gentle. So different from when he tugged me along behind him when we were kids, or held me down until I said boys were better than girls, way back then. But for some reason, just like I did years ago, I feel safe with my hand in his.

How did that freaking happen?

He laces our fingers together and gives me a gentle squeeze.

"Now," Mr. Cates says, "if you'll face each other."

We do as instructed.

Holding the bouquet of flowers to my chest with my free hand, I look at Holden.

"Do we have the rings?" Mr. Cates asks.

My cheeks flame as I bite down on my bottom lip. *Shit!* I drag in a lungful of air, my brain spiraling.

"We're not exchanging rings," I say. "It's not really our thing."

Holden clears his throat. "I have one for Sophie."

"You do?" I ask, whipping my face to his.

"I do." He pulls something out of his pocket but keeps it hidden in his palm so I can't see it.

"I . . ." I shake my head to somehow clear out the confusion. "How did you . . ."

How in the heck did he get a ring? Or did he get a ring? Is it really an ode to the candy ring he used before?

Either way, I have no idea how he found the time but kind of love that he did.

"Don't worry about it," he says sweetly. "We're ready, Mr. Cates."

The judge licks his finger and then swipes a page in the book he's holding.

"Holden, repeat after me," Mr. Cates says. "I, Holden Marcus McKenzie, take thee, Sophia Louisa Bates, to be my wedded wife."

Holden repeats the words easily, his voice strong and smooth. While he vows himself to me forever, I just pray my palm isn't sweaty.

Adrenaline soars through me as he holds my left hand in the air. He opens his palm.

"Holden," I breathe, unable to believe what I'm seeing.

Gramma's wedding ring? The champagne diamond shines under the bright lights where it's nestled against Holden's skin.

As the oldest granddaughter, Liv got Gramma's ring. She never offered it when I married Chad, and I didn't ask for it, although I desperately wanted it. It was the only piece of jewelry I ever remember

Gramma wearing, and she wore it long after Grandpa died. She was so proud of that ring, and Liv was so proud to have it too.

I look up at Holden with a million questions as he slips it on my finger. My throat constricts so tightly that I have a hard time breathing.

"This is so much better than a Ring Pop," I say quietly.

Holden's chuckle is low and deep and resonates through my body. He squeezes my hand.

"Sophie, repeat after me," Mr. Cates says.

I regurgitate everything asked of me without really listening. My brain buzzes and misfires, my body humming as I take in everything happening around me. Holden watches quietly, almost stoically, as I profess my love forever and ever.

My brain tunes out my voice. It refuses to hear myself lying out loud. In place of the vows, my mind keeps reminding me that this will be over in a few weeks.

"I'm sorry I don't have a ring," I say when it would be time for me to put one on his finger. "I didn't think . . ."

"Don't worry about it. I don't need a ring. An animal will just shit all over it, anyway."

Just like that, I'm brought back to reality, and I laugh.

"By the power vested in me by the state of Tennessee, I now pronounce you husband and wife. You may kiss your bride," Mr. Cates says.

Haley takes my bouquet to free both my hands. She wrinkles her nose in excitement as she moves behind me.

A rush of goose bumps breaks out across my skin as Holden takes both of my hands in his. Fire shoots through my chest and limbs, coalescing in my core. My lips part so that I can drag in more air and not pass out.

Holden lowers his lips slowly to mine. Every inch that he moves closer causes my heart to beat faster. I close my eyes as his mouth hovers over mine, and—

"Haley!"

My eyes fly open as Holden jerks back. We all look toward the door, where the tattooed hottie from earlier is standing.

"Oops," he says. "Sorry. Did I interrupt something?"

"Just a freaking wedding, Penn," Haley says, reaching out and smacking him on the forearm. "What do you want?"

"I need help picking out these bulbs. Meredith wants something pink, naturally, and she said these would be yellow. They are not acceptable—her words, not mine."

"Ugh," Haley groans. She looks at me over her shoulder. "Let me help him so he'll get out of here. Do you guys need anything?"

Holden steps closer and wraps his arm around my waist again. I'm not sure whether he thinks this will be our new thing, but I'm not totally mad about it. It's intimate enough to make people think our dynamic is real, but distant enough not to melt me completely.

His fingers dip lightly into my side as he slides me closer to him. I'm not sure it's necessary, really. But I figure it's a normal husband-and-wife kind of thing to do right after a wedding ceremony, so I let it go.

"We're good. Actually, we'll probably head on out after we pay you all for your help today," Holden says.

Haley laughs. "I'll put it on your tab."

"What's that mean?" Holden asks.

"It means you're going to have to pay for it in a way that she can't take it back," I say, shooting Haley a raised brow. "We will pay you eventually."

"Good luck with that. And with him," she teases as she tosses me a wink. "Now let's go, Penn, you dummy."

"Congrats," Penn hollers over his shoulder before disappearing from the doorway. "Dumb? These bulbs are dumb . . ."

"You got the wrong ones . . . ," Haley tells him.

Their voices fade as they disappear into the store.

"I'm going to be going now, too, if you don't mind," Mr. Cates says. "I have a big case tomorrow that I want to read some case law about tonight."

"Oh, absolutely. Thank you for doing this," I say.

He nods. "Haley took care of my bill before you got here. She's a sly one, you know."

Holden releases me to shake the man's hand again. The spot he was touching tingles long after his palm is gone.

I lift the flowers from the bench and breathe them in again. The sweet smell gets lost as I catch the sparkle of my gramma's ring on my finger.

A lump settles in my throat as I turn my hand from side to side. I wonder what she would think of this day, of this man I just married.

With a tear licking the corner of my eye, I look up at Holden. He has a hand in his pocket as he chats with the judge. They go back and forth, a two-way conversation, and I catch myself smiling.

The judge picks up his folder and gives me a little wave before disappearing through the doorway.

It's just my husband and me, standing together in this sweet little flower-filled room.

A shiver runs down my spine.

Holden takes a step back. His teeth come down on his bottom lip. I can tell that he's feeling me out, waiting on me to break the ice.

"What do we do now?" I ask, swinging my flowers back and forth at my side.

He cocks his head to the side and narrows his eyes. "Is this like asking what we are having for dinner? And there's a complete right answer that I have to pick out of thin air?"

"Oh no. Trust me. I'll always just tell you what I want for dinner. I don't play around about food."

His laugh makes me laugh.

"I think we completed our mission." I glance at the arch again. "I'm so glad we came here, though. Can you imagine walking out straight into Honey Creek right now? The whole town would've known by the time we got to our car."

"That would've been awkward."

"You have no idea. They might've staged a parade or something for us before we were out of the courthouse."

He grins. "I've always liked a good parade."

I pull my eyes away from him and focus on my ring. "By the time we get back to town, it'll be seven or so. Should give us plenty of time to get settled and used to all of this before tomorrow hits and everyone finds out." I hold my hand up. "How did you get this, anyway?"

"Liv brought it to me at work. Said she was happy to loan it to us for as long as we needed."

A tinge of regret fills me again for not having my sister with us today. I don't know why. It's not like this is a major milestone in my life or something.

And then I consider Holden's wording. This gorgeous ring on my finger, like Holden, is temporary. *On loan.*

"Uh, yeah . . ." I drop my hand and blow out a breath. "Okay. You ready, then?"

He steps to the side and motions to the door. "Right after you, sugar."

"You're pushing it, Doc."

He opens his mouth as if to say something, but closes it just as quickly. Instead, he halfway shrugs and heads to the door ahead of me.

I remember leaving the courthouse on the day I married Chad. I was so happy on the outside, but on the inside, there was a nugget of uncertainty. My gut was telling me something just wasn't quite right.

But today, right now, watching Holden wait for me at the door so he can hold it like a perfect gentleman, I try to find any sense of wariness about what just transpired. The closer I get to him, the wider his smile gets and the more I'm convinced that the feeling I'm searching for isn't coming.

I don't know what that means. I'm only sure that today was a good day.

I just hope this idea, this means to an end, proves to be a good one too.

CHAPTER ELEVEN
HOLDEN

T hat wasn't too bad, was it?" I ask.

Sophie sits in the passenger's seat. She riffles through the bag of candy as I pull out onto the road. Her hands stir the contents inside the bag over and over, and I kind of think she's doing it as a distraction and not because she actually wants another pack of Nerds.

"Sophie?"

"What? No," she says, flustered. "That wasn't bad at all. I mean, the vows were kind of cookie cutter, but what does it matter?" Her hand comes to a stop inside the bag and she looks up. "What did you think?"

I strum my fingers against the steering wheel. "I thought it was pretty great. Not that I know what a wedding is supposed to be like, but it met my expectations."

"Then your expectations are incredibly low."

"Really?"

"Yes, really." She snorts as she goes back to the bag of candy again. The plastic rustles as she digs through it. "Aha! I knew I saw one of these earlier."

I look over my shoulder to see her holding a Caramello as if it's a gold medal. The excitement on her face is contagious.

"What if I told you I got that for me?" I tease.

"Then I'd tell you that you're shit out of luck." She shrugs with a hefty dose of swagger before setting it on her lap. "You're kidding, right?"

"Yes, I'm kidding."

"Good. Because I wasn't giving you half of this one."

I gasp. "What happened to those vows you just took?"

"I didn't promise anything about candy. I wouldn't even joke about that."

She tears the wrapper and takes a bite off the top before settling back in her seat.

A hundred thoughts fight for space in my brain as we coast out of Dogwood Lane. I scan through all the potential topics—from when Montgomery might show up to what I will do with my apartment in Phoenix if I get the job in Orlando to how serious Sophie was about Jobe killing us both if he finds out what we're up to. As I try to sort them out in my head, my phone rings through the Bluetooth.

Pap's name appears across the radio display.

Sophie swallows hard. "Did you tell him?"

I shake my head as the phone continues to ring.

"Are you going to?" she asks.

"I have to at some point, don't I?"

She nods. "Yeah. I just . . . Shit just got real, didn't it?"

"Shit just got real." I give her my best reassuring smile. "Here goes nothing."

I click the button on the steering wheel to connect the call. Sophie tenses beside me. Her gaze is plastered to the side of my face as I try to concentrate on the road ahead of me . . . and what I'm about to say.

"Hey, Pap," I say.

"Hey, kiddo. What's happening up there?"

"Ah, not much. I was going to call you earlier today."

An amused chuckle fills the car. "Good to hear. I waited for a call for the last two hours."

I look at Sophie. Her brows are pulled together.

"And why is that?" I ask.

"Well, I called the clinic to give you some news. Dottie said you weren't there. And I poked around a little bit because you know it's not hard to get Dottie to talk, and she said that something was going on with you. But she wouldn't tell me what."

Sophie buries her face in her hands, making me laugh.

I try to swallow the nervous energy running amok through my body. Regripping the steering wheel, I blow out a breath.

"Why don't you share your news first?" I ask.

"Okay. Well, I'm on my way home."

Sophie drops her hands to her lap. Her eyes are as big as golf balls as she grimaces. I think it's supposed to be a look of horror or fear, but it's too damn cute to take seriously.

"That is some news," I say, trying to keep the tone light. "Is everything okay?"

"Yeah. The fishing boat we were renting down here had some engine issues. We'd be stuck on land for upward of a week if we stayed."

"Can't you rent another boat?" I ask.

Sophie nods emphatically. "Do that," she whispers.

"We could, but my buddy Pete's wife fell and hurt her hip this morning, so he's flying back to Kansas City. I figure I might as well come home too." He waits a beat before continuing. "Now, what's going on with you? What am I coming back to?"

Before I answer, I glance over at Sophie. Despite her antics, there's a very real anxiety in her eyes. I hate it. A lot.

I hold my hand in the air between us with my palm up. Her gaze falls on my extended fingers for a long couple of seconds before she reaches up and very carefully lays her hand in mine.

A zing winds through me like hot coffee on a cold day. I give her hand a little squeeze before resting them on the console between us.

"I have some news," I begin. "Some . . . bigger news than you're probably expecting."

"I'm waiting."

"I got married today, Pap."

My declaration is met with silence. Total, absolute silence—both from my grandfather and my wife.

Sophie holds her breath, her eyes glued to Pap's name on the radio display, while she waits for his reaction.

I shift in my seat, unable to take it anymore. "Did you hear me?"

"You got married today? Is that what you said?"

"It is."

"To whom? Are you still in Honey Creek? What's going on, Holden?"

I cough to clear my throat. "Believe it or not, but I married Sophie Bates today."

"You married who?" His laugh is loud and throaty, filling the car. "Did you say you married Sophie?"

"I did." I shake my head. "What's so funny about that?"

My eyes stay trained on the road. I don't look at the woman next to me because I'm not sure how to reassure her. I'm not even sure if that's what's needed, because I don't really know how to read Pap's reaction.

"I love you, Holden," he says, getting himself together. "I do. You take after me—smart, good-looking, charming."

"Um, thanks. I think. I want to say thanks, but something tells me there's a *but* coming."

Sophie tries to slip her hand from mine, but I clamp down on it, refusing to let go.

"*But* with that being said, there's no way in hell that Sophie Bates married *you*."

My brows pull together. "Well, she did."

"She did not. What's really going on?" he asks.

"I got married," I repeat. This time, the exasperation in my voice is evident. *"To Sophie."*

"That little firecracker would chew you up and spit you out. She's a handful, that one. Comes into the clinic and gives me hell at least once a week."

I look at her over my shoulder. She shrugs sheepishly.

"Did you know she cleans my shop once a month?" he asks.

"She does?"

"Ever since she came back from college, she has. My girl quit, and Sophie heard me talking about it one day and volunteered to help me out and refused to take a paycheck. If I try to pay her, she just hides the money somewhere in the shop, and I find it eventually. I told her to stop cleaning if she wouldn't take payment, but she finagled a key from Dottie. So I gave up. Sophie does what Sophie wants."

My core warms as I imagine Sophie helping out Pap. When I look at her, she's picking at the hem of her shirt. I want to reach out and bring her attention to me, but I don't.

I have so many questions for her. Why does she do that? Who else does she help? But before I can get too far with them, Pap distracts me.

"What are you really doing, kiddo?" he asks.

"I'm not joking. I really did marry Sophie today." I look over at Sophie and shrug.

"Hey, Fred," Sophie says, leaning on the console.

"Well, I'll be," Pap says. "Is my grandson telling me the truth, Sophie Girl?"

She smiles. "He is. We're family now, Fred. What do you think of that?"

"If that ain't somethin'. I had no idea you two knew each other like that."

"We just reconnected," Sophie says, repeating the words I told Haley. "And we decided not to beat around the bush about it. When you know, you know."

Pap hums through the line. I've heard this a few times in my life—like when I told him I was graduating with honors. When I got accepted into veterinary school. When I agreed to come down to Honey Creek a couple of weeks ago.

I can imagine him sitting back in his chair, his feet up on a desk or an ottoman. He probably has a cigar burning in an ashtray, because he never actually smokes them, and is wearing a button-down shirt with small pictures of an animal repeated on the fabric.

And smiling. He's definitely smiling.

That makes me smile.

"Does this mean you'll let me pay you for cleaning now?" Pap asks.

"This means I'm *really* not letting you pay me now." Sophie giggles. "You know what I will let you do, though?"

"What's that?"

"I'll let you tell Dottie to give me all of Birdie's apple pies. Since we're family now and all."

Pap bursts into a fit of laughter. "Oh no. I'm not about to get in between you and Dottie and those pies. I might be old, but I'm not senile."

"It was worth a try," Sophie tells him.

Pap rattles on with her about pies and Dottie and a myriad of other things I'm not privy to. I just listen to them go back and forth like old friends. There's really no one in the world I can do that with, and it stirs a sense of nostalgia for something I've never had.

I wonder how that feels. What would it be like to be that carefree with someone? To know people whom you don't have dinner with on a regular basis so deeply?

"You still there, Holden?" Pap's question pulls me back to the present.

"Yeah. I'm here. Just listening to you two jabber."

Sophie curls her legs up under her and watches me. She's so cozy next to me, so casual, that I have half a notion to keep driving forever.

"When are you coming home?" I ask Pap as I pilot the car over a bridge.

"Tomorrow. My flight is early. Eight, I think."

"You missed me, didn't you?" Sophie teases.

"Like a pain in my ass," he says. "Where are you two lovebirds now?"

I glance at Sophie as she rolls her eyes.

"We're on our way back to Honey Creek. Should be there in a half hour or so," I say.

"Okay. Drive safe. I'll see you kids tomorrow. Keep that boy in line, Sophie Girl."

"I'll try," she tells him. "You be careful coming home, old man."

He snorts. "All right. I'm headed to grab some dinner. Holden, you caught me a little off guard with this marriage thing, but I'm proud of ya, kid. Good choice. Couldn't have chosen a better wife for you myself."

Sophie beams beside me while pointing at herself. I ignore her as I say goodbye to my grandfather.

Once the call is ended, the cab grows quiet. Sophie rummages around in the candy again while I mull over Pap's words.

"Couldn't have chosen a better wife for you myself."

No matter how I cut it, I think he's right. And if this were a real marriage, I'd be damn proud—not just of having a girl like her agree to marry me but also of getting my pap's blessing like that. That's the gold stamp right there. I've tried to get it on every big decision I've ever made. To know that he would give it to a decision like this, even if it's a not-quite-real one, gives me hope that if I ever do settle down someday, it might work out.

"I always knew I liked Fred," Sophie says, holding a piece of taffy in the air.

"You just like him because he likes you."

She shrugs like my point is invalid.

"Why do you clean for him, if I may ask?"

Her head falls to the side as she thinks about my question. It takes her longer than I expect to answer me. Just as I'm about to press on, she speaks.

"I don't know. I just started doing it when I got back from Florida. Gramma had just died, and I was bored, I guess. Babar got sick, and I took him in—"

"He was a real dog, then?"

She sticks her tongue out at me. "Yes. He was a real dog. I told you that."

"Okay. You also told me he was your current pet."

"I never said that directly. But that's not the point. The point is that I had Babar with me and heard Fred mention to Dottie that he had to find someone to clean. So I volunteered."

She holds her hand up in the air. The diamond on her finger catches the light and shines like it's some kind of beacon.

"Point well made," I say, trying not to focus on the sparkler I just gave her. The sight of it on her finger throws me a bit, and I can't quite nail down why.

Sophie leans forward and flips on the radio. The beat is smooth, the singer's voice soft and nearly hypnotic. I find myself strumming my fingers against my leg as we glide along the highway.

The sun slips on the horizon as we near Honey Creek. Purples and pinks flood the sky, and it reminds me of Sophie's flowers earlier today. I glance at her to see if she might be thinking the same thing, but she's turned toward the window and away from me.

I wonder how much of this adventure will be a mainstay of my life going forward. Will I always think of her when the sky looks like this or

I spot a rose? Will a bag full of candy spark memories of this crazy ride today that began with me as a bachelor and ended with a wife? Will I hear a woman's laugh or a tease in a voice in the middle of a crowd and think of Sophie Bates?

Just like I do my mother.

I regrip the steering wheel as I think about what Mom would say about this. There's a niggling in my soul that tells me she'd love it. She'd love Sophie, no doubt. But I think she'd like this going-off-script idea, doing something off the wall to see if it works. She was fun like that. Always saw the bigger picture. When she was alive, she balanced Dad. Without her, things shifted the other way.

He, unlike her, would chalk this up to a grave miscalculation. Which is why I'm not telling him.

Sophie turns to me as we pass the welcome sign to Honey Creek.

"You doing all right?" I ask her.

"Will you quit asking me that?"

"I'm being polite."

"You're annoying," she says, but softens it with a smile. "It makes me nervous when you ask me if I'm okay. Like, should I not be? What can I even do about it if I'm not?"

I hold a hand in the air. "Okay. Fine. I won't ask."

"Good." She sucks in a breath. "I'm just focusing on all the things I can do once the taxes are paid."

I don't care what she's going to do. It's none of my business, and I won't be around to see it come to fruition anyway. But I get the sense that she needs to talk about it, so I bite.

"Like what?" I ask.

"I want to build a gazebo for weddings. And paint the bedrooms. And fix the pipes upstairs so they don't squeak." She bites a fingernail. "I also have considered getting a fancy marketing package from this company out of Nashville that Haley knows. She hooked up a bed-and-breakfast in Dogwood Lane with it, and their reservations tripled."

"Wow. That's a good sign. What's your vacancy rate now?"

She sighs. "Well, it's very seasonal. We get lots of people in the summer and a fair number in spring and fall. If all goes right, I'll get a little bump in a few weeks once the leaves start to change. It's really feast-or-famine in this business."

"Gotcha."

We pass Tank's and start the final descent to the Honey House. As we get to the bottom of the hill, Sophie sits up in a panic.

"Oh shit," she says, gripping the dashboard.

I ease my foot off the accelerator.

The Honey House is lit up like it's at full capacity. Cars line the streets on both sides. Some are even parked on the lawn. Liv's driveway is full too.

"What the hell?" I scan the porch and try to make out the letters dangling from a colored ribbon. "Oh fuck."

CONGRATULATIONS is spelled out plain as day with balloons capping off each end.

"How did they know?" I ask.

Sophie falls back in the seat, covering her eyes with her hand. "Beats me. Liv, maybe? Jobe? No, I don't think Jobe . . ." She sighs. "Dottie? I don't know."

"What do we do?"

"What can we do?"

I rack my brain for ideas. No matter what I can come up with, the result is the same: we have to face this sooner or later. And although we preferred later, we can't put it off forever.

I whip the car into the driveway into the single slot left open. A WELCOME HOME sign is stuck on a pole that almost touches the bumper as I shut the car off.

The cab is so quiet I can hear Sophie's quick breaths.

My stomach twists in a knot as I try to figure out how to sell this to her.

"Hey," I say softly. "We're okay. This might even be fun."

She slow blinks.

"What? It might. Let's just go in and get it over with."

"It's not like we have a choice," she says.

"Even if we did—let's say we didn't have to go in there at some point—we still should. They're happy for you."

She takes a long, shaky breath and looks out the window.

"Look, we got this," I say, drawing her attention to me. I give her a smile. "Me and you. We're in this together. Nobody in there knows what's happening—"

"Except Liv."

"Except Liv. And Liv gave me your grandmother's ring, so I'm pretty sure she's on Team McKenzie right now."

This helps. A small smile washes across her lips.

"Now let's go in there and live it up. It's a free party," I say, elbowing her in the shoulder. "There might be cake. Who doesn't love cake?"

"I like cake," she says, giving in.

"Right? And music. And . . ."

She gasps. "Pie. Birdie might have made pie."

"Let's hope, because nobody wants her buttercream."

Sophie laughs. The worry lines around her eyes vanish as she shakes her head. "Okay. Fine. You got me. Let's do this."

"Let's do this."

We both pause, unprompted, and exchange a look. I can't put my finger on what it means. Solidarity? Maybe understanding. I don't know. But I do know that tonight might just be the fun I didn't know I needed.

CHAPTER TWELVE

SOPHIE

The house is lit up on the inside, but I can't see anyone through the windows. Noise filters around from the backyard, and I figure that's where everyone has congregated.

At least I hope so. I hope they aren't *in* my house.

Holden meets me at the front of the car. "What do you think?"

"I think my sister has a lot of explaining to do."

"Who are all these people?" he asks, taking in the cars parked around us. "How did Liv summon them all with, what? A few hours' notice? Is she some kind of a magician?"

I laugh. "Hardly. She will get so much enjoyment out of putting me on the spot like this that it's not even funny."

"Well, I'm here if you need me." He extends a hand. "Let's go eat pie."

I place my hand in his. He flashes me a smile—one that's inherently more intimate than any others before it—and we start around the side of the house.

The air smells of pine and fall. The cool evening breeze licks at my skin and makes me shiver. Holden tugs me closer, pulling me into his side just as we take the corner by the kitchen.

"Congratulations!" rings out from the crowd filling my backyard.

My feet stop in place as my jaw drops. The work that must've gone into this at a moment's notice is surreal.

Lights hang off trees like little stars in the sky. Balloons are tied everywhere in an assortment of colors that makes me happy. Tables have been set up along the back of the house. Dishes of every size, shape, and color sit on white plastic tablecloths.

My breath stalls in my chest, because this is more, *much more*, than I even expected.

Drinks are held in the air, whoops of celebration shouted across the lawn by people I had no idea would even consider showing up, albeit at the last minute, for an impromptu wedding reception for me.

I try to see each person, one by one, but it's overwhelming. Debbie from Tank's sits near the tire swing with a beer in her hand as she talks to a girl I went to high school with. The cashier from the Lemon Aid stands next to one of Jobe's friends by a giant speaker. Dottie and Birdie engage in conversation near the tables of food. By the way Birdie moves her hands as if she's stirring something in a bowl, I imagine they're sharing recipes.

"This is crazy," Holden whispers. "Are you sure you didn't plan on marrying me days ago?"

I snort. "You were in Phoenix days ago."

"True."

I scan the crowd as they go back to their conversations until my sights land on my sister. She's standing in the doorway to the Honey House, looking absolutely pleased with herself.

"It's amazing what my sister can pull off when motivated," I mumble.

Holden takes a proffered beer from one of Jobe's friends. I tune out their conversation as my sister comes racing toward us and brace myself for impact.

"You're glowing," Liv nearly squeals. Her grin is so big that I wonder if her face hurts.

"I'm *not* glowing. I got married. Not pregnant."

"You got married. You could be pregnant next."

I gasp. "Olivia!"

"I'm kidding. Well, kind of. I'm just . . ." She holds a hand against her heart. "This is so *exciting*."

I lean forward until my lips are close to her ear. "While I appreciate this all very much, please don't get so excited about this. You know the truth. This is just temporary."

"Yes, I know you said that, but it doesn't mean that's how it has to end."

"Liv . . ."

My argument is cut short when I notice my brother approaching. I step to the side as Liv heaps her giddiness on Holden and I focus on Jobe.

One hand in his pocket, a beer in the other, he moseys his way through the crowd. His face is unreadable. His posture worrying. And his sights? They're set on Holden.

"This is some party you're throwing," Holden says to Liv.

"Well, it's not every day that your baby sister gets married."

Jobe stops a couple of feet in front of me. "Let's hope it's the last time."

Liv jabs her elbow into Jobe's side. The motion knocks him off-balance. But in typical Jobe fashion, he controls it so that anyone watching thinks they're playing.

He's not.

He levels his gaze at Holden.

"Hey, Jobe," Holden says, sticking out a hand. "It's nice to see you again."

My brother takes my husband's hand and gives it a shake. "I remember you as a kid. Spunky little shit. Always talking about baseball."

"I'm not quite as spunky these days, but I still love baseball."

Jobe arches a brow. "You're spunky enough to marry my sister."

I look at the sky and sigh. "Help me. Please."

Holden gently tugs on my hand and draws me closer to him. Our sides nearly touch as we face my siblings.

My brain swirls as he moves his arm around the back of me and places his hand on my hip. The pressure of his fingertips lying on the thin fabric of my shirt is enough to create a ripple of chills shooting across my skin.

Liv notices. She squirms in delight as she watches the two of us together. Jobe, though? Not so much. While his smile exudes kindness, his eyes tell a different story. Holden is on a short leash with Jobe, and I think he knows it.

"I'd like to apologize for not coming to you myself before we left," Holden tells him. "I meant no disrespect. I should've asked for her hand in marriage, but we—"

"It's my fault," I butt in. "I was adamant we go right away. You know how I can be."

My brother looks at me. His face is intentionally unreadable. That makes me nervous.

"Yeah. I do," Jobe says finally.

"So be easy on Holden, okay?" I ask pointedly. "I texted you before, and you said—"

"I know what I said." Jobe takes a long pull of his beer. He looks Holden up and down. "And I stand by it. This might be good for you."

My body sags against Holden.

"But you be warned," Jobe says, pointing at him from around his bottle. "If you make her cry, I'll make you cry harder. Got it?"

"Jobe!" I exclaim.

"Oh my gosh, Jobe. Stop it," Liv warns.

"No, Liv, it's fine," Holden says. "Jobe is doing what any man should do. He's defending his family. There's not a damn thing I can say about that. He's right."

A touch of surprise flickers on Jobe's face. He obviously wasn't expecting that. Neither was I.

Liv wasn't prepared, either, because she swoons. "That's the sexiest thing I've ever heard."

I blow out a breath. Watching Holden's confidence and class makes my knees a little weak.

He stands tall next to me.

"Glad we're on the same page," Jobe says. He studies Holden for a long couple of seconds before a slow grin settles on his face. He claps a hand over Holden's shoulder. "Maybe we can grab a beer one of these days and talk baseball."

"I'd like that," Holden says.

Debbie comes up and starts chatting with Liv. I stand between the two men in my life and wait for the next volley.

Jobe's tongue sticks in the side of his cheek. His mouth opens like he's going to say something, but his gaze lands somewhere behind me.

"I'm gonna . . . go do something that's not this," he says. "See you both later."

"Goodbye," Holden says.

And, with that, Jobe disappears into the crowd. Before I can get recalibrated, Debbie is standing in front of me.

"I knew it," she exclaims. "I knew there was something between you two. Waitresses just know. We watch people all day. It's our specialty. I just . . . I knew it."

"Did you?" I ask before looking up at Holden.

He bites his bottom lip, clearly entertained by Debbie's incorrect observation. I wrinkle my nose at him.

"I knew it too," Liv says. "From the moment this guy walked in— no, before that. As soon as Sophie said she saw the hot vet—"

"Liv, please," I beg. "Just . . . stop."

"What? You said it. Not me. Besides, you married him, so what's wrong with me pointing out that there were fireworks all along?"

"Oh, please."

Holden's fingers strum against my side, redirecting my attention back to him. It takes all I can do to stay still and not lean into his touch.

I can't do that—not even a little. Not only will it make him think I like it, but it will only encourage my sister's antics.

"Yeah, what's wrong with someone saying how hot you found me from the beginning?" Holden's body shakes as he chuckles. "I love hearing how you're smitten with me, sugar."

I fire a warning glance up at him. It only makes him chuckle harder.

"You know what?" I ask, stepping free of his grip. "I need a drink. Excuse me."

I mosey through the townspeople congregated in my backyard. I'm stopped and congratulated, my ring examined over and over. By the time I get to Dottie, all I want to do is scamper inside and run a bath. Alone.

"Well, look at you," Dottie says smugly. "A married woman now. Who would've thought?"

"Don't start with me. Please."

She crosses her arms over her chest and leans against the dessert table. "Start with you? Honey, I'm just congratulating you on your wedding. How exciting."

I quirk a brow. We both know she's not just congratulating me on my wedding—she's pressing for information. She smells something in the air like the hound dogs brought into the clinic. I have half a notion to point out the similarities but stop myself short.

She must sense how tired I am, because she sighs. Wrapping one arm around my shoulders, she pulls me into a half hug.

"I hope this is okay with you," she says. "When we put out the call to come over and celebrate, we asked everyone to bring a quick dish. It is a weeknight, after all. We weren't sure when you guys were coming, so we've been here for a while, eating and drinking. Left you some food, though. Didn't want you to be without energy for later." She winks.

"Wait a minute. You were a part of organizing this thing?" I ask.

She nods. "I called Liv to see what was going on because Holden is a terrible liar. She told me you two were eloping. We couldn't let that go without a party. Although if you'd have thought it through, you might have done it on a weekend so we could *really* have a shindig."

"Oh. Darn."

She snorts. "I can tell you're just upset about it."

"Totally. I—"

I'm cut off by Liv's voice. Everyone turns to see her standing by the tire swing.

"I'd like to thank everyone for coming by tonight to welcome Dr. and Mrs. McKenzie home," she says.

Holden comes up behind me as everyone begins to clap. His breath is hot against my ear.

"Welcome home, Mrs. McKenzie," he teases.

I smile at the onlookers. "Who said I'm changing my name?" I say without moving my lips. "You might end up being Mr. Bates."

Holden can't hide the puff of disbelief that escapes his lips. "Right."

"Now without further ado," Liv says. "Can I ask my sister and her husband to please come forward?"

My heart pounds in my chest. I look at the door to the kitchen—it's only a few steps to my right. I could make it inside and shut the door in just a few seconds. But before I can, Holden takes my hand in his.

"What is she doing?" I ask, swallowing a dose of anxiety.

"No clue." He bends down as if to kiss my cheek. Instead, he whispers, "Let's go before things look suspicious."

"Right," I mumble.

He leads me toward Liv. I shoot her the quickest glare. She accepts it with a sweet smile.

Ugh.

"We don't have time tonight for all the traditional wedding things, like cutting the cake. But Birdie did bring you an apple pie," Liv says loud enough for everyone to hear.

Birdie beams. "You're going to love it, Holden." As if she just realizes that I'm standing here, too, she looks at me. "And you, too, sweetheart."

I lace my fingers through Holden's without thinking twice. Only when he gives me a smirk do I realize I've even done it.

There's no time to mitigate my actions, however. Liv makes sure of that.

"But what we do have time for," Liv says, "is one of the best traditions of a reception. In my opinion, anyway."

"What are you doing?" I groan.

"The first dance. I should've asked you what your song was, but you were off eloping. So I picked one. Hope that's okay." She winks. "Please make room for Dr. and Mrs. McKenzie."

"What?" I stammer as the group surrounding us begins to part.

It's only now that I see her phone connected to a speaker by the kitchen door. My stomach falls as my blood pressure soars.

Ever so slowly, I turn to Holden. I don't know what I expect his reaction to be, but it's not what I get.

As Elvis begins to croon, his voice singing about fools rushing into love, Holden's face sobers. The smirk from earlier is gone. The levity I always see in his gaze has evaporated.

He watches me with hooded eyes.

He raises our interlocked hands and presses a sweet, gentle kiss to our knuckles. I can hear the gasps from Liv and Dottie.

My heart swells in my chest as Holden pulls me close. He wraps his other hand around the small of my back. I let mine do the same to his.

My brain misfires as my body overheats. The combination of Holden's steady gaze and gentle yet intentional touch makes it hard to stay in control of my thoughts.

I have completely given up control of this situation.

Our bodies move together, swaying back and forth in time with the smooth, rich voice of The King. The sun slipping behind the trees paints shadows on Holden's face. It makes him more handsome, if possible.

The greens of his eyes deepen as he guides me in a slow circle. The muscles in his back flex as we move, and I fight the strongest urge to move my hand beneath the hem of his shirt—to feel his back, his skin, his sweat.

The song fades into the background of Holden's embrace. Everything does.

His lips part into a smile that I haven't seen before. It's a hint of something, a promise that's just for me. I don't have time to decipher the meaning because he pulls me closer yet again.

He leans forward and lets his lips hover against the shell of my ear.

My skin breaks out into a fit of goose bumps as the heat of his breath runs across it.

"I'm going to kiss you," he whispers.

I force a swallow through my constricted throat. "Why does that feel like a warning?"

His chest shakes against mine as he chuckles. "We have to make this believable, right?"

I nod. I think.

He pulls back far enough to look me in the eye. I open my mouth to say something—what, I'm not sure. Just something to give myself a few seconds to try to prepare for whatever is about to happen.

But it's too late.

His lips press against mine before I get the chance to even close my eyes.

I inhale deeply, taken aback by the suddenness of his actions. The air is filled with his scent, his *pheromones*, and I'm a puddle at his feet.

He cups my face in his hands, his thumbs stroking my cheeks as he moves his mouth against mine. Just like he took the lead when we were dancing, he takes the lead now.

All I can do is follow along. I'm in no state to make decisions. He's silenced me for the first time, and also for the first time, I'm not mad about it.

We stand still, nothing between us but the fabric of our clothes, and kiss like we've done it a million times before. The crowd cheers.

A whistle screeches above the noise. But nothing stops Holden from kissing me.

I lean against him, my hands dangling over his shoulders. He parts my lips with his tongue. He kisses me like he has all night to show the people of Honey Creek that I am, in fact, *his*.

Finally, but still far too soon, he presses against me one last time. He then lays his forehead against mine. His chest rises and falls. His breath is every bit as ragged as my own.

"That okay?" he asks.

I can feel the smirk return.

"It was okay," I nearly pant. "I don't think it deserved a warning, though."

He bursts out laughing as he steps back. His eyes warn me again, but this time, his humor is back.

My shoulders fall in relief as I regroup my mental faculties.

Holden takes the lead as my friends come up to give us their well-wishes and to tell us they are taking off. I'm glad. Not only because I can't think straight yet but also because watching him in control is a sight to behold.

"All right," Dottie says. "We are going to let these two enjoy their honeymoon. You all will see them around."

"Good night, everyone," I say. "Thank you for coming. It was so sweet of you."

Dottie stands in front of us and spreads her arms. "Now go, you two. Liv and I will clean up."

"You don't have to do that," I say, looking at my sister over my shoulder. "I can do it tomorrow."

"No," Liv says sweetly. "You go consummate your marriage."

"Liv!" I say, my face on fire as Holden laughs next to me. "Are you serious right now?"

"Come on, sugar. Let's go consummate our marriage."

I look at Liv and then Dottie with a slack jaw as Holden guides me inside.

CHAPTER THIRTEEN

HOLDEN

Sophie steps inside the kitchen ahead of me. Her foot taps against the floor as she waits for me to shut the door.

"I'm going to kill you," she says as soon as the latch closes. The apples of her cheeks are flushed as she faces me with her hands on her hips.

Running a hand through my hair, I try to sort out what, exactly, she's pissed about.

Her eyes are a bit wilder than usual as I take her in. Her face is pink, her hair a bit more disheveled than I'm used to seeing. It's clear that the adrenaline of the day is wearing off and exhaustion is settling in.

Also, the reality of the two of us being together, and married, is hitting her.

"Why do you want to kill me?" I ask.

"Let's go consummate our marriage," she mocks, rolling her eyes.

"First of all, that's a terrible impersonation of me."

She lifts a brow. "Close enough that you know I was talking about you."

I lift mine right back. "Or it could also be that no one else is referring to you and consummating a marriage tonight."

She gasps. "I'm not sleeping with you!"

I can't help but laugh at the wild streak in her eyes. And the longer I laugh, the madder she gets. And the angrier she gets, the prettier she gets, and that makes it even harder to stop. It's a vicious circle.

"Sophie," I say, holding a hand out in front of me. "Settle down."

It's too late for that. I know it. And I also know as soon as the words escape my lips that I never should've said them to her.

Now both of her brows shoot to the sky. "First rule of marriage: don't tell me to settle down. That's a surefire way to ensure I just get more heated."

"Noted."

She squints her eyes and wrinkles her nose like she's trying to decide what to say. I could do something and redirect our conversation, but she's too cute.

Eventually, she shrugs. "I don't know. Maybe you're right. Maybe that was the right thing to say."

"Of course it was. You've been married. Isn't that what people do after their wedding reception?"

"Well, I don't know . . ." She toes the tile with her shoe.

"What do you mean that you don't know?"

"Chad and I got into a fight practically as soon as we said 'I do.' And you know, it probably wasn't a normal situation."

I don't laugh. I don't flinch. I don't even crack a smile at this because it's not funny . . . to her.

But it is to me.

For the first time, I'm genuinely happy that Chad was such an epic screwup. He's going to make me shine brighter than I ever could have on my own.

"I'm going to say this, and you can take it however you want." I force a swallow. "If we were actually married, I wouldn't give a shit if we were fighting or not. It would have no bearing on my desire to get you naked and in bed as soon as humanly possible."

If her cheeks were pink before, they're red now.

She lifts her chin. "I don't know how to take that either. So I'm just going to say thank you and then pretend you didn't say it."

She spins on her heel and heads toward her bedroom. I follow, because I'm not sure what else I'm supposed to do. I definitely don't want Dottie coming in and finding me alone with a raging hard-on after just talking about sex with Sophie.

Sophie stops at the threshold of her room. I lean against the other wall and wait for her to tell me what to do. I hate it, not being in charge, but this is definitely a situation in which I need to let her call the shots.

At least some of them.

I watch her tuck a strand of hair behind her ear and remember the sweet smell at the nape of her neck. The softness of the curve of her hip. What it felt like to have her in my arms.

The taste of her is still on my lips. As I lick them again, I realize I'm screwed. Sadly, not in a literal sense. But if I want to maintain any semblance of normalcy, I gotta get the hell away from her.

Now.

"I'll go on upstairs," I say, my voice squeezed by my need to resolve the explosion building in my core.

"What?"

"I said, I'll go on up to my room."

"Oh no. You can't do that," she insists, shaking her head. "What happens if Dottie goes up there and finds you in your room?"

I slow blink. "I'll close the door. I'll be quiet."

She shakes her head harder in defiance. "I hate to tell you this, but you have to sleep in my room. *On the floor,*" she adds.

"Are you serious?"

"Yes, I'm serious. We can't blow it now. If we do, what was the point of all this today?"

While sleeping on the floor in her room is not the best-case scenario, as she's pointed out, it's not the worst case either.

We're both adults. Moreover, we're friends. We can manage this. *I think.*

"Okay. Fine. I'll sleep on your floor," I say.

"You can have the bed if you want it."

"Right. Like I'm going to let you sleep on the floor."

She shrugs as she opens the door. I follow her inside.

"Liv has way too much time on her hands," I say, taking in the scene in front of me.

My bag has been moved from the room upstairs and placed on a chair by the door. There are four or five heart-shaped balloons in the corner. An ice bucket with a bottle of champagne sits by the bed, next to two long-stemmed glasses. It's not the most romantic thing in the world I've ever seen, but it's a lot for the time she had to work with.

"Well, this makes things awkward," Sophie mutters.

She marches over to the champagne and pops the cork like an expert. She fills one glass most of the way. She takes little time in emptying it again.

It's clear she's amped up by this whole thing, and I can't say I'm sorry. Knowing I'm not alone in my over- yet understimulation does help. There's a bit of satisfaction in that, and right now, I'll take all that I can get.

She holds a hand to her mouth to cover a belch as she looks at me. "What?"

"Nothing," I say with a grin.

"Do you want a glass?"

"Nope. I think one of us needs to stay reasonable."

"I'm reasonable." She narrows her eyes before pouring herself another drink. "I don't normally drink like this. Or ever. But since you came around, here I am."

"I don't think a lot of that has to do with me." I take a couple of blankets off the end of her bed and spread one on a rug on the floor.

The sooner we separate and get the light off, the better. "The first time had nothing to do with me, actually."

She shrugs as if the point I've made is moot.

I take a pillow off her bed—one from the farthest side from the door—and plop it down on the blanket. She monitors my progress while downing the second glass of champagne.

The vibe in the room changes, as does the feeling between us. Instead of being playful and lighthearted, veins of uncertainty run amok. She feels it. It's obvious when she goes for the champagne again.

I walk across the room and snatch it out of her hand.

"Hey," she protests. "Gimme that."

"Afraid not."

Her forehead furrows. The champagne starts to hit her full force, because she has a hard time focusing on me.

"Marriage rule number one: don't tell me what I can and cannot do," she says.

"I thought number one was that you aren't doing my laundry?" I grin. "Or was it that I'm not supposed to tell you to settle down?"

She fights a smile but gives in. "Fine. Make that rule number two. Or three. I don't care. Just remember it."

"I certainly will. But marriage rule number four is that I can't watch you do something that I think you'll regret later."

She spreads her arms wide. "My room. My house. My champagne even, probably. And you're now my husband. Pretty sure it's safe." She reaches for the bottle again.

"You're right. This is your room and house, and it probably is your champagne. And I am your husband. But I want you to wake up in the morning and remember exactly what happened tonight."

She grins a lopsided grin. "What's that supposed to mean?"

It takes every ounce of self-restraint that I have not to lunge forward and kiss the hell out of her—self-restraint I didn't even know I had. I run a hand down the leg of my pants and try to sneakily adjust myself in the process.

"That means," I say carefully, willing myself to not give in to the fire rushing through my body, "that you are going to remember that I slept on the floor and you curled up in bed and we went to sleep."

Her face falls. "Oh."

I toss her a wink and set the bottle on the floor by my bag.

"You know, I didn't have you pegged as a party pooper," she says.

I dig through my stuff and find a pair of sweatpants and a black T-shirt. "Yeah, well, I didn't peg myself to be the lame one either."

She gasps. "Are you insinuating that I'm lame?"

I wad the shirt in my hands and stand to face her. "Believe it or not, 'lame' is not one of the first fifty words I'd use to describe you."

She smiles, obviously proud of herself. "I'm glad we're on the same page, then."

"Me too."

A lock of hair falls in her face. She half blows, half spits it out of the way.

I stand and watch her, wondering how someone can be this adorable and this sexy at the same time. It's mind-blowing. Usually women are one or the other—a sexpot or a little-sister type. Sophie is both.

What do I do with that?

She walks across the room. Her shoe catches on the edge of the rug, and she uses the momentum to propel herself into her closet.

"What are you doing?" I ask with a laugh.

Her head pops around the corner. "I'm going to change for bed. Don't peek."

"Only if you don't peek either."

"Ha."

As soon as she's out of sight, I make quick work of changing my clothes. My eyes stay trained on the closet door.

I need a shower. My body is so tense it aches. Sweat trickles down my back. A bit of privacy would probably do me about five minutes of good—just long enough to take care of business. But I'm not about to hit the shower and leave her with the champagne . . . or give up one of the only nights I'll have in this close proximity with her.

Even if I am on the floor.

I need to be on the floor. *Don't complicate this, McKenzie.*

This all might be temporary, but it is enjoyable. I've never experienced something like this. If this is what marriage is, I might not be as averse to it as I thought.

I fold my clothes and set them on top of my bag. Just as I'm turning around, Sophie comes out of her closet. Relief washes over me when I see she's put on a pair of shorts and a button-up pajama top.

Then she turns around and I see the bottom curve of her ass, and I groan. Thankfully, it's covered by the sound of dishes in the kitchen.

Sophie's eyes go wide. "They're doing dishes? Are they freaking serious?"

"Want me to kick them out?"

"I mean, yeah. It's . . . weird. What if we were in here . . ." She giggles. "How embarrassing would that be?"

It's clear the champagne has started to work its magic. She places a hand on the bed as she continues to giggle.

"I don't know that I would be particularly embarrassed about that," I say carefully.

A salacious, sexy grin splits her cheeks. "We should make them think we are. Embarrass *them.*"

I scoff. "Sophie, Liv knows this isn't real. Dottie probably does, too, by now. They might be shit-stirrers, but they aren't voyeurs. They're probably just cleaning up the mess they made."

It's like my words fall on deaf ears.

She wiggles her plump little ass over to the bed and grabs a pillow. It dangles in her hand as she watches me with a sparkle in her eye.

"Watch this," she says before taking the pillow and hitting it twice against the wall.

The sound is nothing more than a gentle thud. It doesn't even shake the picture of daisies she has on the wall next to the bed.

"What in the hell are you doing?" I don't even bother to quell my laugh. "What was that supposed to be?"

She shrugs. "I don't know. My head on a pillow getting rammed into a wall."

My entire body clenches at the thought. My fists ball at my sides as I grit my teeth to keep myself in check.

"I hate to tell you, but that's not what it would sound like."

"What would it sound like then?"

I'm not sure if she's baiting me or if she's serious. Either option is dangerous . . . for both of us.

My brain flashes caution words on repeat as I take in her pouty lips. Words like "temporary" and "Orlando" and "friends." But all the flashing in the world doesn't stop the testosterone from rolling, urging me to get it over with.

To indulge.

"Silence? That's what it sounds like?" she goads.

I should let it go. I need to lie down and let her win this battle of the wits.

But I can't. Because that's not me.

Our gazes locked together, I walk over to the wall across from the kitchen. I twist my knuckles into a ball and pound on the drywall. *Hard.*

Again.

And again.

The dresser next to my fist shakes, rattling around the perfume bottles sitting on top.

I hit it a fourth time.

With every impact, her eyes grow wider. She bites her lip. Her fingers dig into the comforter on the bed.

The sounds from the kitchen halt. It's like the entire Honey House is waiting with bated breath for a reaction—me included.

Finally, Sophie releases the comforter and exhales. Reality washes across her face as she forces a swallow. "I'm going to have to answer for that tomorrow."

I can't do this anymore. I can't play this game with her.

Closing my eyes, I try to take myself out of this situation mentally for a moment. Envisioning Montgomery Farms and weekends at the beach and talking to people who don't know my business, nor care, helps.

I don't look at her as I tap my pillow into place with my foot.

"What am I supposed to tell Liv?" she asks.

"I don't know. You wanted it."

"You're right. I did." She looks me right in the eyes as if to confirm the innuendo I hear is there.

My chest rumbles as a growl gathers at the base of my throat.

"Get in bed," I tell her as I walk to the door.

I hear the box springs squeak as she does as instructed. And fuck if that doesn't make it so much worse.

The need to strip her bare and climb beneath the covers and over her delectable little body is so damn strong that I think I groan.

It's been too long since I was with a woman. And now here I am, married to a little siren, and I can't have her.

I take in a long, deep breath.

The light switch is an easy flip, and I march to the foot of her bed.

I could climb in bed and sink into her sweet little body. She'd be all for it.

But as I grab the bedpost and start to do just that, my brain reminds me that . . . I can't.

She's been drinking. And this is my friend—my friend who is making decisions based on a day full of excitement and emotion and all-around craziness. She deserves my respect, and if I crawl in beside her tonight—whether or not she wants it too—I'm an asshole.

The floor is hard as I get situated in the blankets. She doesn't make a sound.

It isn't until the sound of a car pulls out of the driveway that I finally speak.

"Good night, sugar," I say softly, unsure if she's asleep.

"Night, Doc."

I close my eyes and dream of purple roses.

CHAPTER FOURTEEN

SOPHIE

The sweet chirp from a family of birds mixed with Elvis's faint voice lures me awake.

I reach over my head and stretch until my hands hit the headboard. The thump, reminiscent of fists and pillows hitting the wall, drowns out the chirps and melodic love songs. I jolt upright.

My brain tries to filter through a thick, heavy fog. There are pictures and memories sitting at the edge of my consciousness, but I can't quite make them out. My palm presses against my temple as I try to discern what I dreamed and what is reality.

Did I drink too much at Liv's last night?

I glance around my room. Everything looks untouched. Nothing is out of place.

I must have. But how funny that I dreamed I married Holden McKenzie.

Dropping back against the pillows, I reach for my phone. And that's when I see it.

Gramma's diamond ring.

On my finger.

As if the stone has magical powers of clarity, the fog rolls away in one swift motion. Yesterday comes barreling back to me.

A PayDay in the car. A judge standing in front of an archway of beautiful flowers. Holden saying, "I do."

To me.

I force a swallow.

Holy shit. I did it. I went through with it.

My chest rises and falls as I reconcile the next wave of memories.

The warmth of his breath against my neck.

The taste of his kiss.

Him sleeping on the floor . . .

I rip off the blankets and crawl down the center of my bed. I don't breathe until I grab the footboard and peer over the top like a child looking over a banister to see if Santa has arrived.

And see nothing.

A mixture of confusion and relief floods my veins as I leap off the bed. The wooden floor is cool against my feet. My heart races as I swipe my robe off the bedpost, thankful I'm at least dressed in a decently modest set of pajamas, and locate my worn slippers. The toe of my right foot snags on the rug as I race toward the door.

I let out a squeal as I fly forward and catch myself against the chair. Whiffs of Holden's cologne filter through the air as his bag rattles on top of the cushion, and I come face-to-face with a piece of paper propped against the black leather.

My eyes roam over his handwriting. It stays within the lines of the white notebook paper but slants terribly to the right. Something about that makes me smile.

Sophie,

Didn't want to wake you but felt like I should say good morning. I hope you feel all right. I'm heading to work.

Not sure what the protocol is for something like this. Should be interesting. Call if you need me.

Holden

And I'm locking the door on my way out.

I begin to reach for the letter but stop short. The last line tickles something in my chest, and I laugh out loud.

"Of course you did," I say.

A dose of warmth spreads across my body.

I tug the tie around my waist a little harder as I make my way through the house to the front door. The lock is engaged. I flip it free before stepping onto the porch.

Pieces of decorations litter the lawn. Tire tracks mar the grass near the road where cars pulled off to join the party last night. If I try hard enough, I can still hear the clapping and celebration.

It's . . . *surreal.*

Pulling the robe tighter against the cool morning air, I head across the road to Liv's. The house is quiet as I step inside.

"Liv?" I ask, closing the door behind me.

"In the kitchen."

I walk around the vacuum still in the middle of the living room and find her at the kitchen table. She looks up from the newspaper with a cheesy grin on her face.

"How's the bride this morning?" she asks, wiggling her eyebrows.

"Will you stop it?"

The paper rattles as she sets it on the table. "No, I won't stop it. I saw that kiss. And I heard a little somethin'-somethin' while we were cleaning up."

My face feels like I've been walking in the desert. I sit across from my sister. "What you heard was your own fault."

"Am I supposed to feel bad about that? Because I don't. I'm jealous, in fact." She looks at the ceiling. "The way he kissed you—"

"Liv."

She lowers her head and looks at me. I meet her gaze with my own no-nonsense glare. She's unaffected. I, however, am not.

I, too, remember Holden's kiss. *Vividly.* And how soft his lips were against mine. The heat of his breath as it mixed with mine. How his hand nestled at the small of my back.

If all that were real, I'd be one lucky girl.

But it's not.

And I have to remember that little bit of unfortunate truth.

"Why are you still home?" I glance at the clock in the hope that we can change the subject for a while. "It's . . . nine thirty. Crap. I should've been up hours ago."

"That's what happens when you're doing the dirty all night."

She giggles at my ill-fated attempt to glare at her again.

"I'm home," she says, "because Henry is at company headquarters in Nashville this morning. I hope this means I'll get transferred to the Rockery office. I also hope it doesn't mean Henry gets transferred elsewhere without me, because I love working for him."

"Good luck," I offer.

"Thanks. Anyway, back to you and the good doctor . . ."

"He's a vet."

"Your point?"

I shrug. "Just . . . clarifying."

She tucks her legs under her and gets comfortable. Liv getting situated is a solid indication that she's in this conversation for the long haul, meaning she has questions and wants to prod.

I start to get up but am frozen to my seat by a cocked brow.

"All jokes aside," she says. "You doing okay this morning?"

The question is full of sincerity. There's no teasing implied, no ribbing ready to fall out of her mouth. She means it.

And this is why I love her.

I settle back in my seat and contemplate how to answer her question. Am I okay? *Yeah. I think so.*

"I mean, I need a little coffee, but yeah, I think I'm good," I say.

She slow blinks.

"What?" I ask.

"I don't understand how you can be *good*. It's such a . . . nondescript word."

"That's not true. *Good* means I'm . . . fine."

Her head tilts to the side. "Which is another meaningless word."

I scoff before getting to my feet and heading toward her coffee maker. Well aware of her eyes on my back, I pour myself a cup. Slowly. Because I get where she's going, and she's not wrong.

But trying to pinpoint the emotions that I'm just beginning to really feel is harder than I expected. I need to rationalize them to myself before I go spouting stuff I may or may not regret later.

That's a lesson I've learned the hard way—more than once.

Think first, speak later. Figure it out in your own mind before projecting it into someone else's brain.

Except that's easier said than done with a sister like Liv.

"I'm waiting," she says.

I grab a spoon and make my way back to the table.

"Gramma's ring looks pretty on your hand," she says softly.

My stomach tightens as I sit. "Well, I'm sure it'll look just as pretty on yours when you get married someday."

"If I never get it back, I'll be just fine with that."

I raise my mug but pause as it hovers in front of my mouth. I watch my sister over the brim. There's a glimmer in her eyes that makes me uneasy.

"Anyway," I say, changing the subject, "I need your help. Now that I'm not drowning in financial obligations, I get to focus on sprucing up the Honey House. Did you know the homecoming festivities got pushed back to late October this year?"

"No."

"Well, they did. And that means I have time to try to draw in new business. You know how many people come by and make reservations for the holidays and Valentine's Day and spring break during homecoming."

Liv nods. "I know. I have to make sure I don't write stuff down on sticky notes this year and actually put it all on the calendar. You'd think I'd learn."

I chuckle before taking a sip of my coffee.

The clouds break and the sun begins to stream through the kitchen windows. Sitting back, I prop my feet up on the chair next to me. I work my toes back and forth and feel the stretch up my calves.

My whole body hums. I have a sudden urge to get up and . . . do. Go. Paint, build, and plan. It reminds me of how I felt many, many moons ago.

It reminds me of . . . me. The old me. The capable me. The me who has shit under control.

Man, I missed her.

"What?" Liv asks.

"Huh?"

"What are you thinking right now? You're off in your own little happy world."

I set my mug back on the table. "You want to know what I was thinking? I was thinking that I'm happy."

She opens her mouth and then closes it. "I'm not going to say it."

"Look at you, learning new tricks. I didn't think it was possible."

"So funny."

My feet plant on the floor, and I sit up. "I'm happy because I feel like I'm finally on the right path. I always make decisions and wake up the next morning and second-guess myself. And it's now"—I look at the clock again—"nine forty-five. I've been awake a whole thirty minutes, give or take, and I haven't had my fight-or-flight instinct kick in one time."

"Because he's hot."

I fire her a warning glare that I mean with every bone in my body.

"Well, he is. And he's nice. And he was *so* good with Jobe last night." She leans against the table. "Gramma would've loved him, sis."

I force a swallow and get to my feet. Turning away from Olivia, I take my mug to the sink.

She's right. Holden is hot, and Gramma would've loved him. Heck, I halfway think she sent him here in the first place. But it doesn't matter. This isn't real.

"I'm really going to need you to remember that Holden is leaving as soon as he gets the job in Florida," I say evenly with my back to her. "So if you could just hold on to that little factoid and consider it when talking about this whole thing, the me now and the me when he leaves will really super appreciate it."

I wait for her to respond. To bark some witty or annoying observation back my way, but she doesn't.

I make a meal out of rinsing my cup and setting it on the rubber mat in the sink. Drying my hands on a paper towel is stretched to take a solid twenty seconds. But no matter how long I give her to come up with a response, she bows out.

"Do you want to go with me to pick out paint today or tomorrow?" I ask.

"Sure."

I turn around. She's watching me carefully. Her attention is still rooted in the conversation from two minutes ago—the one where Holden is all the things. If I don't address this now, it will become the elephant in the room.

Or the hot vet who would take care of said elephant.

Instead of sitting back down, I lean against the counter.

Adriana Locke

"I know you like Holden," I say as clearly as I can. "I like him too. But please, Liv, for the love of all that's holy, stop with your incessant . . ."

"Hope that the flames between you catch fire?"

My shoulders sag.

"Look, Soph. I get it. You know the rules. You operate so well under rules, and I get why you want to stick to them." She stands up. "But you can't stop me from wanting the best for my little sister. And Holden is the best. You just . . . come alive around him."

"I'm about to show you how alive I feel right now," I warn her.

She just laughs. "Fine. All right. I'll stop being so loud about it. But I refuse to stop saying a prayer for it to happen when I go to bed at night."

"Don't waste God's time." I shove off the counter and head toward the doorway. "If you want to go paint-shopping with me and can keep your romantic opinions to yourself, send me a text."

"Ooh, speaking of texts, did you get Haley's message this morning?"

My step falters. I pause and look over my shoulder. "No. Why?"

Liv's grin grows wider. "She sent pics of your wedding."

My insides squirm. I turn away from my sister so that she doesn't see the look I'm sure is painted on my face. It takes everything I have not to grab my phone out of my pocket and look now. But I don't want to look as excited as I feel in front of anyone. Not even Liv.

"Fabulous. Can't wait," I say with my back to her.

"Bye, Sophie."

"Bye."

I walk around the vacuum and back out the front door.

CHAPTER FIFTEEN
HOLDEN

"You're late." Dottie grins smugly over a cup of coffee. "But I'll cut you some slack today."

She takes a slow, deliberate sip and waits expectantly.

I knew this would happen but failed to resolve the situation on the drive over. Every quarter mile I got closer to the clinic, the heavier the certainty felt. But as my mind raced to get a hold on the potential questions Dottie would undoubtedly ask without the crowd of the party, my brain would just as quickly skip back to Sophie.

Writing the note—deciding whether to even write it at all—was harder than marrying her. *What should I say? Should I say anything? Is it out of pocket to say I'm worried she'll feel like a wreck after all that champagne? Would it be rude if I didn't?*

Should I stay home today?

Fuck if I knew. All I did know for sure was that I was locking the door and she needed to know that.

Maybe it was an excuse, some juvenile way of equating my decision. But it worked.

Dottie pulls me back to the present with an arched brow.

I flash her a half smile.

My bag hits the counter with a thud. I make a point of taking a long, deep breath before heading to the coffeepot. My stomach curls as if to warn me that the bitter acids aren't going to go over well.

Yeah, well, neither is Dottie's prodding.

She can't take the silence.

"I'll have you know that I didn't expect you at all today," she says. "With that beautiful wife at home and all."

"Yes, well, my beautiful wife is at home asleep, and my grandfather is coming in today."

It's a shitty explanation. I know it. And as I look up at Dottie, I can see she knows it too.

"And I wanted to see you," I say, pouring on the sweetness. "I have an inkling that you helped Liv put that whole thing together last night, and I wanted to thank you. In person."

She smacks her lips together as if to say, "Sure."

It occurs to me briefly that trying to fake all this in front of Dottie is pointless. Her bullshit meter is exceptional. I'd forgo it all and just tell her the truth, but Sophie will be here long after I'm gone. That will be her ball to play however she chooses.

I take my coffee and walk over to the appointment book. My eyes scan the records, glossing over dates and times. All the while, I try to ignore Dottie's stare on the side of my face.

The longer I go without looking at her, the more pointed her gaze gets. And the deeper she digs, trying to work out what's really going on, the more amused I become.

I lift my mug and take a sip.

"Are you planning on having kids soon?" Dottie asks.

The coffee goes down the wrong tube. I leap back from the desk before I choke all over the notes about a cat named Scotch.

Struggling to catch my breath, I pound on my chest with the palm of my hand.

"Is that a no?" Dottie asks, tongue-in-cheek.

I clear my throat. My face heats up, and I'm not sure if it's because of the lack of oxygen or from Dottie's question.

I've always wanted kids—two, to be exact. But I've never considered having them. Not even with Jessica. Despite my being engaged to her, life never got that real. Never on that kind of level. It didn't strike me as odd until now.

Because the idea of having kids with Sophie doesn't seem that strange.

My weight shifts from one foot to the other as I conjure up images of Sophie's belly, swollen. Of a little girl running around with her mother's mischievous smile. Of a little boy carrying in snakes and lizards for me to inspect.

"Or maybe that's a yes," Dottie teases.

I wipe my mouth with the back of my hand. "We got married yesterday. Give us some time."

"Oh, you've had time."

"What's that supposed to mean?" I ask as I watch her spray down the counter with a cleaning agent.

She shrugs. "Nothing, really. Just that I've envisioned the two of you getting married since you were little kids."

"You did not."

"You're damn right I did." She takes a cloth and wipes the spray away. "And I also saw the way your eyes lit up when she walked in here and you seemingly forgot I was standing beside you."

My skin itches as a vulnerability takes over. Her gaze is knowing as she looks at me, and it makes me feel exposed.

"You're crazy," I say in an attempt at covering myself again.

"Oh, handsome. It's like you forgot it's me you're talking to."

"What's that supposed to mean?"

She tosses the rag on the counter behind us. The movement causes the scent of lemons and bleach to waft through the room. Memories of my grandmother strike me out of the blue, and of how her living room always smelled exactly like this.

My heart twists around a hollow spot deep inside my chest.

"It means that I've been a vet tech for longer than you've been alive," she says. "And I know a thing or two about pheromones."

"We aren't having this conversation."

Her laugh is full and bright. "You can't hide attraction from an expert in the field."

"You're right," I say, grabbing my coffee again. "That's the exact methodology I used to determine that you have a thing for Jake. Jack. What was the floor mat salesman's name?"

"Joe? You're out of your mind, Holden."

I wink. "It's okay. I won't tell."

Her jaw falls to the floor, a wicked glimmer in her eye. She tosses her long braid off her shoulder as she prepares a comeback that I'm sure will have *my* jaw hitting the hardwood. But before she can do that, the chimes on the back door—the one no one uses—ring.

"Now that's a sight for sore eyes," Pap says.

His smile is bright and white, much like the color of his hair these days. Of course, they could just look snowier thanks to the apparent tan he got because of the Florida sun. His navy-blue scrubs complement his fit frame, and the running shoes on his feet are worn. Probably from running. Because he's still a three-miler-a-day, even at his age.

All bickering is forgotten as I take in my grandfather.

"Hey, Pap," I say, walking toward him.

He pulls me into a deep, unabashed hug. Despite the fact that I'm a good five inches taller than him, I still feel like a little boy in comparison. My heart fills with emotions I can't quite name. And when he leans back and looks straight into my eyes, I hold my breath.

It's funny how you can forget what people really mean to you until you're standing face-to-face with them. I've always loved my grandfather. I have the best memories of spending time with him, growing up.

No matter where we went or who we encountered, everyone loved him. Respected him. Talked to and about him as if he were a legend.

That's what I wanted, growing up. Even as my dad would make fun of the hick town and hillbilly people, calling them backwoods and simpletons, I didn't care. I wanted that. I liked it. While I remembered those things as I went through college and forged my own way, I think it all got a little blurry, because right now, I remember. Vividly. And those feelings I had as a ten-year-old kid are the same emotions flowing through me now.

He pats me on the shoulder. "I have to say that walking in here and seeing my only grandson at the helm makes me prouder than a peacock."

I look away so he doesn't see the silly grin on my face. "Thanks, Pap."

"He didn't do too bad while you were away," Dottie says. "I had to set him straight a few times, but he did all right."

She and Pap exchange a grin.

"I'm going to pretend like I have some sorting to do in the back so y'all can talk in semiprivate," she says, starting toward the storeroom. "But you know I'll be eavesdropping when I can."

We chuckle as we watch her go, her braid swishing behind her.

Pap turns to face me again. "So does this mean you're going to stick around?"

The question throws me off. I open my mouth, but nothing comes out. The anticipation in his eyes, the hope, clobbers me.

"I just thought since you got married and all that you'd want to take over the shop for me," he says, puzzled. "I mean, if you don't want it, that's fine, but . . ."

I blow out a breath. It's shaky as it passes my lips, and I can feel my chest tighten.

"Sophie and I are still talking about that—about what to do," I say as gently as I can. "We, um, sort of jumped into this pretty quickly."

He ventures over to the coffeepot and pours himself a steaming cup. "I just figured there was no way Sophie would leave the Honey House."

"Yeah, I'm, um, I'm not sure." I pick up a pen and tap it against the counter. "How was Florida?"

"Really nice. I could get used to spending some time down there on the water."

Seeing an opening, I take it. "Well, if I move down to Orlando, you'll have a place to stay."

He sips his coffee, watching me carefully over the brim. "You are still thinking about taking that job?"

"Yeah. I guess it's more complicated now with Sophie in the picture," I say, dancing around the topic. "But she knows that's what I've always wanted to do. And she respects that. There are no secrets between us."

"That's good. And it's good you're not ignoring what your dreams are. That's important for a successful marriage—not hiding things from your spouse or yourself, no matter what it is."

I think about my situation with Sophie and how honest we are with each other. My chest shakes with a suppressed chuckle as I consider what a good start we've gotten on our marriage.

"Take me, for example," he says. "Veterinary medicine was my passion. Your grandmother loved the beach. We'd go there every year so she could get some salt in her system. And every year she'd talk about how she'd do anything to live by the ocean."

"Why didn't you just move down there and work?"

He smiles. "Our roots were here."

"So?"

He swirls his coffee around in the mug and looks pensive. "You'll understand that more as you and Sophie build your family."

I stand, frozen, as his words wash over me. I try not to live in them, to really take them to heart, knowing the truth.

My chin dips as I keep my grandfather from looking into my eyes. He, however, carries on as if he has no indication that I'm hiding anything.

"There's something to be said about walking the same streets that your family has for ages. When I walk into Tank's and remember taking your gran for breakfast there—or into the Lemon Aid and know my father used it as his pharmacy too—there's something special about that. It's secure and real. It's hard to explain. But you'll know. I promise you'll know."

A silence that grows more uncomfortable by the minute fills the space between us. Pap just sips his coffee like he has all the time in the world for me to consider his thoughts. After a couple of minutes and a dropped box from Dottie in the storeroom, I can't take it.

"Well, Sophie and I will have to talk about it," I say. "We aren't sure what we're going to do."

He shrugs. "That's marriage for you. Taking two people and their hopes and wishes and passions and creating one life out of all of it." His head twists to the side. "Can I give you some advice?"

"Please."

He sets his mug on the counter. His features wrinkle, his brows pulling together.

I force a swallow. The uncertainty of what he's going to say is like a wet blanket on a blazing-hot day. My chest struggles to take in enough air as I watch him choose his words.

"Everyone says that love is the key to marriage," he says quietly. "But it's not."

"It's not?"

He shakes his head. "The key is respect. If you don't respect Sophie and yourself, it doesn't matter how much you love each other."

I lean against the counter and let his words sink in. It makes sense. I can see what he's saying, even if it doesn't matter.

"Think about it," he says. "You can love someone, but if you don't respect them, will you take them seriously? Will you take your union seriously? Probably not. And if you don't respect yourself, it's the same scenario."

"I respect Sophie," I say matter-of-factly.

He nods. "That's good. Always respect her. Prioritize her. She gave you her heart. If you have children, she's giving you a part of her body. Don't take that for granted."

A bang rings out from the storeroom, followed by a string of profanities from Dottie. My heart stops pounding hard enough to cause a heart attack.

There's no way he knows what Sophie and I are up to. His words are just words of wisdom. Logic. The same stuff people tell newlyweds every day.

"That Dottie . . ." Pap laughs. "Anyway, if you decide to stick around here, I'd love to have a conversation about turning this place over to you." He starts to head toward the back but stops. "I'd be honored to, actually."

"Thanks, Pap."

"One more thing before I go." He tries to cover his smile. "What's the best thing about Switzerland?"

I laugh at his joke, and I don't even know the punch line. "No clue."

"Well, the flag is a big plus."

He cackles as he disappears into the storeroom, leaving me with the taste of a bad joke and a headache.

I glance at the clock. I could probably run to the Lemon Aid and pick up one of those mini tequila bottles and down it before anyone noticed I was gone. This is much, much more complicated than I thought it would be.

People care. They're pulling for us. They want to see this thing between Sophie and me work, and I don't know how to box that off from reality.

It never occurred to me that Pap would think I might want to take over his clinic. He knew I was heading to Orlando if at all possible. So . . . *What the fuck?* Did I somehow give him the wrong idea? Will it hurt his feelings when I leave?

I didn't want this. I didn't want him expecting me to stay.

And the whole town will hate me when I leave, because I didn't love and protect one of their own. Sophie is adored here. Am I going to shatter that? Because that's not what I want—from any of them. I don't want to lose their respect, either, and something tells me I might.

One thing is certain, though: once I leave, that will be it. I won't be able to come back.

I hadn't considered that. In my haste to figure out how to get this damn job, I hadn't thought about what it might mean . . . or that it might mean anything to me. That I might care about not being welcome in this little town.

I run a hand through my hair as my phone buzzes in my pocket.

There is no name on the screen, just a phone number with a Florida area code. The knot in my stomach tightens as I press the green button.

"Hello?" I ask.

"Is this Dr. McKenzie?"

"Yes."

"Hello. I'm Angela from Montgomery Farms. Mr. Montgomery wanted me to give you a call this morning. He's had a change of plans and expects to be in"—the sound of papers shuffling fills the line— "Honey Creek, Tennessee, in two days' time to complete the final round of interviews. Will that work for you?"

My stomach sours, the acid in the coffee building a wall in my throat.

"That will be great," I say, my voice lacking the excitement that I hoped would come naturally.

"Awesome. He will see you then."

"Great. Thanks for calling," I say.

"Goodbye."

The line goes dead as I hold the phone to my ear. Pap's and Dottie's laughter sneaks up on me as it slips into the room.

When Pap asked me weeks ago if I could come and cover for him in Honey Creek, the timing was impeccable. He needed some rest. I needed some time to lick my wounds and prepare for my next adventure.

I expected it to be a sweet sort of a month with a slow pace and good southern food. I was finally right where I wanted to be—on the precipice of acquiring everything I ever wanted.

So why does it feel like I'm about to lose something in the process? And why does that hurt so damn much?

CHAPTER SIXTEEN

SOPHIE

O oh, those are pretty," I whisper.
I scan the website for a thread count. Things like that have never really meant anything to me—soft is soft, scratchy is scratchy. But an article I read recently about expectations in bed-and-breakfasts said that while I might not care, guests do. And guests will pay premium dollar for the little touches like homecooked meals, nice soaps, and thread counts.

Which is what I hear they offer in Rockery.

I pull a leg up onto the chair and take in the options before me. It's nice to be able to do this—to make plans for the future. Even though Holden hasn't actually come through on his end of the deal, he will.

"He will," I tell myself as if I need to hear the reinforcement.

The timer buzzes on the oven. I get off the stool and check on the meatloaf baking away. It's browned and perfect and will hopefully get me back in Jobe's good graces. As I take it out of the oven, scents of tomatoes and spices fill the air . . . right before the sound of Holden's voice takes over.

"Honey? I'm home," he says from the doorway.

I glance over my shoulder. His dark-green scrubs skim the edges of his body and make the grassiness of his eyes even deeper. His hair is sticking up as if his hands have been run through it a hundred times. He grips the frame of the door with one hand, the muscles in his arm flexing.

It takes everything I have not to bite my lip.

"Is it weird to call this place home? Even if only symbolically," I ask.

His hand drops from above his head, and I'm kind of sad to see it go. I turn my attention back to the meatloaf.

"I feel like this is the place my mom was trying to create at home as a kid," he says, coming up behind me.

The fork in my hand stalls midair. "Really?"

"I mean, I'm not sure she would've chosen sunflowers as her kitchen decor, but I think she was going for this kind of lived-in feel."

I pick up a knife and poke at the sliced onions on top of the hamburger. "You know, using 'lived in' to describe a place probably won't win you any favors."

"What kind of favors are up for grabs?" he jokes.

I ignore the way my stomach tightens and shut off the oven.

"I don't mean it in a bad way," he says.

His eyes don't leave me as I work around the kitchen, getting plates and glasses and silverware out of the cabinets. Even though I feel completely comfortable in his presence, his attention on me makes me hyperaware of everything.

The way my shirt covers my backside. How my pants are a little loose in the leg and probably make my thighs look big. The crazy strands of hair that I had planned on taming before Holden got home from work.

I gulp back my self-consciousness and hold a plate out to him.

"Here," I say. "If you want dinner."

"I thought it wasn't included in my rate."

His grin is adorable. I get now how women say they want to kiss a smile off a man's face, because that's exactly what my instinct is to do—reach up, cup his face in my hands, and kiss the heck out of him.

But I won't. Because I don't hate myself.

Too much.

He takes the plate from me. "Thank you."

"You're welcome." I bat my eyelashes at him and then bump him with my hip. "I do draw the line on making your plate for you, which is a total thing around here. And I'm also filling my plate first, because I'm starving."

He laughs as I take a slice of meatloaf from the platter. Next to it, I add some mashed potatoes and baked beans. He trails behind me, taking a scoop of each, and then follows me to the table.

"What did you do today?" he asks.

"I booked two reservations for next week. Washed down the staircase. Priced some sheets." I fill both glasses up with ice. "Do you have any idea how expensive sheets can be? It's crazy."

"I love good sheets," he says, taking a glass from me. He fills both with tea before leading me back to the table.

We sit across from each other like we've done it a hundred times before. It seems so normal to have this man sitting in my kitchen, the evening sunlight dancing across his face for only me to see, while we have a conversation about our day.

It's strange and sort of great if you like that kind of thing. I could like this kind of thing. The concept has me looking away from him in case he's a mind reader.

I shake my head. "Well, I suggest you keep your expectations low around here, because I'm not shelling out that kind of money for a damn sheet. I don't care how many customers I might be able to attract."

He opens his mouth and then closes it. The corners of his lips curl toward the ceiling.

"What?" I ask.

"Nothing."

"You were going to say something."

"I wasn't."

"Liar."

He sits back in his chair and crosses his arms over his chest. "My comment, while true, was probably inappropriate, and I'd like to have this evening go smoothly. Especially since you're trying to seduce me with meatloaf and potatoes instead of luxury linens."

I snort. "Is that what you think this is?"

"I mean, I can't say it's a bad plan."

I scoop a spoonful of mashed potatoes into my mouth and shrug. The move is more about putting myself into a position where I *can't* respond, because I don't know what to say to that.

He leans to the side and plucks a piece of paper out of his pocket. "Here. I paid your taxes today."

Sure enough, the bright-red ink at the top of the sheet of stapled papers proves my taxes are paid in full. As in, until the spring of next year. Meaning a zero balance.

I fall back in my chair and sigh. "Talk about seduction."

The tension I've carried at the base of my skull melts away. My body is looser, my smile wider. My brain shoots endorphins through my bloodstream like nobody's business.

Suddenly, I'm not hungry. I don't care if the dishes get done. I just want to . . . celebrate.

"You think *that's* seduction?" he asks.

There's a gravelly timbre to his voice I tune out. Instead, I get to my feet and dig a pint of ice cream out of the freezer.

"How's that not seduction?" I ask. "Isn't seduction when someone does something that has an attractive element?"

He stretches his legs out in front of him. I try not to focus on how his shoulders fill out his scrubs when he flexes and instead scoop ice cream into two bowls.

"Is that how you define it?" he asks.

"No. That's how *Webster's* defines it. I think." I carry both bowls back to the table and hand one to him. "The art of seduction is a process of making someone attracted to you, right?"

He quirks a brow. "Yes."

"Well, Doc. I find the fact that you stayed true to your word and helped me out of a bind very seduction-y."

He snorts as he lifts a brow. "Seduction-y, huh?"

"Seduction-y," I affirm. "I mean, there was a part of me—a teeny-tiny one—that considered that you could completely bail out on your part of this deal and I'd be screwed."

I take a big bite of ice cream and watch him watching me. There's a lot going on across his features—confusion, amusement, questions. And sexiness. But I think he wakes up like that.

File that under "things I'd know had I woken up on time today."

"You thought I wouldn't have paid the taxes after I agreed to?" he asks.

"If I would've *really* thought that, I wouldn't have agreed to this. But I find you to be a respectable man, so I took a risk."

I scoop another bite of ice cream into my mouth as a shadow passes across his face.

"What?" I ask with my mouth full of dessert.

He shakes his head.

I shrug. "So, what happened at work today?" I ask. "How was Fred?"

Holden takes a long, deep breath. He starts to speak a couple of times but stops.

"He's jealous you got to marry me, huh?" It's a joke, clearly, but I'm trying to give him an opening to play off whatever he's thinking. Because an inkling in my stomach tells me he's avoiding my question.

"I got a call from Montgomery," he says carefully.

My spoon pauses for a half of a second before sinking back into the ice cream again. "That's good, right?"

"He'll be here this week."

My throat burns as I focus on the black flecks in the vanilla. "That's awesome, Holden. I'll help you however I can."

He laces his fingers together on the table and works them back and forth. His teeth rest on his bottom lip as he seems to wrestle with something in his head.

I can't make heads or tails of it, so I just take another bite. Finally, his hands break apart.

"I know. I never second-guessed you for a minute," he says.

"Because that's me. Dependable."

I take my time getting another spoonful. There's no rush as I bring the utensil to my lips and wrap them around the cool metal. As the ice cream melts in my mouth, I close my eyes and pretend like I'm not here. That I'm not having a conversation with Holden about him leaving. I imagine instead that this is just my normal life with a cute guy and no worries.

A girl can dream.

But when I open my eyes again, his are fixated on me. His eyes burn with an intensity that chills me way more than the frozen cream.

I shift in my seat, needing the fire inside me to stop. But when I look into his heated gaze, the warmth only spreads from my core.

My head starts to cloud, as one's does in this kind of circumstance. I've been in them enough in my life to know this is the moment where things can go one way or the other. Good decisions versus bad ones. And I know I have to get ahold of myself right now, or I'll be on the dark side of things.

I lick the melted ice cream off the spoon and wrinkle my nose as a distraction.

"Are you trying to seduce me again?" he asks, a faint smile on his lips.

"Want the truth?" I ask, sticking the spoon in the bowl.

"Sure."

My throat feels thick as I hesitate. "I couldn't seduce you if I tried."

Although I meant it, he doesn't seem to think so. And the embarrassment I expected to feel—the mortification I was counting on to disable the moment—isn't there.

He laughs, but not *at* me. His grin isn't at my expense. Instead, it feels like the two of us are on the same side of a joke or story. Together. Which is not what I had in mind.

This was supposed to be a wedge between us, not a glue.

Damn it.

"Do you believe that?" he asks.

I nod. "Yeah. For sure. I don't know anything about seducing someone."

His chuckle is gritty as he sits back again. Even though it's only an extra few inches between us, I'm grateful for it. I need it. I need to disable the explosion ticking inside my body.

"Don't laugh at me," I say.

"Oh, sugar. I'm not laughing at you."

I point my spoon at him. "Yes, you are."

"Why do you act like it's impossible for you to seduce me?"

I want to say, "Because you're you and I'm me." That I don't have the experience or confidence to go after a man who obviously doesn't need me. I want to explain that I wouldn't know where to start at actually trying to attract someone like him. But I don't say that because it's humiliating and probably fairly obvious.

My spoon clinks as it hits the china. I get to my feet, cheeks pink, and head to the sink. I'm rinsing the bowl when he speaks again.

"Are you going to answer me?" he asks.

"No."

I think he laughs again, but I don't turn around to make sure.

"Do you know what I find seductive?" he asks.

My body stills. I try to shake my head, but it barely moves.

The chair squeaks as he gets up. The legs scratch against the hardwood as if he's pushing it in.

"Kindness," he says. "Humor. Class. Beauty."

I tuck a piece of hair behind my ear. "So not lingerie and sweet nothings whispered in your ear?" I joke.

"Hardly. Underpromising and overdelivering are what turns me on."

I gulp. "Good to know."

"What turns you on, Sophie?"

"That sounds like a loaded question."

He stands behind me. I can't feel him or see him, but I definitely am aware of his presence. The energy bouncing off him collides with my back and almost whirls me around to face him.

I shut the water off and grip the edge of the sink.

"It's not," he says. "So, answer it. *Please.*"

The added "please," filled with sweet sarcasm, makes me grin.

I should answer with some self-deprecating mishmash of qualities and then slip outside for some fresh air. I'm in quicksand and I know it. But instead of grasping at a branch overhead and trying to pull myself up and out like any rational person would do, I just breathe evenly. Slowly. And then, with deliberate movements, I turn around to face him.

His eyes are hooded, his teeth nibbling at the corner of his lip. The locks of hair that have fallen on his forehead are darker, the shadows against his skin broodier. The testosterone that ripples off his body and pummels mine is intense and intoxicating, and I grab the counter behind me to keep steady.

"This is doing it for me," I say, my gaze pinning his.

He seems to be as surprised that I said that as I am. His brows shoot upward before his mouth dissolves into the sexiest, most "You sure you want this, Sophie?" smirk that I've ever seen.

"You're making it very hard to be a gentleman," he says.

"Who are you kidding? You've dangled spit in my face before. You're hardly a gentleman."

His chuckle tugs my laugh along with it. He wipes a hand down his angled jaw and watches me from a couple of steps back.

My body hums under his attention. And while I'm usually second-guessing things at this point in the game—Does he just want to get laid? Does he specifically want to sleep with me? What will this mean, if anything, if we act on all this?—I'm as cool as a cucumber.

Maybe it's because I know this might be over sooner than I even really thought. Maybe I just want this one memory of him.

As his tongue slips along his bottom lip, I sigh.

Maybe it's simply that I'm only human and I want that tongue on me.

CHAPTER SEVENTEEN

SOPHIE

He drops his hand. "In normal situations, I'd construe your behavior as consent. But this is not a normal situation, and you are not a normal woman."

I lift a brow. He grins.

"What do you want to hear?" I ask.

His Adam's apple bobs in his throat. I think I might explode.

"Is that a trick question?" he asks.

"Nope."

"So 'you panting my name' would be a sufficient answer?"

I snort. "Trash answer, Doc."

He shrugs. "Look, I'm not functioning on all my brain cells right now. Thinking with two heads is hard."

"Especially if they're both hardheaded."

He flashes me a look, making me giggle.

"Look, maybe this isn't the right thing after all." I start to turn around, but he cages me against the counter with both hands.

His breathing is shallow, his body warm as it *almost* touches mine. I stand still and wonder if he can hear the speed of my blood roaring through my veins.

If I moved, even a little bit, our skin would make contact, and that would be it for me. I'd dissolve on the spot. But I don't twitch a muscle, and neither does he. He doesn't even flutter those ridiculous lashes.

"I want this to be the right thing," he says. "But I don't want to complicate things between us."

I search his eyes for the truth. It's not hidden; it's right there on the surface.

He wants me as much as I want him. That feeling alone is heady as fuck. But there's also a stroke of concern, of care and caution, because he's looking at me. And while that should make me rethink whether this is a good decision, it instead makes me want him that much more.

There will never be another Holden McKenzie waltzing into my life. There aren't many men like him. I know that's a fact. And while it might be a good thing in its own way, it also makes it an opportunity. One that I don't want to pass up.

"Things are already kind of tangled up, aren't they?" I ask.

He grins. "Does this mean you want me?"

My legs ache. The apex of my thighs burns. My stomach squeezes so hard I nearly yelp for mercy.

I reach out and touch his cheek. A smattering of stubble dots his skin. The coarseness of it against my palm is the final shot to my libido.

I look him in the eye and smile. "Only if you agree that I wasn't the one trying to seduce you."

He leans forward, his breath hot against my neck. "But you were."

"I . . ." Words fail me as he presses kiss after kiss along my throat. My head falls back as he touches his lips in a trail along my jawline. A moan escapes my lips seconds before his mouth finds them.

I arch my back as his lips work against mine. With each second that passes, his kisses become more frenzied. It's as if he's waiting for my consent—some kind of confirmation that I really do want this. Or maybe it's that he's giving me time to change my mind. But what is crystal clear is that *he* wants it.

It's a good thing that I do too.

His tongue parts my lips. He grasps my head in both hands, and his tongue enters my mouth. I lean against the counter, my knees going weak, as he slowly and expertly demonstrates exactly how into this he is.

I grip his hips and tug him closer. His hardened cock presses into my stomach. I whimper as he slips out of my mouth and sucks on my bottom lip, letting it spring free only when I open my eyes.

"See?" I say, gasping for air. "It's you who's seducing me."

He grins as he lifts the hem of my shirt over my head. Taking a step back, he looks me up and down. "I'm not too sure about that, sugar."

Our eyes meet. As if a clock is ticking down the seconds, we watch each other to see who will make the next move.

I can taste his sweetness on my lips. My skin blazes from the caress of the backs of his knuckles. My core shakes with desperation, needing a release from the energy building.

"Last chance," he says.

"Do you want me to back out?"

"Fuck no."

"Good."

With a confidence I didn't know I had, I reach out and raise his shirt up over his head. His grin deepens as he assists me in my venture.

The fabric of my bra brushes across his chest. My nipples pearl, begging for his touch.

I take a step back and assess.

His abs are cut into six imperfect squares. A line of dark hair trails from his belly button to below his waistband. His shoulders are impeccable, his pectoral muscles rock solid.

If this is a dream, I hope I never wake up.

"You know what?" I ask. "Screw it. Maybe I am trying to seduce you."

He laughs, the sound full and loud, as I dig my fingers into the sides of his scrubs and shove them down his legs. As if this were the cue he was looking for, he jumps into action.

We become a living, breathing, frenzied mess of movements. Our hands fly everywhere—undoing clasps, stepping out of pants, throwing fabric to one side or the other. My bra hangs from the handle of the microwave. His scrubs lie atop the bowl of fruit on the counter. My fingers are in his hair, pulling his head to mine. His hands dig into my behind and drag my body into his.

His lips press, his tongue laps, leaving a trail of his warm saliva all over my skin. My brain tries to process the sensations one at a time but misfires as his nails bite into my ass and he lifts me onto the counter.

I scoot myself to the edge, the stone cool beneath me. A condom appears from his wallet and he slides it along his thick, hard shaft. I watch, applauding myself for not springing off the counter and climbing him like a freaking tree.

"Ready?" he asks, holding himself in his hand.

"I was ready ten minutes ago."

He grins as he approaches me. "Only ten?"

"Fine," I say, positioning myself so he can enter me. "I wouldn't have turned you down when I was seventeen."

He shakes his head as he rests a palm on my shoulder. His cock hovers over my opening and he watches me with the most alluring grin.

"I wouldn't have turned you down either," he says.

"I—*ah!*"

He slips inside me in one slow, deliciously smooth move. I scoot closer to the edge, wanting, needing, willing to beg for more.

"Holden . . ."

His eyes roll to the back of his head as he fills me completely. "That. That's what I've been dreaming about, right fucking there."

"As you slept on the floor?" I tease, wincing as he rolls his hips.

He opens his eyes. "You're going to tease me *now*? While I'm inside you." He pulls back until the head of his cock is almost out before filling me again.

My body shivers at his words—"I'm inside you." I'm not in any position, in any sense of the word, to deal with that kind of language. So I just stick with it.

"I'll always tease you," I moan. "Whether or not you're *inside me.*"

He stills. His palm on my shoulder tenses before he grips me again. I think he whispers, "I hope so," but I'm not sure. Before I can think about it too much, he's driving into me again.

The air fills with a mixture of his cologne and the smell of sex. My hair sticks to my back as it topples from the haphazard knot at the top of my head.

He runs a palm down my chest and over each breast, rubbing each nipple against the calloused skin of his hand. It's sensation overload, and I whimper as it all boils together in one crazy, hot cauldron deep in my core.

"Damn you . . . ," I say, each word uttered in a hiccupped breath.

His knees hit the cabinet doors with each thrust, knocking into the wood with a force that has me vaguely concerned about repairs. I can feel his fingers in the skin of my backside as he drags me so that I'm half-off the stone. I twist my leg around his waist, my top half barely propped up on my elbows.

As I gaze up at his face, it's like gasoline has been added to an already burning fire.

"Holden!" I shout, the flames licking through my veins.

He doesn't say a word, just watches me fall apart beneath him.

I thrash my head back and forth, the explosion barreling through my body almost too much to take. Colors paint my sight, the sound of our bodies coming together ricocheting through my ears. I can hear, smell, taste nothing but Holden McKenzie. It's incredible.

He eases his thrusts slowly, deliberately, taking his cues from me. Finally, when there's nothing left to coax from my body, he stills.

His hand comes out and brushes a strand of hair off my face. The tenderness in his eyes makes me shiver.

I wait for him to speak, to say something to break the ice. I don't even care if it's something annoying right now.

Instead, he pulls out and then surprises me. He slips one arm under my back and the other behind my legs.

Before I know what's happening, I'm being carried through the kitchen.

"What are you doing?" I ask, my throat tight and raw.

"Taking you to bed."

"Why?"

He grins down at me as he kicks my bedroom door open. "Because I haven't finished yet."

I rest my head on his shoulder, my arm draped around his neck. Sweat dots his skin and coats his hair, and I don't tell him, but I could stay right here for the rest of the night.

He lays me in the middle of my bed before climbing in with me. On his knees, he hovers over me.

The air between us shifts. The lust from earlier seems to have disappeared, and in its place is a reverence that settles heavily on my chest.

He touches his lips to mine before rolling me on top of him. I straddle his waist and watch him smile up at me.

"You're enjoying this, aren't you?" I tease.

"You have no idea." He raises his hips until his cock digs into my skin. "Now will you please sit on me so I can enjoy you again?"

I nod in appreciation. Guiding him to my opening, I pause before I sit down.

"I would like to say that I appreciate your use of 'please.' Good manners, Doc," I say.

He moves himself, trying to shove into me again. I stay lifted ever so slightly so he can't.

He fires me a faux glare before gripping my hips. "Please."

I drop down in one swift, fluid movement until he's sunk completely inside me. We move together, moaning in unison. It's a dance that feels familiar, yet so foreign at the same time. Each movement is matched perfectly, a push for a pull. Sometimes slow, sometimes fast, but always *right*.

I had no idea. Not a damn clue that sex could be . . . *like this*. So good. So hot. So . . . everything I've never had before.

It's not a completely fair apples-to-apples kind of comparison when considering the men I've been with before, but still. This sets the bar. *High*.

He takes care of my body, makes me laugh, treats me like both his friend and his lover. It's the wildest experience I've ever had and one I'm sure I'll never forget.

Even when he leaves. Especially when he leaves.

When I'm snuggled next to him hours after the sun has gone down—and after Holden has gone down . . . twice—and our dinner is cold and mostly untouched, that unfortunate little reminder rears its head. *This is so very temporary.* Magnificent and incredible, but still so impermanent.

And I fall asleep with my cheek against Holden's chest and my heart safely inside mine.

CHAPTER EIGHTEEN

SOPHIE

The morning sun shines brightly through my office window. Steam rises from the cup of coffee on the corner of my desk and lures me in with its heavenly scent. I pull the mug closer and take a deep breath of the aroma with the hope that it will ground me. Put my feet on the floor. Lure me back into reality.

Because after last night? My head is in the clouds.

I floated from my bed to the kitchen—where I found a freshly brewed pot of coffee waiting for me. Somehow I drifted toward my office—where I discovered that Holden had locked the front door on his way out this morning. Then I sort of danced to my desk with not a care in the world, and that's concerning.

I have cares in the world. Lots of them. It would behoove me to remember that.

"It's just because I got some sleep last night," I say before taking a sip of coffee. But even I don't believe that. The only part that sleep plays in how I feel this morning is because I slept on Holden, after sleeping with him.

"It's not a big deal," I say, letting the warmth of the mug soak into my palms. "I'm a big girl. I can separate sex from . . . emotions."

I set my mug down and wish it were that easy to set aside feelings. Particularly the ones that I have an inkling are going to get me in trouble.

In the center of my desk lies a receipt from the elderly couple who stayed with me. Mr. Ingram's signature is shaky. So are the words "Bless You" that he carefully printed along the bottom of the paper when he checked himself and his wife out early one morning.

I settle back in my seat and gaze out the window. The Ingrams have such a beautiful relationship. He'd hold her hand when they walked to their car, and I'm not sure she ever opened a door for herself. She laughed at his jokes, which, by the little wink she'd toss me, I'm sure she's heard a hundred times over their years together. It's as if the years they've spent together have drawn them even closer.

All I can figure is that they got married in a different day and age—when attention spans were longer. People valued things differently back then. The top of the totem pole wasn't a shiny car or a fancy college degree. It was a life well curated with people who love you.

I pick up a picture frame from beside my computer. In the photo, Gramma is bursting at the seams with pride as my brother, my sister, and I stand beside her.

My thumb runs over the glass.

"I'm sorry I didn't understand in time," I whisper to her.

My chest tightens as I think about how I let her down. I shunned her advice. I was so determined to leave, to do something bigger and better than anything in Honey Creek.

The truth is that life outside my hometown was filled with shiny objects and dazzling promises. But what it lacked was something even better: the simple things.

S'mores on paper plates in the evenings with neighbors. Dottie's chicken noodle soup when you're sick. Your sister coming over in the middle of the night because she watched a crime documentary and is too scared to sleep alone. The ability to pick your brother up from the bar when he's had too much to drink.

"Shake this crap off," I mumble.

The crunch of gravel grabs my attention, and I look out the window. My brother's car pulls next to the flagpole.

The front door of the Honey House squeaks open. By the time the door shuts, Jobe is standing in my office with a grin as wide as Tennessee.

"What?" I ask, raising a brow.

"What do you mean, 'What'?"

"I mean, what are you looking at me like that for?"

"What am I looking at you like?"

"Like you want me to throw my stapler at you."

He chuckles.

I jiggle the mouse on my computer. The screen comes to life with a beach scene, prompting me for my password. I type it in as my brother makes himself at home. He sits across from me and props a boot on the edge of my desk.

"Get your foot down," I tell him.

"Sorry." He sits up with both feet on the ground. "Better?"

"Yes."

"Great."

He holds my gaze. The corner of his lip slides up as if it's trying to slide something out of me.

"Wanna tell me what this is all about?" I ask.

He relaxes back in his chair. "How's married life treating you?"

"Good."

"Just 'good'? I didn't come over last night in case you were getting some—"

"Jobe!" I sit back in my chair so hard that it rolls a little from the force. "What are you doing?"

My face heats as I look into my brother's brown eyes. There's a twinkle of roguery, of the troublemaker I know him to be. But despite his antics, he's the one man I've been able to count on my whole life. He might come to my aid with a hangover or with a girl I don't know—or even two, sometimes—on his arm, but he comes. Every time. It makes it hard to be irritated with him for too long.

"What?" he asks. "Is it that crazy to assume you might be screwing your husband?"

"I'm not talking about my sex life with you. That's just . . . no. Ew."

"Sounds to me like you might not have a sex life to talk about. Because if you aren't fucking like rabbits on day . . . whatever it is of your marriage, then something might be wrong."

My face is in flames. I can tell by the heat radiating from it and from Jobe's triumphant grin.

Jerk.

"Oh my gosh," I groan. "Can you just please go to the kitchen and get breakfast and get out of here? Don't you have someone in this county to sell a house to?"

Instead of getting up, he settles in. I consider how much damage my stapler would actually cause. Emergency-room kind of damage I can't handle, but he could probably superglue a wound shut himself without too much of a problem.

It might be worth it.

"I actually don't have an appointment until noon. And I was supposed to go fishing with Aaron this morning, but he canceled on me. Lucky for you," he says with a grin.

My head falls to the desk, and my forehead rests gently on the edge. "Please tell me you just remembered that's not true and have to leave."

"I—" Jobe begins but is cut off by another voice coming from the kitchen.

"Hey," Liv shouts down the hallway.

"In here," I call.

Jobe looks over his shoulder as our sister comes barreling into the room. She plops down in the chair next to Jobe with a hefty sigh.

She looks from me to Jobe and back to me. "Did I miss something?"

"No. Just Jobe interrogating me on my sex life, of all things," I say, firing him a dirty look.

He grins. "Of note—there isn't much of one to discuss."

Liv snorts, throwing a hand through the air. "I'm going to have to call bullshit on that. There's no way, when a woman is alone in a house with that man, of all men—no offense, Jobe. Especially when he looks at Sophie the way he does." She leans against the armrest and looks at our brother. "She just doesn't want to tell you the dirty details."

"Good, because I actually don't want them."

"Then why are you asking?" I ask.

"I'm just trying to rile you up a little bit. It's so easy these days." He leans forward and rests his elbows on his knees. "He's good for you, I think. I might have to actually like the bastard."

"You don't?" Liv asks. "There's not much not to like . . ."

Jobe rolls his eyes as he gets to his feet. "You're insinuating . . . dirty things about your brother-in-law, Livvie."

"Yeah, Livvie," I tease.

"Whatever. I was only stating things that are general knowledge. Facts, if you will." Liv shrugs. "Anyway, my boss is getting transferred to Rockery. So if either of you are hiring, I'll take the job."

Liv gives us her best practiced smile.

"Yeah, I'm good," Jobe says. "But thanks anyway."

"What?" Liv asks. "You don't think I'd be a good personal assistant? Every Realtor needs a personal assistant."

He winces as he looks down at her. "I'd like one I can fuck. Thanks."

Liv's jaw drops open as I laugh.

"You still have your job, right?" I ask.

"Yeah," Liv says. "But Corporate is sending Henry's replacement next week, and I don't want to work with anyone else." She sticks out her bottom lip. "Henry spoils me."

Jobe chuckles as he heads to the door. "I'm grabbing breakfast and then heading out. Chin up, Liv. Call me if you need me, Soph."

"I will," I say.

"And tell that husband of yours to call me too. I want to take him out for a beer."

I narrow my eyes. "A beer?"

"A beer," he repeats, grinning.

"Just a beer, Jobe."

His grin grows wider. "That's what I said, isn't it?"

"I know what you're thinking," I warn.

"Me too," Liv chimes in. "This never ends well."

Jobe shrugs as he starts down the hallway. I roll my eyes as he disappears from sight and sound.

Liv gets to her feet. "I have to get to work too."

"Have a good day," I tell her.

"You too."

The door closes roughly behind her.

I swivel in my chair and watch as Jobe climbs into his truck. He revs the engine as Liv walks in front of it, earning him her middle finger.

Despite the antics and irritation of my brother, I find myself smiling as he pulls away. I turn back toward my desk when Gramma's—*my*—wedding ring catches the light. It sparkles, shining beautifully just for me.

My chest squeezes as I think of the way Holden's eyes shone similarly the moment he placed it on my finger. And how similarly, too, my heart feels when I think of him, compared to when I think of my family.

It's like he's my family.

And while that might not technically be true, it feels real. Genuine. True. And it warms me to the core.

While I let it.

I live in that place for a few minutes—a place full of locked doors before work, shared meals after, and kisses in bed that feel . . . special.

It gives me hope that those can be a part of my life one day. That someone will want to share those things—their life—with me, no matter what.

A love like the Ingrams'.

That's what I want.

Their relationship is something I have always dreamed of but have never really seen. I've only imagined what a connection like that might look like. Now, after spending time with Holden, I have an inkling of what it might *feel* like.

I know the agreement we made about our marriage. It's no great question what his plans are. But as I study the ring on my finger and think about the way his lips feel against my forehead in the morning when he thinks I'm sleeping, a sliver of hope settles in my heart, anyway. Against better judgment, I let my heart and head consider that maybe, in an unbelievable twist from the universe, Holden will pick me.

A burning sensation flows through my core—a warning shot from the part of my brain saddled with protecting me. The jolt is uncomfortable, searing in my chest like a drink of hot coffee right from the pot. It serves its point to remind me of the dangers of hope. Of just how destructive the pain can be if I daydream too much.

Because at the end of the day, that's what a life with Holden is: a daydream. And I'd be smart to remember that.

My hand falls to my side.

I clear my throat.

"Don't get too ahead of yourself," I say and get back to work.

CHAPTER NINETEEN

HOLDEN

The song on the radio is a country tune. It's something about spray-painting cars and spending summers stacking hay—about growing up in the middle of nowhere.

I pilot the car onto the street. The warm afternoon sun kisses my face. The lyrics filling the car could easily be describing Honey Creek.

A man waves from the post office as I drive by, and I wave back. It makes me laugh, because no one from Phoenix waves unless it's to tell you to slow down or hurry up. It's more of a signal there to move. It's more of a hello here.

My good spirits have made today fly by. Dottie was rather upbeat too. We made a contest about who could come up with the worst joke that my grandfather would eventually repeat. I won, but I bet Dottie would disagree with that.

We also disagreed on the source of my mood.

Dottie was sure it was because of Sophie. She said marriage looks good on me. I told her my optimism stemmed from Montgomery's visit tomorrow. I told her that I've been waiting on that day for weeks.

"That's true," I tell myself as I come to a stop sign. "But she's not wrong either."

I grin as I glance all four ways and then proceed through the intersection.

My mood probably has something—or a lot—to do with Sophie. It's hard not to feel good when you're with her. She's a boost to the ego. She makes you feel good. Sophie has a way of making you feel like a light has been turned on inside you and that she sees you. It's incredible. I can't quite figure it out.

I lay in bed last night and watched her sleep against my chest. She slumbers so peacefully. She curls up next to me and wraps her leg around mine like she needs me to stay put.

It's cuddling in its rawest form. It's an act I've never been into . . . until now. Jessica and I used to build a wall between us with pillows because neither of us liked to touch while we slept. But now I look forward to going home and ending the day with Sophie up against me.

I glance at the clock. I have only twenty minutes before I need to get back to the clinic so Pap can head out to Birdie's. A sign sits to my right, informing me that the Lemon Aid has deli sandwiches.

With a sigh, I pull in. There's no way I can get to the Honey House and back to the clinic in twenty minutes if Sophie is home. I'll find myself wanting to stay with her instead.

I have to be an adult.

Damn it.

�

I park the car and get out. The Lemon Aid sits in between a hardware store and a building that isn't open anymore. It appears to have hosted music lessons or something at one point in the past.

My phone rings in my hand, and I look down at the screen. My dad's number flashes as if it's warning me not to answer. To not destroy my mood. I slide it back into my pocket.

Chimes ring against the door as I swing it open. Two cheery faces greet me with a wave and a hello as I step inside and inhale scents of cinnamon and vanilla.

A long counter runs the length of the building on my right. Behind it is a deli-style operation with a grill, a fountain beverage machine, and ice-cream freezers. On my left are tables and chairs and a booth or two.

In the back of the building is a pharmacy that looks like it came right out of a television show. It extends the width of the building and has little chairs in front for people to wait.

Walking inside here gives me a feeling of nostalgia. My mother worked here in high school, and her picture hangs somewhere on the wall above the tables and chairs. She used to bring me here for sandwiches when she'd pick me up in late July. Sophie and I would come in here, too, for milkshakes, as often as we could get money from our grandparents.

"Can I help you?" A blonde teenage girl smiles at me from the fountain beverage machine.

"Yes. Please. I'd like a turkey sandwich with lettuce, tomato, and pickle."

"Sure. Would you like a drink? You can get a bag of chips and a drink for two more dollars."

"That sounds great. Throw some plain chips and a cola on there for me."

"You got it."

I take a seat toward the back and fight the urge to get it to go. The Honey House is so close that I could still get my food and swing by there to say hello.

Instead, I get out my phone and flip through the news feed. None of the headlines are interesting, and I find myself mostly staring off in a daze until the chair across from me is rattled.

I look up to see a man about my age. He has reddish hair and a wide, friendly smile.

"You must be the vet," he says.

"I am."

"Nice to meet you. I'm Aaron Andrews. I'm friends with Jobe Bates."
He grabs the back of the chair and slides it out. "How do you like it here?
Jobe said you were from Arizona. Must be a big change, huh?"

"It is. But I came here a lot growing up, so I knew what I was in for."

"That's right. You're Dr. Fred's grandson."

He smiles again. This time, it triggers a memory.

"Let me ask you something," I say. "Did you try to bungee jump off
that bridge south of town with a paracord back in the day?"

Aaron's eyes light up. "I might've done something stupid like that."
His brows pull together. "You were there, weren't you? You were the kid
there with Sophie."

I can't help but laugh as I recall the afternoon I watched Aaron try
to re-create a stunt he'd watched in a movie. Only in his case the cord
didn't recoil—it broke, and he ended up going for a direct dive into
the water below.

"That was me," I tell him.

"You were the one that talked me out of jumping off the cliff."

"I figured that the odds of your feat weren't great and that at least
the bridge was lower. Your chances at survival were much higher."

His laugh is loud, filling the building. The two men sitting by the
door look at us before going back to their sandwiches.

"You saved my life, man," Aaron says. "I've always wondered who
that kid was. Or if you were there at all. I thought I might've imagined
you. Had a headache for a couple of weeks after that." He rubs his head
absentmindedly.

"I don't know about saving your life, but I'm glad it worked out
okay."

"Believe it or not, that wasn't the dumbest thing I ever did," he
says with a laugh. "But that'll be my legacy, I guess. The guy that did
the dumb shit."

I join him with a laugh of my own.

My food is placed before me. I decline anything else. Tina, according to her name tag, has a quick conversation with Aaron before scurrying back to the counter.

Aaron sits back in his seat and folds his arms over his chest. His face is painted with amusement.

"I heard you went and married Sophie," he says finally. "Can't say I blame you."

My hands stall over my sandwich. He's being friendly and making conversation. I know this. But something about the smugness in his tone—like he's thought about Sophie *like that*—prickles something deep inside me.

"You are correct," I say, looking him in the eye. "We got married a few days ago."

"Good for you, man. Good for you."

If he catches my warning, he doesn't care. I'm not convinced he does, though, because he reaches his arms over his head and stretches with a loud yawn.

"Okay, well, I better get out of here," he says, sitting up again. "I'm glad we got to say hello."

"Yeah. Me too."

He gets to his feet. "So now that you're here and basically family, we play poker at my house the first Friday of every month. I live on County Road 500 just north of the turkey barn. The game usually starts around seven and goes until we run out of money. Fifty-dollar buy-in. Bring your own beer."

"All right," I say, thrown off a little by the sudden invitation.

"Gonna run. See you next week." He walks backward toward the door. "Tell Sophie hi for me."

He flashes me his smile again before disappearing as quickly as he arrived.

I'm not sure what to make of Aaron. He was nice and friendly, if not a little impulsive. I wonder if he always says what he's thinking or whether he ever ponders it first. By the way he jumped off that bridge, I'm thinking he just goes for it.

I take another bite and wonder if this is what life is like here. Random pop-ins from people just saying hello. Invitations to poker games just because. Sit-down lunches instead of drive-through windows.

Life here goes at a different pace. It crawls instead of barreling down the fast lane. The things here that are important to people—things like community and celebrations—feel completely different from what's important to the rest of the world.

It's something that I think I could get used to. Especially if it meant that Sophie would be at my side.

I grin as I take another bite of my sandwich.

Maybe if this job with Montgomery doesn't work out, it won't be the end of the world.

Just maybe it'll all work out.

CHAPTER TWENTY

SOPHIE

Warm water runs over my hands as I give them a final rinse. Concentrating today proved impossible. I gave up on paperwork an hour after Jobe and Liv left and focused my attention on cleaning the kitchen tile.

Cleaning when stressed is a habit I picked up a long time ago. Apparently, cleaning gives me the feeling of being in control. It relaxes me to have things on the outside look orderly when my insides are chaos.

My bathrooms aren't complaining, even if my fingers are.

I gaze out the window as I let the water soothe my skin. The sun hovers over the tree line at the back of the property. A handful of birds pitter-patter beneath the tall oak tree that grows at a slant in the middle of the yard. The rope swing that Gramma hung for me when I was a child—and that Jobe repaired last summer—moves lazily in the breeze.

I rinse the sink out before shutting off the water. Grabbing a towel, I dry my hands before looking up.

Oh!

Holden's reflection in the window startles me, but I catch myself before making a show of it. I continue to dry my hands while keeping my back to him.

It takes a long couple of seconds to settle my breathing and trust my reaction enough to take another peek. When I do, I get a glimpse of him leaning against the doorframe with his strong arms crossed over his chest.

It's a view all its own. I'd be hard-pressed to look away under normal circumstances. But the fact that I know intimately the feeling of those arms around my waist, his shoulders under my palms, his lips on my body—it makes it even harder to stay composed.

I force a swallow. "Are you going to stand there like a weirdo, or are you going to say something?"

"Are you going to stand there and pretend like you don't know I'm here, or are you going to turn around?"

Tossing the towel on the counter, I spin on my heel . . . and am wholly unprepared for the sight in front of me.

He's shucked his work scrubs for a pair of gray sweatpants and a white cotton shirt that skims the ridges of his body. The shirt looks like it's made of the softest fabric, and the color highlights a set of tanned forearms that are muscled and thick.

Shit.

Turning around again, I pour myself a drink of ice-cold water from the refrigerator. Being thirsty, whether from dehydration or desperation, is not what I want to be, and the temperature in the kitchen just rose to a dangerous level.

"You okay there, sweet pea?" he teases.

Asshole.

"Me?" I ask, clenching my hands so I don't fan my face. "I'm fine."

"That you are," he mumbles under his breath. He shoves off the doorframe with a grin as wide as the kitchen. "So what are we going to do this evening, Mrs. McKenzie?"

You.

No. No, no, no, Sophia Louisa Bates. Get a grip.

I shake my head to clear the errant thoughts.

"I don't know," I say as casually as I can. I try to force the flutter in my stomach from the "Mrs. McKenzie" comment to stop. "I'm trying to decide what to do for dinner. How was your day at the clinic?"

"Not bad. I saw two dogs, and a cat with three legs, thanks to a lawn mower. But that thing could run, let me tell you. Oh, and the highlight of my day was a guinea pig named Toots with an impacted bowel." He makes a face.

"The cat with the three legs has been alive longer than me. Its name is Midnight, and it's kind of the town cat. Everyone sort of takes care of it."

He furrows his brow. "Cats have a life span of two to sixteen, seventeen years, give or take. There's no way that cat is older than you."

I cross my arms over my chest. "Well, it is."

"Well . . . *fine.*" He laughs. "On another, more neutral note, is it wrong of me to say that I was hoping you were going to cook? Maybe something with chicken? Because I'm getting used to home-cooked food, and I kind of like it."

I grin at the compliment. "Don't bother trying to charm me now."

"If I was trying to charm you, you'd know it."

My face heats in response to his smirk. "I was going to fry some chicken breasts, but my hands hurt." I hold them up for him to see the wrinkled pads of my fingers. "I scrubbed the bathrooms all day and didn't wear gloves."

"I could've helped you. And I totally have rubber gloves in my bag."

I back away slowly. "That's an odd thing to carry around."

He chuckles. It's low, smooth, and melodic and strums that little chord in my body that none of the blind dates that Liv and Jobe set me up on ever seem to hit. Probably because Holden is absolutely unrelated to me, no matter how far back you look, and has all his real teeth. And because he's absolutely gorgeous and . . . my husband.

"They're in case I run into an emergency animal situation," he says, rolling his eyes. "But back to more pressing topics—dinner. Can I help you make it? Or should we just go to Tank's?"

"I could totally go for a salad with ketchup dressing." I smack my lips together. "I can taste it now."

He makes a face. "I'm sorry. I thought you just said *ketchup dressing.*"

"I did."

"The idea of eating ketchup on a salad is enough to make me want to vomit."

"That's only because you've never had it," I say, wagging a finger his direction. "Don't knock something until you've tried it. Didn't your mother teach you that?"

He works through the concept by biting on his bottom lip. A whiff of cologne, something peppery with the warmth of leather, billows through the air. It dances through my body and taunts my brain.

"My mom taught me not to curse in public. Especially the word 'fuck' in church. That's a lesson I won't soon forget." He widens his eyes for effect.

I laugh as I head into the hallway. "I bet you were a handful to raise."

"I don't think I was bad, actually. I mean, I had moments. But generally I was pretty levelheaded."

He follows me as I shuffle down the corridor. He leaps ahead and tugs the front door open before I get the chance.

"Thanks," I say, dipping my head to hide my smile and slipping outside.

The chirp of crickets welcomes us as we take the few steps across the porch. We stay quiet until our shoes hit the gravel of the driveway.

"Aren't you going to lock up?" he asks.

"No."

Shock registers across his face. "You can't just leave your doors unlocked like that. I know that it's Honey Creek and all, but you still gotta lock your doors."

"No, I don't." I laugh. "No one is going to bother the place. Besides, if they do, Liv will see."

"What if she doesn't know we're not there? Our cars are there."

"She will." I glance at him out of the corner of my eye. "Even if she doesn't, someone will call her after they see us at Tank's and want the scoop."

He slows his pace and shoves his hands in his pockets. "The scoop, huh? What will that consist of?"

"Just that the new vet in town was having dinner with me. You and I getting married is somewhat of a scandal around here," I joke. "I mean, I was sort of the Most Eligible Bachelorette, you know. And you slide in here and put a ring on me."

I look across my shoulder.

The dimple in the center of his chin creases as he mulls over whether I'm kidding or not. That little indentation used to be my go-to when he would tease me about my freckles. I'd tell him at least my chin didn't look like a baby's butt. But now, I kind of like it. It gives him a playfulness, and it's a warning that he's chock-full of trouble.

He turns and catches me looking at him.

"Were you really?" he asks.

"What?"

"The Most Eligible Bachelorette."

My cheeks split into a wide grin. "I was kidding, Doc."

This seems to satisfy him. He worries his bottom lip back and forth as we mosey our way up the road.

"I hope our scandal is really good," he says finally. "There's something fun in getting to be the bad boy that leads you astray."

"Sorry to burst your bubble, but our scandal is more of a low-key thing. We'll probably only get one, maybe two more good days out of it, because the scandal mill is pretty busy right now."

"Ooh. What are we gossiping about?"

"Well," I say, digging my hands into my pockets too. "The mayor of the town next door got drunk, stole a police car, and parked it on the courthouse lawn last week. So I'm pretty sure everyone is still dishing about that."

His eyes light up. "The town next door? Is that where we used to go to the Fourth of July festival every year?"

"Yes. Barnstable. Same place."

"Wow. I haven't thought about that for a long time. Do you remember those Popsicles we used to get that looked like red, white, and blue bombs? And then we'd climb up on the—"

"Hill by the bank and watch the fireworks," I say, finishing the sentence for him.

He nods, a look of satisfaction painted on his face. I'm sure I have something similar on mine too. I can't believe he remembers those silly Popsicles and our Fourth of July tradition, but there's something acutely wonderful about the fact that he does.

"I tell everyone I'm with on the Fourth every year about the time the fire department let them off and the one came sailing right over our heads," he says with a laugh. "No one ever believes me about that."

"I was scared of fireworks for years afterward."

"Logically," he says, shaking his head. "Man, we had some good times around here. Do you remember the summer when I was into baseball cards and you were into the bubble gum that came in the packets?"

I let my head fall back. "I loved that stuff. It had the best flavor. I'd forgotten about that."

"And you used to go into . . . was it called Harvey's?"

"Yes," I say with a laugh. "He blamed you for throwing that baseball through his window."

"The old codger. That was . . . Aaron that did that," he says, his face jerking toward mine. "I saw him today. What a coincidence."

"Not really. This is Honey Creek, you know."

He half shrugs. "True."

We step over a broken piece of sidewalk and around a bicycle whose rider is nowhere to be seen.

"I'd forgotten about Harvey's," I admit. "You would give me the money, and I'd go in and buy them since he wouldn't let you in."

He bumps me with his shoulder. "And then I'd split the gum with you. Pretty good plan, if you ask me."

"Hey, it was a business arrangement," I say, bumping him back. "We both won in the end."

"Yeah, I guess."

He makes a face I can't read as we reach the top of the hill. A silence fills the space. All I can think of is how we've always been good business partners. A yellow sign in the shape of a beehive welcomes passersby to Honey Creek. Holden stops and points to the small font beneath the trio of bees smiling that spells out the town's population.

"You know, I thought the rest of the world would've caught up with Honey Creek by now," he says, almost to himself.

"We check the rest of the world at the county line, don't ya know? Just to make sure you city people aren't trying to sneak in all that modern hocus-pocus stuff."

He laughs. "One of the reasons I always liked visiting here was that it really was so different from Phoenix. But I was just as happy to get back home."

I scoff like his statement offends me somehow. "We were just as glad to get rid of you."

He takes his hands out of his pockets and runs one through his hair. The look on his face is animated. I can almost see the wheels turning in his head. I just don't know what they're turning about.

"I get why Pap loves it here so much, but I get why Mom wanted to leave too. It's a great place to visit, but I need . . . I don't know what I need," he says, his voice drifting away.

We exchange a smile as we find the sidewalk that starts in front of the old deli. Slowly, we make our way into town. Holden doesn't seem to be in much of a hurry, so I just walk alongside him.

We pass the gas station with two pumps—one unleaded and one diesel—and the butcher shop. Finally, the little red metal building comes into view.

"My grandma used to bring me here for breakfast," he says.

"It used to be more of a breakfast place, but we never went there until Tank took it over because my gramma thought that the woman that ran it before stole her crepe recipe, and Gramma refused to set foot near that place."

He chuckles as he picks up the pace toward the restaurant.

The church bells from a few streets over ring a new hour as I make it to the front of Tank's. Holden stands next to a muddy Jeep with a bumper sticker outlining what will happen to the person who mistakenly rear-ends them.

He turns quickly, extending an arm to point toward something. Instead, his arm collides with my side and knocks me sideways.

My foot catches on the curb, and I topple toward the ground.

"Ah!" I squeal as panic flashes through my veins. I turn to the side to try to catch the ground with my hands when I'm snatched upright . . . and into Holden's arms.

My stomach wiggles around as his grin grows warmer . . . and more mischievous.

Our breathing is ragged as we stare into each other's eyes. My heart pounds in my chest so loud that I think Holden can hear it.

Adriana Locke

Holden's fingers press into my side, his cologne washing over me and drowning out the fear that just surrounded my senses.

He forces a swallow. His Adam's apple bobs in his throat.

My lips part as my gaze lands on his mouth. His tongue swipes along the bottom ridge and makes it appear even more kissable.

Damn it.

I drag in a lungful of air.

He releases me from his grip, but not completely. It's as if he wants to hold on to me as much as I want him to.

"What do you say we get our food to go?" he asks, his voice rough.

I grin. "I think that's a good idea, Mr. McKenzie. Or we could say forget it and just go home."

His eyes burn with a mixture of heat and amusement. "When is the last time you've eaten?"

"Um, breakfast? Maybe."

He releases me. "Then you're going to need some sustenance. Let's get a sandwich and eat it on the way home."

I laugh and head for the door. "I'll race you."

His laughter follows me inside.

CHAPTER TWENTY-ONE

SOPHIE

Here." Liv shoves a coffee from Tank's into my hand. "I had to get some caffeine, or I wasn't going to make it through the day."

We stroll down the center of Grigg's Hardware. Old Man Grigg waves with one hand from the front counter as we pass by. His other hand is stuck in the front of his bib overalls.

The Styrofoam is warm in my hand, and I have half a notion to let it sit against my hips in the hope that it works out some of the kinks in my muscles. But I don't. Because doing something like that is the first clue to your nosy older sister that something is wrong.

And nothing is wrong. Actually, everything is very, very right, and that's what scares me.

"What do you think?" I ask, pointing at the paint chips in all colors of gray. "I'm thinking of redoing all the bedrooms upstairs in gray."

Liv wrinkles her nose. "Then how will you keep track of them? You can't say, 'Check on the couple in the yellow room' if they're all gray."

"I know that. But everything I'm reading online says that gray is the color right now." I take a sip of the coffee and eye a particular shade in something called Dove. "I usually have another five or ten reservations for next month. I know the Sweet Tea is stealing them from me."

"Well, it's not stealing them *from* you. They're just stealing what could be yours."

"Not helping."

She rolls her eyes.

I sort through the paint samples and find a sage-green one that's not on the Hot Colors list, but I do love it. Although I wonder whether that's because it reminds me of someone's eyes.

My weight shifts back and forth as I fan the paint card in my hand.

I pretended to be asleep this morning when Holden got up. He didn't know I peeked as he came into my room after a shower and got dressed at the end of the bed. I'm sure he didn't know that I felt him watching me out of the corner of his eye or that I held my breath while he pressed a ghost of a kiss to my forehead before he left.

Goose bumps break out across my skin as I remember waking up last night in his arms. He held me tight, as if he were afraid I'd get up and go. Little did he know, I wouldn't have left if the house caught on fire.

These mornings are too sweet. The evenings ridiculously fun. The nights too . . . *everything* for any of this to be good for me.

But that's the problem. It feels too good.

When I look in his eyes or feel his touch, I almost believe it's real.

The rational part of my brain says to play it safe. But the rest of me points out that it doesn't feel dangerous. It feels exactly as it should.

I sigh.

"What's going on?" Liv asks.

"Huh?"

The paint sample that has been swinging back and forth stops in my palm as my gaze connects with my sister's.

"Oh my gosh," she almost squeals. "I get it. Or, *you got it*, rather, but I get it."

It's my turn to roll my eyes. "Can you not make a spectacle, please?"

"Oh, who cares? It's just Old Man Grigg. What's he care?"

"Everyone in this town gossips, Liv. Even the man born before our grandparents."

She pops her hip to the side. "You slept with your husband. That's not weird."

"You just made it weird."

She fights the grin that spreads across her face and fails. "Was it good?"

"Olivia!"

"Okay, no more. I promise. But one of these days . . ."

I shove the green card back in its slot and choose three separate gray samples. They all look the same to me, really. One might be bluer, but that's only because I saw on the website that some grays have more blue tints in them.

"Do you like Earl or Dove?" I ask.

"Neither."

"You're so much help."

She shrugs and sips her coffee.

I leave her standing there and walk a few aisles over. I have no clue what I'm doing, but I pick up a roller, a tray, and some painter's tape. If nothing else, it'll be a good distraction.

I chuck a paintbrush into the tray.

"Okay," Liv says, walking up beside me. "What's bothering you?"

"Nothing."

She blows out a breath. "Let's try this another way. What is Holden doing today?"

"He's working."

I twist my lips around, willing myself to just be quiet. I don't need to talk about this. Talking will only make it worse. Except when I look at Liv and sees she cares, it prickles something in my heart. And I need to tell her if only so she'll be on my side. Because even though there aren't sides in this, and there won't be, I need someone to reassure me that it'll all be fine.

"And," I say, looking back at the paint supplies, "meeting with Montgomery today or tomorrow."

"Who is that? Wait. He's the guy from Florida or wherever, isn't he?" I nod.

Her eyes grow wide. "Is he still going?"

This is the question that I've been avoiding. Hearing it asked out loud feels like someone stabbed me in the heart with a pickax.

"Yes," I say softly.

If hearing the question out loud hurt, hearing my answer spoken into the universe is torture. A pain that I've been trying so hard to keep contained breaks free inside my soul.

My chest splits in half as I take in my sister's pity—a pity I don't want.

"Oh, Sophie. I get it now," she nearly whispers. "I'm sorry."

"It's fine," I say, reassuring her . . . and maybe myself. "Honest."

"It's not fine."

"Nothing has changed," I say, my voice dead. "I mean—"

"So, sleeping with him changed nothing for you?"

I give her the best blank stare I can muster. "Does it always mean something to you when you have sex with a guy?"

"No. But I don't marry my childhood bestie first and then have sex with him. I just pick random guys up at the bar in Rockery."

I sigh, turning my back on her as I move toward the plastic drop cloths.

"It's not the same, Sophie."

"Maybe not. But it is the same situation as it was before. I mean, the whole objective of this little caper was so he can get the job in Florida. That's still the objective."

I force a swallow and ignore how hot my skin feels. I tell myself to breathe, that everything will fall into place soon, and that I will realize it's for the best. But as I stand in front of Grigg's sale rack and stare at opened packages of drop cloths, it doesn't quite feel that way.

"Maybe he won't get the job," Liv says. "Is it wrong to hope that?"

"Yes."

"Well, I can't root him on when I know it will hurt you."

I tear my eyes away from the shelves and look at my sister. "It won't hurt me. It might sting a little, because . . . I might miss him a little. He's . . . fun."

"I bet he is."

Her grin snaps me out of my funk.

The pity I've felt from her already today is the first of what will come when he leaves. I don't want her—or anyone—to look at me like I lost another husband. Because to everyone else, he *is* my husband. It's the real deal. But Liv knows how I feel. I can see it on her face. And having her feel sorry for me will be embarrassing too.

I have to stay levelheaded about this. I need to take things one step at a time. At one point, I had this all figured out. I just wish I could get back there.

"I need you to listen to me." I set my pile of things down on the floor before giving Liv my attention again. Taking a deep breath, I try to find the right words to explain how I feel. "It would be really easy for me to just go all in with hope and rainbows here. Holden is fun and *fun*. He's smart and funny and sweet. But he's not mine, Liv."

"Why not?"

"Because that's the truth. It's what I always do. I hear what I want to hear. I see what I want to see. I feel what I think I feel, and before I know it, I'm all screwed up." I brush a stray hair out of my face. "I can't see and hear in my head he's going to stay. And now that we're talking about it, I . . . it sounds so rational. I have to accept it, Liv. Somehow."

Olivia takes a sip of her coffee and silently pleads with me to see things her way. I can feel her brain waves trying to permeate mine, but I hold tight. Eventually, she gives up.

Her shoulders drop. "Fine. I hate it when you're all logical."

"You know what?"

"What?"

I smile sadly at her. "At least now I have some idea of what a relationship can be like. I know what I want now. I'll just have to find it with a guy that wants it with me."

Liv returns my smile. We stand face-to-face for a long time, neither of us saying a word. There's really nothing to say. I've basically admitted I have real feelings for Holden and he doesn't for me. Surely, that's the first baby step in getting through this minefield.

She reaches out and taps the Earl sample.

"What?" I ask.

"Go with that one. It's the less depressing of the two. More pink than blue undertones."

I grin to myself as I put the Earl card in my paint tray. "Decision made. Now, do we have a ladder tall enough to reach the top of the walls?"

She looks at her watch. "I don't know, but I need to get back to work. My lunch hour is almost over."

"Already?"

"Yeah." She presses a kiss to my cheek. "Call me if you need me, okay?"

"I'll be fine."

"That's not what I asked."

I smile at her. "I will. I'll call if I need you."

She tosses me a wink before heading out the door.

The room is quiet. The longer I stand alone, the more alone I feel.

I fish my phone out of my pocket and dial my brother. It rings four times before he picks up.

"Hey," he says.

"I was starting to think you were avoiding me."

"Nope. I only avoid girls I've slept with who want to marry me."

"So no one, then?"

He laughs. "What do you want, you little pest?"

"Well, two things. First, I made a meatloaf if you want some. It's in the fridge."

"Damn right I do."

"And second, do we have a ladder tall enough to reach the top of the walls and ceilings?"

He pauses before answering. "Why didn't you call your husband about it?"

My jaw sets in frustration. "You're right. What am I doing calling my brother? I'll start excluding you from things now. My bad."

A low groan rolls through the line. "I didn't say that."

I balance the phone on my shoulder and put my things back in the tray. It takes a bit of Tetris skills, but I manage.

"It's in the shed in the back," he says.

"Thank you." I make my way to the front of the store. "Want to come by tonight and grab the meatloaf?"

"I'm actually heading to Liv's tonight to change her oil. I'll swing by after that."

"Deal."

"I have a prospective buyer pulling up right now, so I gotta run. Wish me luck."

"Good luck, Jobie," I say, using his nickname from childhood.

"Love you."

"Love you too. Bye."

I get to the counter. My phone goes back into my pocket, and I ask Mr. Grigg to whip me up a sample of Earl. He disappears into the back, leaving me alone in the store.

I mosey around, checking out the shovels and hoes. My fingers dust along the green tines of a rake, and I wonder offhandedly when the leaves will change this year. It's my favorite part of the season. I like it much better than when they start to fall from their limbs and leave a mess all over my deck.

Maybe Holden will be here to help out this year.

My fingers stop on the edge of the handle.

I shake my head, my body squeezing in preparation for the moment when he leaves. I don't know when that time will come. Even if he gets the job, as I'm sure he will, it might be a month or two.

I take a deep, calming breath.

Easy, Sophia. You'll figure this out.

I hope.

CHAPTER TWENTY-TWO

HOLDEN

"You definitely have a problem on your hands," I say.

Patrick takes Fidget from me. Relief is evident on his face as his prized pet squirms until she's up and under his chin.

"I don't know what to do with her," Patrick says. "She just sniffs out all of my candy now. It's like she's addicted."

"Sugar is addicting."

I smile to myself. Just like everything else today, the word "sugar" reminds me of my wife. And boy, is she ever addictive.

The more I'm around her, the more I want her time. Every touch leads to an itch of my fingers that I can barely stand. Each laugh or joke, every poke and prod, creates a need for another go-round.

It's a problem. I know it. It's a situation I didn't expect—one I don't think I could've expected if I'd tried. Sure, she's always been pretty. No doubt she's sexy. But I've encountered pretty, sexy women before and not felt like . . . *this*.

Pinpointing the exact cause of my predicament is tough. Impossible, even. No matter how long I stay awake after she falls asleep against me, I can't decipher it. Am I just nervous and appreciating having someone wait this out with me? Is it just a case of proximity making me want her? It could also be that we make a really good team and that lends itself to other crazy thoughts that are more smoke screens than reality.

Because Sophie and I don't really want an actual marriage.

We can't.

Our lives and goals are different—so different, in fact, that we had to get married to achieve them. There's no way to get around that.

"Anyway," I say, as Fidget tries to climb back up my arm, "just try to keep your goodies where she can't get to them. I know she likes all that stuff, but candy and chips aren't any better for her than they are for you."

"Got it. Thanks, Dr. Holden."

"Anytime, Patrick. Anytime. Go see Dottie before you leave, okay?"

I open the door, and he exits the room. I, on the other hand, pull out my phone.

No missed calls or texts from Montgomery Farms.

I consider calling his office and seeing what his status is, but I don't want to appear desperate. And I'm not desperate. Not really. I'm not even sure what the hell I am anymore.

The thought of getting the job in Orlando comes with mixed emotions. There's an elation I can feel at the idea of hearing the words "You're hired." But right on the heels of that feeling comes something else. It's painful and depressing, and the thought of working that out makes me not want to even think about it.

If I could pause time forever and just stay here, thinking that I might get the job, I'd do it. Just to have both worlds in some way.

My phone buzzes in my hand, and I answer it without looking.

"Hello?" I ask.

"Well, hello, Holden. I finally caught you."

My dad's voice sends an immediate dose of tension through my spine. I work my neck back and forth and will myself to stay calm.

Breathe.

"Hey, Dad. What's going on?"

"Oh, nothing," he says in a way that lets me know that he's lying. Something is definitely going on. I'm probably not going to like whatever it is. "Heard anything from that job you were waiting on?"

"I have a meeting about it today, actually. So I'll hear soon."

"That's good. I'll be interested to find out what happens."

"Me too."

He doesn't say anything right away. I don't either. I wait on him to direct the conversation, because there's clearly a place he wants to go and I'd rather just go there and be done with it.

"I golfed with Bob Grundel yesterday," Dad says. "He said he thinks he can find you a job at one of his offices."

I hold my temple with my free hand. He means well. In his own way, he's trying to help, and I have to remember that.

"I appreciate it, but I really don't need it," I say.

"Why the hell not? You don't even know if you got that job in Florida yet."

It takes everything I have not to raise my voice. The tone of his words triggers my reaction, and I can just imagine the look of disdain in his eyes like I'm some errant child who won't listen to reason.

"If I don't get it, I'll find something else. I don't need charity from one of your friends."

"You better be appreciative that my friends like me so much that they would extend a hand to my son," he says, stroking his own ego. "You better get your ass out of that little Podunk town and away from those small-minded people and get back here before they poison your brain."

My jaw hits the floor.

Anger courses through me, and I have a hard time controlling it.

"I'm not going to sit here and listen to you talk about this town and these people like that," I spit.

"Oh, please."

The vein in my temple pulses with each beat of my heart. "The people here have shown me more kindness than you ever have."

He sighs. "They've gotten to you, haven't they? Just tell me you aren't staying there. Please, for the love of God, tell me you aren't staying there. Don't throw away the education I paid for to play tiddlywinks with your granddad."

The muscle in the back of my neck throbs. As my shoulders sag, reality sets in, and I know one thing: I won't change his mind. It's useless to try.

I drop my hand to the side. "I don't want to do this with you."

"Well, I don't want to have to pick you up by the bootstraps, either, boy, but you just keep getting yourself into a pickle—"

"When?" I ask, my jaw ticking. "When have you ever had to clean up a mess I made? Name one time."

"Right now, if you don't get your shit straight."

"Right now? Right now, I'm on the precipice of the biggest thing of my life. I'll be working for the most prestigious animal hospital in the world. I'll have risen to the top before I'm thirty. Did you do that in your field?"

I pause to let my words sink in. I've never spoken to him like this, never come back at him with a tenth of the ferocity that I feel.

"The answer is no," I tell him. "You didn't. But I will have. So you can take your advice and your—"

"Don't disappoint me, Holden."

The laugh that comes out of my mouth is not from amusement. It's from a place buried so deep inside me that I can feel the reverberation in my toes.

He's said these very words to me over and over again throughout my life, and every time I tuck my chin and try to do better. I try to make him proud.

This time, though, what I'm going to do—come hell or high water—is make *me* proud. And he will get no glory in it.

"I have to go, Dad. Take care."

I end the call.

Patrick walks by the exam room and waves. I nod as I stand by the sink and try to even out my breathing.

The door chimes as Patrick leaves. I take a long, deep breath and turn around . . . and come face-to-face with Dr. Montgomery.

It has to be him. I've seen his face on the company website, on interviews, even on the news.

He's shorter than I expected, but with a face that matches his voice. He's clean shaven with intelligent eyes and a polite yet slightly reserved professional smile.

"Hello, Dr. Montgomery," I say. "It's so nice to meet you."

"Holden, I'm sorry I'm so late," he says. "I had an emergency at the office this morning and had to take a later flight."

I extend a hand. "I'm just honored you'd come all this way to talk to me face-to-face. It's usually the other way around for a job interview."

He gives my hand a firm, steady shake. "I like to see potential team members in their element. It makes so much more sense to me." He drops my hand. "I would've been here earlier, but I got caught behind a tractor."

"What color . . . Actually," I say, shaking my head, "say no more. Those tractors and I have had a few run-ins ourselves."

He grins. "I'm glad you're still here. I was afraid you'd be closed before I arrived."

"We are actually done for the day, but I'm happy to stick around."

A hand waves through the air as he sighs. "To be perfectly honest, I'm tired. Traveling exhausts me these days. I'm happy to go through everything tomorrow, if that works for you."

"Yes. Of course."

I walk through the doorway, and he follows. Dottie is nowhere to be seen. She mentioned earlier that she'd be gone right at five tonight for some bingo fundraiser at a church. Pap is at Birdie's. That leaves just Mr. Montgomery and me.

A sense of trepidation wiggles through me. It feels unnatural to be standing in my grandfather's clinic talking to another vet about leaving after Pap offered me a permanent place. I shake the chill away and refocus.

"May I ask where you're staying?" I gather my keys and bag from behind the counter.

"At a place over in Rockery, I believe. I need to check my secretary's email."

"Well, my wife and I run a bed-and-breakfast here, and we'd love to have you stay with us tonight. It'll save you a twenty-minute trip to Rockery."

"Oh, you got married?"

"I did."

"That's wonderful. Congratulations." His eyes light up. "If you have a vacancy, I'd be thrilled. Thank you."

"Of course. Just follow me through town. It's not far."

"I'm parked out front," he says.

"Great. Let me lock up. I'm driving a little silver car. Watch for me to pull up the alleyway, and then get behind me."

He nods and leaves me to lock up.

So far, so good, I think as I tug my phone from my pocket. I find Sophie's name.

Me: Dr. Montgomery is here. He's going to stay with us. Are you okay with that?

I look at the words on the screen. An uncertainty fills my body as I realize what this means: it's do-or-die time. And I don't know if I do want the job or if it'll cause a part of me to die.

The chat bubble blinks immediately. Her message pops up in seconds.

Sophie: I have the yellow room, and dinner, ready.

Me: See you soon.

ॐ

"Something smells incredible," Dr. Montgomery says, setting his overnight bag by the door.

He stands next to me in the foyer. Sophie's office is to our right, and to our left is a formal dining room. Three places have been set—complete with linen napkins. Two taper candles glimmer on the mantel. The reflection of light in the large mirror hanging just above the wicks creates a warm, cozy setting.

Down the center of the burl wood, antique table is a blue runner. Sitting on top of the fabric are white dishes filled with food.

I'm floored. Utterly speechless. When Sophie texted me that she had dinner ready, I didn't expect . . . this.

Sophie comes down the hallway. "Well, hello. You must be Dr. Montgomery."

He nods appreciatively at my wife.

So do I.

She's wearing a pale-pink dress that cinches at her waist. Her hair is down in a style that makes me think she got out of bed like that, except I know better. A pink stain tints her lips, and her cheeks are flushed.

She's *fucking gorgeous*. Like, wife-mode gorgeous. A "this woman chose me and I'm wholly undeserving" kind of gorgeous.

I'm not expecting it, nor do I deserve it. Hell, it's not even technically true. But that doesn't stop me from puffing up like some asshole with a trophy wife.

Because *damn*.

I hold a hand toward her. She takes it as she reaches us with a wide smile. I slip my arm around the small of her back and try to will myself to behave.

"You must be Mrs. McKenzie," Dr. Montgomery says. "I'm Timothy."

"Well, Timothy, I'm Sophie, and I'm so happy you're joining us tonight. I've made roasted chicken. I hope you're hungry," she says sweetly.

"I love roasted chicken. As a matter of fact, my wife made that the night I proposed to her," he says as he follows her into the dining room. "I always tell her that it was the final nail in her coffin. I couldn't possibly not marry a woman that could make a chicken like that."

Sophie laughs. "I'm not sure that Holden married me for my cooking skills, but I must have done something right."

"He must have," Dr. Montgomery says, offering his elbow to my wife. "Hosting such a nice gathering is an art lost to most."

I stand in the doorway and watch Sophie charm Dr. Montgomery— or "Timothy," to her. I hope my jaw isn't on the hardwood floor, but I'm not sure.

How did the woman who fought me over a PayDay a couple of days ago turn into this?

I must have missed something, because when I look up, Dr. Montgomery is seated with a glass of wine. He looks more relaxed and at home in this space than I probably do, and I don't quite know what to make of that.

"Would you like a glass of wine, *love*?" Sophie looks at me and tries to tame her smile. Her pet name throws me off, and she clearly delights in it. Her quiet, contained giggle is at my expense but music to my ears.

"I would love one," I say.

She pulls out a chair across from Dr. Montgomery and hands me a glass of wine.

"This is a lovely place you have here," Dr. Montgomery says. "There's so much charm. You can feel the history. I bet that if walls could talk, this place would have stories for years."

"My grandmother inherited the Honey House from her grandmother," Sophie says, sitting to my right. "My great-grandfather kept honeybees. He had a locally famous beekeeping farm way back when."

I walk around to the chair she's standing in front of and pull it out for her. She seems surprised but covers her shock quickly.

"Thank you," she says.

I sit at the remaining chair with a plate. "This looks amazing, Sophie."

"Thank you. It's nothing, really. Just some roasted chicken and vegetables. I threw in some biscuits and a salad to round it out." She flashes me a nervous smile. "Now let's eat before it gets cold."

We begin to fill our plates with the aromatic contents of the dishes in front of us. It's a comfortable silence interrupted only by the occasional ding from silverware hitting porcelain. The wind blows outside, and the Honey House creaks with it. It all works together to create a storybook-like environment that I think my potential employer might appreciate.

"So, Sophie. Tell me about your husband," Dr. Montgomery says, spearing a piece of chicken. "What's he like?"

Sophie sets her fork down beside her plate. Her gaze falls to mine. Her lashes flutter as she eyes me with mischief.

I can't help but grin. She could roast me right now—carry on a spiel of things that are unflattering at best. But she won't. She might have a bit of fun with this, but I trust her.

The realization that I do, on this level, *in real time*, is a wonderful thing.

"Well," she says, "I don't know where to start."

"Start with the good stuff," I whisper loud enough for Dr. Montgomery to hear.

He laughs. "What made you decide to choose him?" He busies himself by smoothing a square of butter on a biscuit. "I often find that's the best way to get to know the truth about a person—finding out why the ones closest to them choose to be with them."

My stomach rumbles as I manage my breaths. I hope Sophie has something good, and false, to reply.

She sits tall, shoulders back, and looks right at Dr. Montgomery.

"When he asked me to marry him, I thought he was joking," she says. "It was so out-of-the-blue and spontaneous that I contemplated that he'd lost his mind."

"Oh no," Dr. Montgomery says, lifting a brow.

Damn right, oh no.

"But the more I thought about it," she says, "the more I realized that it was such a logical progression in our relationship. We've known each other for years. We got married once under a maple tree after a Wiffle Ball game when we were ten or eleven. So doing it again at this age didn't seem all that crazy."

Dr. Montgomery chuckles, but my heart squeezes at her words. She's right. My proposal was a natural move because it solved a problem for each of us, but it was not because we were in love. And I'm sure that's what the doctor thinks.

I watch Sophie's profile and the way her little nose turns up at the end. The way the apples of her cheeks sit high, perched on the ends of her cheekbones. Her lips form the sweetest rose and beg for a kiss . . . from someone who loves her. Someone who would do for her so much better than me.

Her head turns and she faces me. Her eyes search mine with a concern and kindness that hits me in my already-sensitive heart.

"I could tell you that he worries obsessively about me locking the door or that he goes out of his way to take care of the little things that mean a lot to me," she says, spinning her wedding ring around her finger. "He refuses to put me in a situation until he's one hundred percent sure I want to be there, and if he gets any inclination I'm uncomfortable or worried, he stops what he's doing and asks me to talk about it. He gets . . . creative when I have a problem to solve with my business."

We exchange a smile so soft that it takes everything in me not to reach out and pull her into my chest.

"But the thing I love most about him, Dr. Montgomery, is that he's a good man. He's genuine. Holden is a man you can respect, and that's really, truly hard to find. I know. I've looked."

She blinks rapidly as the color in her eyes blurs. Looking down at her plate, she dabs at her eyes as discreetly as possible. I reach out and take her hand in mine and give it a gentle squeeze.

My heart swells in my chest. I want to tell her all the things I admire about her, all the reasons why she's a great friend and a great wife. But I don't because her words swim together with Pap's—words like "respect" and "love" and "marriage" all colliding together and making me confused and tongue-tied.

Sophie talks about me like my gran would've talked about Pap. Like she really does care for me. I guess on some level she probably does; we're friends, after all, but if she did want me to stay here with her, why would she speak so glowingly about me?

It's counterintuitive. I can't rationalize it.

Before I can sort it out, Dr. Montgomery speaks again. "That's quite a referral," he says. "And from the heart."

"You would be crazy not to hire my husband, Timothy. He's the best man I've ever known." She looks at me and smiles. "This job is all he's ever wanted. And seeing him get the things he wants most is what I want too."

Dr. Montgomery sits back and places his napkin on the table. His plate is clean, polished of the food Sophie thoughtfully prepared.

"I appreciate your thoughts, Sophie. And I hope your husband does as well. I'm sure it won't be easy for you to leave this place behind and come to Orlando if he's selected for the job. Many spouses put up roadblocks. I've seen it many times over the years."

Sophie looks at me. She raises her chin. "Holden's dreams hinge on this one opportunity. I'm just a piece of a much larger puzzle. This marriage isn't only about what I want. It's about what he needs to be happy too."

The hair on the back of my neck stands as my chest squeezes. Of course she's right. She is a piece of a much larger puzzle. But as I sit and look into her eyes, I wonder how big this puzzle might actually be.

Her words roll around my head. I want to believe there was a veiled meaning in what she said, but I'm not sure I have the right to hope for that.

"Very well." Dr. Montgomery pushes away from the table and gets to his feet. "I'm a fast eater. It's a product of growing up in a house without much food. It was delicious, Mrs. McKenzie. Thank you for sharing your talents with me tonight."

"Oh, of course," Sophie says. "Thank you for making the trip up here for Holden."

He gives me a tilt of his head. "I'm going to retire for the evening. It's been a very long day, and a good night's rest will do me a lot of good, I'm afraid. Can you tell me where my room might be?"

"I'll show you," I say.

He waves me off before I can even get to my feet. "Nonsense. Enjoy your dinner. Just point me in the right direction."

"It's up the stairs, the first door on your right," Sophie says. "I'm happy to show you."

"That's quite all right," he says. "Towels are in the bedroom?"

"Yes, sir," she says.

He nods in approval before turning to me. "I'll see you in the morning. Around eight?"

"Sounds great," I say.

"Good night, Sophie," Dr. Montgomery says.

"Good night, Timothy."

With a nod of his head, he exits the room. The stairs squeal as he takes them slowly. Before long, we hear the bedroom door shut.

I look at Sophie, unsure as to what I should say. There are so many things on the tip of my tongue, but they all feel wrong.

She scoots her chair back. "I need to go to the ladies' room."

"Wait," I say.

She pauses, her eyes darting to mine. I think she's holding her breath as well.

I force a swallow. "How did you do all this?"

"I made it for you." Her shoulders fall. "You said you wanted chicken last night," she adds as she bows her head and gets up from the table.

I start to speak, to ask her what I really wanted to say, but don't because . . . she might be afraid of that. There's a chance that she'll be scared that I'm going to ask her what she meant earlier. There's a greater chance that she doesn't want to explain. An explanation could be something she can't give me, because she may be as confused as I am about what's happening between us.

If she's feeling anything like I'm feeling right now, she'll need a second to herself.

She disappears around the corner, her pace quicker than necessary. I don't go to her. Instead, I take a bite of the chicken and wonder what in the hell just happened.

Things with Dr. Montgomery went well—very well, actually. He seemed to like me and Sophie. He looked comfortable and a bit impressed by dinner and our interaction.

So why is there this pit in my stomach?

Why do I feel like something is terribly fucking wrong?

CHAPTER TWENTY-THREE

SOPHIE

I open the bedroom door to find Holden already in bed. He's awake, his forehead wrinkled as he looks at something on his phone. He glances up, takes me in, and gives me a small smile before going back to whatever had his attention before I walked into the room.

Making my way to the empty side of the bed, I pore over what I should say to break the ice. And why there's ice to break in the first place.

My plan was to give him time to fall asleep before I came to bed. I insisted on cleaning up dinner myself. He was typical Holden and insisted just as adamantly that he help. We moved around the kitchen quietly. It was a comfortable silence, albeit ripe with a conversation of unsaid things.

What things, though, I'm not sure.

I fulfilled my part of the agreement tonight. I made Holden look like the perfect candidate he is. So why it feels like he wants to say something to me about it, I'm not sure.

I'm also not sure I even want to know.

As I take off my robe and hang it on the bedpost, I can feel him watching me. And I wish for the first time that things between us could be different. How? I don't know. There's so much I don't know. But I do regret that I like him so much—that talking to him is so easy, and working with him on things from crazy marriage plans to seducing a CEO is so much fun.

Because he's going to leave. I can feel it. And that's that.

The mattress sinks with my weight.

"How do you feel like tonight went?" I ask.

He rustles beside me. The sound of him setting his phone on the nightstand pops through the air.

"I think Dr. Montgomery likes you," I say as I get settled beside him, being careful not to bump or touch him in any way.

"Oh, I think Dr. Montgomery is smitten with *you*. If he were thirty years younger, he'd give me a run for my money."

He looks at me across his white cotton T-shirt. Our eyes meet somewhere in the uncertainty between us as we realize the words he spoke.

Holden's eyes divert to the blankets. "Well, you know what I mean."

"I do. You mean theoretically."

He rolls over onto his side to face me. I tug the blankets up to my waist and tap them snugly around me. Maybe it's because I'm nervous, and when I get nervous, I get cold. Or maybe it's to put a barrier between his body and mine, I don't know, but I tuck those suckers around me tight.

"You really like it here, huh?" he asks.

"Where?"

"In Honey Creek."

My throat feels dry. "Yeah. This is home for me. My brother and sister are here. All of my memories. Why?"

He shrugs as if it were some random question that just popped into his mind. But the way his forehead creases makes me think that's not true.

"No reason," he says. "I've just been thinking . . ."

He wiggles around in the blankets, sticking a leg out and then pulling it back in. He shoves an arm under his pillow and then uses it to prop his head up. It's like watching an overgrown child not want to go down for a nap, and I can't help but giggle.

"What?" he asks.

"Nothing. You're just moving around like you have ants in your pants."

His grin is subtle. "I assure you that ants are not what's in these pants."

I look away, embarrassed at walking right into that one.

"So back to my thinking," he says. "If I get the job with Montgomery, we don't have to get divorced right away, you know."

I press my lips together as a physical block to keep from speaking. I'm not fully confident that my language will match the instructions sent from my brain.

The command center in my head is shouting at me to proceed with caution. My mouth is ready to spill some kind of crap that will indicate that I kind of like being married to him so far and that maybe we can try out one of those newfangled marriages where the couple lives apart. People do it all the time.

Lucky for me, I'm aware that my mouth is a traitor to my best interests.

He searches my eyes. "I'm just saying that there's no rush."

My throat burns with a tightness that comes just before tears. I force a swallow and plead with myself not to go there.

I part my lips and test my restraint. So many things, questions, and possibilities are coursing through my brain, and I'm not sure which will shoot into the air if I open the gates. But I can't sit here and not say anything at all.

"What will you do if you don't get the job, Holden?" I ask.

My fingers dig into the blankets, curling the soft fabric in my hands. I can feel the material scrape beneath my fingernails. I try to keep my face free of any of the emotions that well up inside me.

But hope is building in my heart. The painful experience of it swelling has me holding my breath.

I hope outright, without telling myself not to. I allow my heart to wish that he will choose me. This. Us. That for the first time in my life, someone will think I'm worth fighting for.

It's risky and potentially devastating, but it's where I am. I'm hopeful. I've been quietly hopeful all along.

I guess I'm more like Liv than I thought.

"I don't know," he says carefully. "I'll have some decisions to make, then, I guess."

"I guess so."

"There's something I didn't tell you."

The fabric clenches harder in my hands. "Oh yeah? What's that?" I slip my gaze up his torso and to his face. His eyes are mossy, like a storm is rolling in, and a smile plays on his lips.

My heart thumps in my chest because I don't know where this is going, and by every indication, it's going somewhere interesting.

"Pap offered me the clinic." His voice is quiet, soft, but edged with what I think is a tempered excitement.

I unclench my fists. My shoulders twist so I can face him more head-on.

"He did?" I ask.

The surprise in my voice somehow tugs at the corners of his lips. They rise higher and higher until he's in a full-blown smile.

"Would you consider that?" I ask, aware of how excited I sound. It completely defeats my efforts to not show him exactly how I feel, but I can't hide it. I don't want him making a decision because of me and then resenting me for it.

I want him to want to stay on his own.

My palms begin to sweat against the blankets, and my legs are suddenly too hot all tucked into the sheets.

I free my legs from their confines and scoot one foot to the edge of the mattress. I watch his handsome face for any indication as to what he's thinking.

"Would you want me to?" he asks carefully. "If I stayed here . . . I mean, we're married. What does that look like for the two of us?"

"I . . . I don't know . . ."

My brain races almost as fast as my heart as I try to get a grip on all this.

"Well, if I lived here," he says, forcing a swallow, "things might get more complicated. It's not like I can just move out and get out of your hair. I mean, unless you wanted me to—"

"No," I say quickly, much too quickly. I clear my throat and then carry on in the hope that it distracts him from my interruption. "I'm just saying that if you moved out, then the rumor mill would turn on, and neither of us need that. Right?"

He nods, biting back a smile. "Right. Could you put up with me for a while? I mean, I don't mind living here. With you."

I try not to return his grin but fail epically. "I don't mind you living here. Too much. With me."

"I can see why. I'm an easy guy to get along with."

"Oh, whatever," I say, rolling my eyes. "It's really just that I'm terrific at dealing with assholes. I married Chad. There are—ah!"

I yelp as Holden grabs me by the arm. He untucks my body, swirls me around, and has me lying with my back to his front and his mouth hovering over my ear before I realize what's happening.

His breath is hot against my neck. "No more Chad."

"Huh?"

A spatter of goose bumps slip across my skin, and it has absolutely nothing to do with being cold.

My core tightens as Holden's body ripples behind me. An arm comes around me, caging me against him and the mattress. I hold my breath for fear that I might moan.

"No. More. Chad," he whispers.

"What do you mean, 'No more Chad'?" I ask with my eyes pinned to the blue curtains framing the window.

"I mean that I'm sick of hearing about him."

"Well, when we talk about marriage and behaviors associated with our experiences in relationships, he's my frame of reference."

Holden sighs and lies back against the pillows. Just as I sigh in relief that I can breathe again, his hands guide me backward too.

My head lands on the curve of his shoulder. My brown hair splays in a harsh contrast to the white shirt stretching across his broad shoulders.

Instead of doing anything that could remotely be construed as having underlying motivations, he just lies still. He brushes the hair out of my face with one hand. The other wraps around me and holds me to him. That palm, his right one, is heavy on my abdomen. But he doesn't move it. Doesn't drag it north to my breasts or south between my legs.

A quiet peace tucks itself in around us and brings us closer together. I have questions—so many questions—but I don't ask them. It feels like I might be jinxing myself if I do.

We lie together in the still of the night. Eventually, he lifts his left hand and shuts off the lamp.

"Thank you," he whispers. "For tonight. For everything."

"You're welcome."

He pulls me closer and rests his head on top of mine.

The Honey House sways in the wind, as if it's luring us into a sweet slumber.

His breathing evens out as his chest rises and falls to a consistent, smooth rhythm.

I close my eyes, surrounded by Holden, and try to sleep. I try to ignore the solidness of his body, the comfort his proximity brings. I attempt to block out the way his leg crosses over mine at the ankle.

But, most of all, I try to ignore the idea of Holden staying in Honey Creek. Because against my own good advice, my hopes are soaring. And that has never gotten me anywhere good.

CHAPTER TWENTY-FOUR

HOLDEN

W hat's this?"
Sophie's voice makes me jump.

I turn around to see her standing in her robe. She leans against the doorway, her hair a wild mess piled on the top of her head, a curious, sleepy look on her face.

Her cheeks are pink, and there is a line extending from her temple to her jaw from having her face pressed against my shirt all night.

I like it. I like it too damn much.

The feeling clouds my head and mixes with the remnants of the conversation I had with my father yesterday and the day I'm about to have with Montgomery. I need to focus.

Clearing my throat, I turn away from her. "I made breakfast."

"You did?" Her bare footsteps patter against the wooden floor. "What did you make?"

"Breakfast quesadillas."

She peers over my shoulder. "Never heard of it, but it looks delish."

"My mom used to make them. As a matter of fact, she used to put everything in a quesadilla." I slide one onto a spatula and transfer it to a plate. "Here you go."

"What's in it?"

"That's no way to say thank you," I tease.

She pulls her eyes from the plate and up to me. "Dare I say that I didn't know you can cook? So I'm . . . nervous."

"I'm a man of many talents." I shake the plate. "Here. Take it. I gotta get going."

A light in her eyes dims as she does as I ask.

"What about Dr. Montgomery?" she asks. "I got up early to make him breakfast."

"Already took care of that."

She slow blinks. "I thought y'all were leaving at eight?"

"Well, I got up around six to go to the bathroom, and he was up. We thought we'd just get the day started early."

"Oh." She looks down at her plate. "Well, thank you for breakfast. And for doing my job."

"Guess you owe me."

She grins as she heads to the table but doesn't comment. It's just as well.

I carry the pan to the sink and give it a quick rinse. The small cut I got while slicing the onions this morning burns under the water.

That's what I get for being a pussy and letting my hands shake.

I grab a towel and dry them off, careful to blot and not rub the injury. If Sophie weren't watching from the table, I'd inspect it more closely. But I'm not about to raise her suspicions that I'm anything but steady by showing weakness.

Steady. My insides ripple with suppressed laughter at myself.

I'm never good on little sleep. And although I slipped into dreamland without a problem, staying there proved to be much more difficult. Hell, even if I could've gone back to sleep, I probably wouldn't have. I couldn't have appreciated having Sophie nestled up beside me, her hands wrapped up in my T-shirt as if she were holding on to me for dear life, if I hadn't been awake. I've never felt so . . . wanted. Needed. Content with all that. Happy about it, even.

But if today goes well . . .

The knot that took up residence in my gut last night twists a little tighter.

I have no idea how today will go. Will I pass his inspection? Will he be able to see me in the future of Montgomery Farms? Will he think I might be a good fit?

Will I feel like Montgomery Farms is the right fit for me?

I force a swallow and try to clear my brain.

"This is really good," Sophie says. "I'm definitely impressed."

"It's an Arizona specialty."

"I approve." She blows on another bite before putting it in her mouth.

Footsteps down the hall redirect our attention. In a few seconds, Dr. Montgomery appears in the doorway. "Well, good morning, Mrs. McKenzie," he says.

"Good morning, Timothy."

"Thank you again for letting me stay. I left my card on your desk for you to please invoice my secretary."

Sophie nods. "We were happy to host you. You can stay again this evening, if you'd like."

Dr. Montgomery looks at me for a split second and then back to Sophie. "I'll be heading to Kentucky today for my final interview. But I might just bring my wife back here for a visit this fall. She'd love it."

Sophie gets to her feet and walks across the kitchen. She busies herself at the island. Out comes a container and a big apple pie that she got from Birdie for dessert last night. Only no one ate any of it.

"Here you go," Sophie says, handing the container to Dr. Montgomery. "You can't leave Honey Creek without Birdie's apple pie."

He looks quite pleased as he takes the container from my wife. "I do love me some apple pie."

"I hope you have a safe trip." She stands next to me. "And I hope we get to see you again soon, Timothy."

There's a ribbon of trepidation in her voice that I'm afraid to linger on too long. Whatever it is has a straight shot to that knot in my stomach and pinches it until I almost bend in half to relieve the discomfort.

"As do I," Dr. Montgomery says. "I'll see you outside, Holden."

As he leaves, I look down at Sophie. There are a hundred questions dancing through her eyes. I wonder if she can see them in mine.

I reach out, tucking a strand of hair behind her ear. Her skin is so soft. The way her head shifts in the subtlest way and leans into my hand almost has me grabbing her and hugging her.

But I don't. Because this has already gotten more complicated than it should've.

"See you tonight," I say softly.

"See you tonight."

I press a kiss against the top of her head, and it hits me . . . This really could be my life. This could be my every day. With Sophie.

Someone to say goodbye to each morning. Someone to let me hold them through the night. Someone who wants to cheer me on.

Someone to come home to.

Our bodies stay separated, our hands to our sides. My lips linger a few seconds longer than necessary as I say a silent prayer for whatever is the best answer to this quandary to happen.

I back away, giving her a final smile, and watch her move backward toward the table. With a final wave, I turn down the hallway and walk out the front door.

Dr. Montgomery is waiting for me on the porch.

"I'll see you at the clinic?" I say, running a hand over my hair.

He sets his bag on the floor and looks at me. "No."

"No?" My head spins. "I . . . Okay. Um . . ."

He sticks out a hand. I take it, my brows furrowed, and give it a shake.

"Holden," he says, blowing out a breath. "I've seen enough to know that you would make an excellent asset to Montgomery Farms. My gut tells me that you and Sophie are good people—the kind of people I seek out for my team."

My mouth goes dry as his words permeate the confusion in my brain.

"This is not public information," he says, "but I have been looking for someone for a very specific position. I need someone to mold, to shape, to take over the CEO position in five, maybe ten years. I can't work forever."

I join his merriment, chuckling along with him. But in reality, my heart is trying to climb out of my body and find Sophie.

Why? I don't know. I just need her. Now.

My temperature rises, something inside my head starts screaming, and I can't make sense of it.

"My children have carved out their own ways in life. I'm so proud of them. Both of my daughters and one of my sons work at Montgomery, but none want my job. None want to be CEO. John, my oldest, is expanding into aquatics. My daughters are working in social outreach. That leaves no one to keep everything together, and I'm not just going to hire someone off the street to take over my life's work. That leaves me in a predicament."

"Dr. Montgomery . . . ," I begin, but he waves me off.

"If you would prefer to take the role that you applied for, it's yours."

My head spins. I try to make sense of all the information, and opportunities, that were just dropped in my lap. But the longer I try to come up with something coherent to say, the harder it becomes to speak intelligently.

"Okay. Thank you. I just, um, I'm not sure. This is a lot to process."

He nods. "I know it is. Take a couple of days to think about it. In the meantime, I'm still going to Kentucky to see the final applicant. It's always good to know who is out there."

I try to speak, but nothing comes out. Luckily for me, Dr. Montgomery laughs.

"Please give my secretary a call and let her know what you've decided. I fully expect you to talk this over with your wife. I make no decisions without my wife's—Rose's—approval," he says. "I called her last night and told her about you and Sophie and dinner, and she had the same reaction I did: 'These are our people.' *You* are our people."

"I . . . Dr. Montgomery, I'm honored. A bit shocked, I have to admit, but so honored to have someone of your caliber say such nice things and have so much faith in me. Truly. Thank you."

"Holden, of course." He picks up his bag. "If you have any questions at all, get in touch with me. I'm happy to talk things out and answer any questions you may have. But time is of the essence here. I have a trip to Africa next week, and I really hope you can join us."

Africa? Is my passport up to date? Does Sophie even have one?

Shit.

My throat squeezes shut as reality hits me.

This job means Sophie stays here. And I go to Orlando.

I look over my shoulder.

Taking this job means leaving Sophie. It means we move on like we planned.

But what if I don't want to move on without her? What if leaving her feels like a grand fucking mistake?

It's not that easy, though, because the Honey House means everything to her. She was willing to marry me to save it. I would be a complete and utter asshole if I asked her to leave it.

Would she, anyway?

I look back at Dr. Montgomery. "I'll get in touch soon. Thank you again."

He nods and heads to his car. The gravel crunches as he backs out of the driveway and speeds off toward Tank's.

I stand on the porch like an orphan with nowhere to go. Somehow, going back inside feels wrong. It feels like an asshole move. But going to the clinic feels wrong too. Like I don't belong.

Rubbing my temples, I realize that no matter what I do from this point on, I'm screwed. Somehow, I've gotten to the point where I've bent over backward to acquire a job offer better than the one of my dreams, and now I feel shitty about it.

I glance over my shoulder again.

Maybe because I woke up this morning and realized that maybe, just maybe, I have other dreams too. Dreams of things like having a partner in life. Dreams I didn't even really know existed.

Until now.

And it might be too late.

CHAPTER TWENTY-FIVE

Sophie

H ere you go." Jobe plunks the ladder against the wall in the foyer
before coming inside my office. "Anywhere you want me to put
it, specifically?"

I sit back in my chair and watch him take a seat across from me.

His red flannel shirt makes him look slightly older and wiser than
he is. It reminds me of a picture I found of my dad in my mom's Bible.
He was probably Jobe's age in it and wearing a similar shirt. He had
the same smile and same build, and I wish every time I think about my
father that I'd known him more.

Would my life be different with a strong male presence? I don't
know. Jobe has done his best—more than he ever had to or probably
should've—to make sure I was protected and loved. And Gram was
strong enough for both her and my grandfather, a man I never knew.
But would having a father, a guiding male force in my life, have given
me a better understanding of the male mind? A little insight on how
to read men?

Men, meaning Holden.

I sat all day and wondered how it's going with Holden and Timothy.
It's going amazingly well, I'm sure. And I'm happy for Holden. He

deserves this. I can't help but feel like a jerk when I daydream that he won't get the job. It's not fair. I know that. But still . . .

I've willed myself not to put too much into Holden saying that his pap offered him the clinic. He said it offhandedly, after all, and not like it was something he genuinely wants to do. Over and over, I keep reminding myself that Dr. Montgomery is here to recruit Holden for a position that he wants. That he's dreamed of. That he's been pining for longer than I've even known him as an adult.

It's a mistake to want something you have no control over. I know this. So why can't I pop the bubble of hope growing inside my stomach that Holden will choose to stay here?

"So . . . ," Jobe says.

"Thank you for getting the ladder. I know it killed you."

His lips form a lopsided grin. "It did. But I did it for you."

"And that's why the meatloaf I made for you is still in the fridge."

A shadow crosses his face. "Hey, yeah. Thanks. I didn't get over here to get it. I got . . . sidetracked."

"Sounds like there's a story there."

"One you don't want to hear."

Jobe picks up a picture frame off my desk. It's of us, our parents, and Liv. It was taken just a few months before they passed away. We were in the backyard, having a barbecue. Dad cooked salmon on the grill. For some reason, I can remember so many details about that random day—the smell of the mesquite chips, the feel of the sun on my face, and how it was almost too warm for an April evening. Mom's laugh never seemed to stop that night, and she chased Liv and me around with a water gun, making us shriek.

This house is full of memories like that—memories that I can't make anywhere else. Memories I can't leave, because if I do, I'll be walking away from the only parts of my family that I have left. The people who love me for me, regardless of anything else. The promises I made my grandmother.

The person I am.

Jobe sets the picture back down. He runs his hands down his jeans.

I take in the lines around his mouth and the way his jaw flexes. Figuring he's right, that I don't want to hear his story, I change the subject.

"How's the real estate market?" I ask. "Selling any houses?"

"I'm closing on a house out past Shiloh Church tomorrow. The red one just past the cemetery. Remember that one?"

"Ah, yeah. It's cute."

He nods. "So is the woman buying it."

"Oh, Jobe," I say with a sigh.

He just laughs. "So what's going on around here? I saw paint cans out back and all kinds of shit. What are you doing?"

I scoot back from my desk and stretch my legs out in front of me.

Usually, projects like this would end up being a family affair. It would start with Liv traipsing over because she can't stand not to get involved in, well, everything. And then she'd end up calling Jobe for advice or help, depending on what she was doing. He'd bitch and moan about it. But a little while later, he'd come over, too, and we'd spend all night refinishing floors or hanging new curtains.

Now, though, I'm not sure how it works. Holden is still here. It would be weird to ask Jobe for his help, although I could totally use it, but I can't ask Holden either. For one, it's not his place. And for two, I don't know his time line for staying.

"I'm painting," I say simply. "I'm starting in the hallway leading upstairs because I feel like it's the worst. So many suitcase dings and dirty hands and traffic smudges. Then if I like the color, I'll work on the bedrooms and stuff."

"Ah, don't paint the bedrooms, Soph." He makes a face. "It's a part of the Honey House lore."

"Yes, but no one knows that lore but me, you, and Liv. No one else cares. Everyone else wants fresh and fancy-named paints."

He looks unfazed.

"I don't make the rules, Jobe. I just have to work within them if I want to get this place going again at full speed."

He leans forward and rests his elbows on his knees. "Is this your husband's idea? Because it sounds like something a city slicker would say."

"What? No." I laugh. "This is all mine."

"He's rubbing off on you, then. I'm going to have to take him out for a drive sooner than I thought."

I give him a look that makes him laugh.

"So, really, what's going on?" Jobe asks. "Something is happening in your head, because the house smelled like bleach a couple of days ago and now you're painting."

I bite my bottom lip.

"Just spill it," Jobe says.

I take a deep breath and study his face. Beneath his debauchery and totally womanizing ways, I know he'd understand my predicament. He wouldn't like it, but he would get it. And right now, that's what I need.

Forcing a swallow, I shift in my seat. "When you married Shelby—"

"We're not talking about that."

His words are abrupt. Cold. Hard. It's a topic, a person, that we never, ever talk about. Shelby Laine is the only thing my brother has cared about outside of our family, and she broke his heart into a million jagged pieces.

His eyes are as chilled as his words as he stares at me with a warning not to proceed.

"Fine," I say. "I won't ask."

Irritation swirls across his features, muddying the usual softness he has for me. He leans back in his chair, his shoulders rigid, as his internal fight over what to say plays out on his face.

"I'm sorry. I shouldn't have brought her up," I say with a frown.

"Why did you?"

"I wanted to ask you something. But I won't. Forget I said anything about it."

His jaw pulses. With each movement, it gets lighter. Finally, after a few minutes, he sighs.

"What did you want?" he asks.

Guilt swamps me for making him so obviously miserable. "Don't worry about it."

"You know I don't wanna talk about her. So if you brought her up, you must have something you wanna talk about. And being that you just married Holden, I have to know."

I tap a foot against the floor as I piece together my question. I had it worked out, but his response threw me off and made me forget.

"When you married Shelby," I say, starting again, "did you feel like it was forever? Like if she hadn't left, you'd still be married to her?"

He furrows his brows, obviously confused. I know he wants more information—the root of why I'm asking, but I can't give that to him.

I can't tell him that I'm wondering if I'm in love with Holden. There's no way to explain that I'm worried it is love and that if he leaves I'll be alone forever. Because I've never felt this way about anyone, never been able to actually imagine lifetime milestones with someone else at my side. I might've hoped for it and tried to mentally Photoshop faces at my side, but I've never seen it like a movie, as I can with Holden.

Jobe clears his throat and sits up. His eyes shine with sincerity. "If she hadn't left, I would've still been with her," he says. "I loved that girl."

"Then why did you let her go?"

A small, sad smile slips across his lips. "Sometimes when you love someone, you have to let them go do their thing. It hurts like a motherfucker, and everything inside of you screams to hold on to them. But what are you going to do? Keep them around and have them resent you?" His laugh is more at himself, more a sigh, than anything.

My heart hurts for him. He's never been serious about anything except work and Shelby Laine. Half the time he's not even totally serious about work. Seeing the sadness in his face, imagining the pain of letting the woman he loved go hurts *me*. It also flames an ember of fear in the bottom dregs of my soul that I, too, will know that kind of pain soon.

Because he's right. If Holden wants to go, I'll have to be happy for him.

I don't have the history with Holden that Jobe had with Shelby. We didn't grow up together, going to the same schools, loving the same friends, attending the same bonfires. And even though I'm catching glimpses of what could be so good between Holden and me, that's all they are. Glimpses.

This is Holden's future. That was the deal. He's given me what I needed for my future—for the Honey House to be solvent. If I try to keep him here, I'll be the irrational one. The one in the wrong. The one who'd be resented. And I like myself too much to be the bad person. I like him too much to pull a stunt like that.

Maybe I love him too much too. Or maybe I love the pretty picture of marriage to a man like Holden presents.

I don't know. It's too much to freaking think about this early.

"On that note, I'm heading out," Jobe says around what sounds like a lump in his throat. "You need anything else?"

I shake my head. A lump in my own throat swells. "Don't forget your meatloaf."

"I won't. Love you, sis."

"Love you, Jobe," I tell him as he walks out of the room.

The room feels vacant all of a sudden. The light coming through the windows is less warm. The Honey House feels big, maybe too big, with just me inside.

There is still a smidgen of hope that I can't extinguish, a flame buried in my soul that wishes things will work out.

Somehow.

CHAPTER TWENTY-SIX

HOLDEN

"Dottie?"

I glance around the clinic. The door shuts softly behind me. Sunlight streams through the windows. I can't help but see the irony of walking into a place so sunny when I feel so . . . not.

"Dottie?" I call again.

She's not at her usual perch behind the counter. And while that's not a necessary requirement of her job—to be here to greet me in the morning—I miss it. I was hoping for her admonishment over my being late, even when I'm not, and her knowing eye. I was even secretly hoping she'd toss me some insightful advice that I didn't ask for.

Because I could use that right now.

I'm setting my bag on the counter when my grandfather pokes his head around the corner.

"Hey, kiddo. Good morning," he says.

"Where's Dottie?"

"She's home sick today, so it's just me and you . . ." He cranes his head farther out the door and swipes his gaze behind me. "And Montgomery. Where is he?"

I hear his question, but I'm less worried about it than I am about Dottie.

"Is she okay?" I ask. "She seemed fine yesterday."

"She's fine. She likes to pretend she's your age, running around here like a chicken with her head cut off. I've been telling her to get some rest before she wears herself completely out, but she refuses to listen."

"I wonder who she learned that from?"

He tosses me a wink. "No clue. But anyway, she had a checkup this morning. Routine, yearly thing. I called Dr. York across town and told him she needed to stay home for a few days. And being that I saved his wife's Siamese cat a few months ago after he fed it the wrong food and it had an allergic reaction that nearly killed the little thing, he owed me a favor."

I head to the coffeepot, letting that scenario sink in. "It's amazing what you can get away with here. That kind of behavior is illegal in most places."

"Eh, it's for her own good." He dismisses me with a wave of his hand. "Anyway, where is Montgomery? Is he coming in this morning?"

A lump settles in my throat. I add a dash of sugar to my coffee in the hope that it makes it go down more easily.

"He's, uh, he's not coming in," I say, pussyfooting around the answer.

Pap's feet shuffle. "And why not? Is everything okay, Holden?"

I blow out a sigh that's as heavy as my conscience.

I don't want to turn around and face my grandfather. Dread fills me as fast as I filled my mug with coffee.

I'm sure he'll be proud that I got hired by Montgomery Farms. Pap understands what this means for my career. He's a vet too. But he's also my grandfather. I'm his only child's only son, and I know that having me here would mean a lot to him.

But does that mean I give up on what I want out of my life? Haven't I done that enough throughout my life with Dad? Haven't I taken cues from my elders and let their voices affect me enough?

Montgomery Farms is what *I* wanted. *I* worked for this. *I* started putting these pieces in place a long time ago.

My heart aches as I turn around. Pap's demeanor changes as he takes me in.

"I see . . . ," he says.

"Pap, I . . ."

I stumble over my words, unsure as to what to say. This isn't how I planned for this to work. Not in the least.

This is the day I've been waiting for. I've put so many ducks in a row so that if and when this opportunity came my way, I could grab it by the horns. And now, here it is, the horns dangling in front of me, and I have Pap on one side and Sophie on the other, and I don't know what to do.

This is an opportunity to show what I'm capable of—to prove to myself, and to my father once and for all, that I can do it on my own credentials.

"Montgomery not only offered me the job but also an amazing position that would put me in top-level management soon."

Pap clears his throat. The disappointment filtering across his face floats away, and his game face is on.

"I'm not surprised in the least," he says. "Good for you. It's an amazing opportunity, kiddo."

"Thank you."

He walks over to me and places a hand on my shoulder. His grip is firm, cupping the end of my clavicle, but his touch is gentle. It's just like I remember him from when I was a little boy. Tough, yet loving. Expectant, yet kind. It's a feeling I've forgotten, and feeling it now, in this very moment, makes my knees want to buckle.

"You are so bright," he says, looking me in the eye. "Gifted. Your mother would be so proud of you."

My eyes sting as his words fill holes in my soul that I wasn't aware existed. I blink rapidly, willing tears not to spill down my cheeks.

Pap swallows hard. "And I'm proud of you too. Never forget that."

"Thank you," I say, pulling him into a hug. He smells of the licorice jelly beans that are probably in his pocket. That, too, brings back a wash of memories from years ago.

Pap pulls away. "So what's Sophie thinking about all of this? I can't imagine the Honey House in other hands."

I clear my throat. "I have to talk to her about it tonight."

"You haven't told her you got the job?"

I shake my head.

"Holden . . . ," he says, eyeing me warily.

My hands rub down my face. The top of my head might explode from the pressure building inside it.

I know I have to tell Sophie. *Clearly.* I also know I don't want to.

My stomach churns as I try to imagine the look on her face when I tell her. Will she be sad? Angry? Will she cry?

I don't know how to do this. How do you do something you don't really want to do?

How do you break your own heart?

The idea of walking away from her causes me physical pain. Bile creeps up my throat. My shoulders get so tight that I wince. My chest threatens to cave in on itself.

But no matter how I think about it, there's no way to have both. I can't have my cake and eat it too. I can't get the job and future in veterinary medicine that I want, that I've dreamed of for my entire life—the job I promised my mother I'd get someday—*and* have Sophie here so she can keep the Honey House too. There are too many obstacles down an already bumpy path.

She deserves a man who will be with her day or night and help her live her best life.

That man's not me.

I don't think.

Pap watches me with the eye of a man who's trained to discern every tiny detail about behavior. Of course, he's particularly good with animals, but he's not bad with the human variety either.

"How do you think she'll take it?" he asks. His tone is careful, cautious, as if he's feeling me out. He suspects there's more to the story.

"Good, I think," I say with much more certainty than I feel. "Montgomery stayed with us last night. She's completely aware of what's going on."

"And she's all right with it? It's so hard to believe that she'd leave everything she's ever known."

I shrug. "I guess so. I mean, she knew all of this before we got married." *That's why we got married, but I can't tell you that.*

Pap walks by me and toward the coffeepot. He pours himself a cup and adds a teaspoon of sugar. He stirs it slowly, as though if he keeps doing it, some magic answer will be written out in the steam.

Hell, if that were the case, I'd fill a bathtub up with the stuff to get a clearer answer faster.

I try to take a drink of my coffee and nearly choke.

"You know what?" he says. "The only thing I can tell you is to follow the sun."

"Do you mean your heart?"

He grins. "No. I do not. I mean follow the sun." He takes a sip of his coffee and lets that sink in. "Most mammals find their way home by scent. But many animals, everything from birds to dung beetles, follow the sun."

He moves around the counter and stands in front of me.

"When I met your grandma, something happened inside of me that I couldn't name. It was like a light turned on deep inside my soul. Whenever I was with her, I felt warmth. It's the only way I can describe it."

I nod, understanding that feeling. It's the same thing that happens when Sophie is around. I haven't been able to label it, but warmth? That sounds about right.

"The same thing happened to me the first day of vet school," he says. "I felt lit up on the inside. Like . . . somehow every part of me was brighter and better. Things made sense when I was working with animals too."

"Yeah. I get it," I say. "You remember that I almost went to medical school, right?"

He laughs. "Yes. And you called me and said you hated people, so you wanted to know more about veterinary medicine."

"And when I walked into that building on campus, it was like everything clicked."

I take a drink of my coffee and remember that day. I had a meeting with a professor to see if it was an avenue I wanted to pursue, and I walked out of there knowing it was exactly what I wanted to do for the rest of my life.

So why is this decision not as easy?

"Follow the sun, kiddo," Pap says. "Go where your soul feels warm. Cause the least harm to those around you, and bring the sunshine to those that you can. You'll know what choices you need to make in life if you follow the sun."

The door opens behind us, and Grady walks in. Pap tosses me a final smile. Then he cuts Grady off and ushers him into an exam room.

"How's that garden today, Grady? Any tomato plants left?" Pap asks before the door closes.

I sit on a stool behind the counter—the one that Dottie usually uses. I grab her pen and find a sticky note and write her a little message.

You were really late today. Good thing some of us can be on time.

Handsome

I toss the pen down and sit back in the chair.

Follow the sun, huh?

But what if it's a cloudy day? What if I can't feel the sun at all?

236

CHAPTER TWENTY-SEVEN

SOPHIE

"What's for dinner?" Liv asks.

I pin the phone between my ear and shoulder. "Pizza. I'm not cooking tonight. Every muscle in my body hurts."

"Ooh. Sounds like a good story there."

"Hardly," I scoff, taking glasses out of the dishwasher and putting them into the cabinet. "Unless you want to hear me tell you about taping off trim and patching dings in the wall."

"Yeah. Not interested."

"Didn't think so."

"So, any news on your husband?" she asks, not missing a beat.

I know her question stems only from her wish for me to be happy. She still thinks in her misguided but well-meaning way that he will make the right choice. But the situation with Holden is what I've been avoiding all day.

Of course, it was impossible to completely block it, and him, from my mind. In such a small amount of time, so much of the Honey House now reminds me of him.

I can see him sitting at the table when I look into the dining room. The warm glance of appreciation he cast my way for the meal I'd prepared for Dr. Montgomery. And him. I really made it for him.

As I gaze out of the kitchen window, I see the backyard alight with the string lights someone hung for our wedding party.

Our first dance.

The first moment I was in his arms.

Our first kiss.

His cologne lingers in my bedroom. The bathroom has traces of his presence, and I can barely even look at the kitchen counter without blushing.

One minute, and I'm smiling and giggling and convincing myself that he's enjoyed this too. And I'm picking out every sliver of a sentence that he's said that could be construed as meaning that he might want to stay. He could work for Fred. He'd still be doing what he loves. And . . . he'd be here. Where I am.

That minute is fleeting and replaced just as fast by another. *That* moment is filled with dread and a foreboding fog swirling around my head. The notably rational, obvious reasons that he will be going to Orlando if he gets the job elbow the hope away, and I'm left feeling like I just lost my best friend.

Just knowing would be easier, regardless of the outcome. The indecisiveness is what's killing me, and I don't know how long I can do it.

"Soph?" Liv asks.

"What? Sorry. I was . . . trying to unload the dishwasher."

"I just asked if there was any news on Holden."

"Not yet. Montgomery came, and I think it went well. So it's probably just a matter of time before he gets the job offer."

She pauses. "You still think he's going to go?"

I close the cabinet and blow out a breath. Conflict wars inside me. My brain tells me that he will go. My heart says he won't.

"Honestly? I don't know." I bite my bottom lip and worry it between my teeth. "He did say that Fred offered him the clinic. Or a job there, at least. So maybe that helps."

"So you want him to stay?" she asks softly.

"I don't know, Liv . . ."

"You know what? I know you do. And that's okay. It's okay to have hope, Sophie. When you lose hope, you pull back inside your shell. You forget that there's more out there for you than dickheads and maintaining a bed-and-breakfast."

I sag against the counter. "I know. You're right. But I don't know if I'm strong enough for this. I mean, I know I'll be okay, but"—I force a swallow—"it'll freaking hurt. A lot."

"Listen to me right now," she says. "If he leaves, it's because his hopes didn't align with yours. It has nothing to do with you. We're Bates girls. We aren't victims."

Her words make me smile. It's something our mother used to say when we were little. I haven't necessarily carried that thought process in my pocket, but Liv has. And every time she brings it back out, it hits me in the heart.

"You have to be honest with yourself about what you want," she says. "Embrace that. Validate your feelings. And then we'll deal with the end result when we have it."

I take a deep breath and lift my chin. Liv's right.

The front door opens, and I hear Holden's feet coming down the hallway. I close my eyes as my body flips on, anxiety pulsing through my veins. The force clears out my brain, removes the fog, and I know what I want: I want him to stay.

"Liv," I say, "I gotta go. I'll call you later."

"Okay. Good luck. I love you."

"Love you. Bye."

I end the call before she can reply.

Holden comes around the corner. He looks as divine as ever with his slightly mussed-up hair and green eyes. Lines mar his forehead but somehow just make him look wiser and more sophisticated.

"Hey," I say carefully.

"Hey." He gives me a half smile. "How was your day? The paint in the foyer looks great."

"Do you like it? I only did a few sample patches going up the stairs, because I want to see it in different light. You know, morning, after-noon, evening . . ." I shrug. "Anyway, how was your day?"

His eyes dart around the room.

"Are you hungry?" I ask. "I thought we could order some pizza."

Each second that passes pumps another blast of cortisone into my body. Fight-or-flight instincts begin to kick in, and I can feel my body wanting to move. Press. Prod. To end this. Once and for all.

He walks across the room and takes the final two plates from the dishwasher. I step back and watch. He places them in the cabinet slowly, as if this one chore means something special to him.

"My mom always made me unload the dishwasher," he says out of nowhere. "It was my one constant chore."

"I had about twenty constant chores."

He dips his chin but stays silent.

The air in the room is thick, full of anticipation of what's to come. Because something is about to happen. I see it all over his face. I feel it from the energy coming off him. I hear it in the blood that gushes over my eardrums.

The longer I watch him stand in my kitchen and not look at me, the more definitively I know that he's made a decision. And as that realiza-tion sinks in, as I realize how consumed I've been with him today, about what he'd think about the decisions I've made for the Honey House, another truth becomes evident too: I love him.

I know by the way I want to grab his face and make him look at me. The way my heart breaks as I see the struggle in his eyes is unlike any empathy I've ever felt toward a man before.

I don't want him to hurt. The last thing I want is for him to be miserable . . . especially if the cause has anything to do with me.

When he raises his eyes and the emotion in them is enough to knock me back a few steps—when it's enough to draw tears to the corners of my eyes without a word being spoken—I know what he wants to do.

And I know what I have to let him do.

I can't ask him to stay. Jobe asked Shelby to stay, and it ended so awfully. I did my best to finagle Chad into being happy, and it ended up a wreck.

I won't put Holden in that position. I won't put myself in it either. I respect both of us too much to do that.

Taking a deep breath, I say a silent prayer that I'm wrong. That he's going to tell me he wants to stay and is worried about how I'll respond. *Please, God. Please.*

"When my mom was dying," he says, the words barely audible, "I used to sit by her bed. At first, we'd watch television. And then we'd just talk. But as time went on and she got weaker, I'd do most of the talking. I'd take her hand in mine and hold it, hoping she'd feel it somehow and know I was there."

I walk across the room and wrap my arms around him. He sags against me, resting his head on mine.

"The last time she really said much that made sense, she told me to promise her that I would remember that everything happens for a reason," he says.

Tears pool at the corners of my eyes. I don't reach to knock them away because it won't matter. More will take their place again and again.

I know what's coming. He's going to go. And I have to find the strength Jobe had when Shelby left and the strength Gram had when I left for college, and let him go too.

Because the truth is, Holden McKenzie isn't mine. He was on loan to me. He was sent here to teach me something, maybe just to have hope again. To understand love. To know it in its realest form.

Wetness streaks down my cheeks as he presses a kiss on the top of my head. His chest rumbles next to me, but I don't have the ability to look up at him. I can't.

"For what it's worth," I say, the words blurred by my emotions, "you were a good husband."

He laughs, his lips pressed against my hair. "Oh, sugar."

My laughter mixes with his, a sad melody that feels like a punch in the gut. My heart bleeds as he holds me for what will be the final time.

"When are you leaving?" I ask.

"I don't know." He takes my shoulders and spins me. When I don't look at him, he lifts my chin with the pad of his finger. "Montgomery offered me a position today that will consist of him grooming me to be an executive."

"That's great," I say, tears sliding down my face.

He catches the wetness with the pads of his thumbs. It's such an intimate gesture that it only makes me cry harder.

"I don't want you to think this is about you. Because it's not. It's about . . . me. I guess. About the things I need to do and the promises I need to fulfill." He looks at the ceiling and sighs. "I know you won't go with me, but if there's any way . . ."

I shake my head. "My home is here."

He looks down and nods. He takes me in, his gaze boring into my soul. I stand before him and let him see what he wants to see.

"What should I do?" he asks. "Do you want me to stay? Go now? What will be easier?"

Never leave.

I suck in a hasty, shaky breath and then clear my throat. "You might as well take the Band-Aid off and just go. Why delay the inevitable?"

His eyes fill with a sadness that kills me. A surge of pain envelops me, and I want to wail—full-on sob until my voice becomes too weak and my body too tired to expel that kind of energy.

I don't want him to see that. I'd like to maintain some sense of dignity, and I don't want him to second-guess his decision because I'm a crybaby.

"I'll go to Liv's," I say. "You can leave tonight or tomorrow. I'll just stay gone until then."

"You don't have to do that." He grabs my shoulders, panic flitting across his face. "Stay with me tonight. Stay here one last night."

It's too much.

Panic rises in me, too, as I take a step back. His hands fall to his sides, his face broken.

"I'm sorry, Holden. I can't. I . . . I can't." I wipe the tears off my face with the backs of my hands. "I wish you all the luck in the world. I do. But this . . . you know . . . there's no reason to . . ." I give him the best smile I can conjure up, and despite being blinded by the tears in my eyes, I turn and walk toward the door.

"Sophie!"

I pause at the doorway but don't turn around. If I do, I'll get stuck in this cycle that's going to end the same way no matter how many times we hash it out.

He needs to go.

And I have to let him.

I face my bedroom door. Snot drips down my lip, and I wipe it away with my sleeve.

"I didn't mean for it to end like this," he says.

"I didn't either."

And with that, I run out of the Honey House and don't look back.

CHAPTER TWENTY-EIGHT

HOLDEN

What in the hell just happened?
I sit on Sophie's bed and put my head in my hands. Never, ever did I think I'd feel this way about getting what I want.

Except maybe I didn't get what I want.

I don't even know anymore.

I lift my head and look around her room. It's typical Sophie—quirky, silly, but inviting. All the things I love about her are displayed here. And just last night, I lay here with her snuggled up next to me like all was right in the world.

My head spins as I sort my feelings. It's a confusing mishmash of pros and cons—of feelings and dreams and promises and intentions. But every time I try to sort them out and put it all in tidy little boxes in my head, one thing pops out: she didn't ask me to stay.

Surely, if that's what she wanted, she would have.

Sophie isn't shy. She's opinionated and forward and will ask, maybe even demand, to get what she wants.

The thought makes me smile.

Damn it and damn her.

Half of me wants to march across the street and barge into Liv's house—and potentially duck anything Liv throws at me—and scoop Sophie up and bring her home. But the other half of me sits back with a cigar and points out that there was a reason this wasn't real. And I'd be smart to remember that.

Getting too comfortable in situations leads to an acceptance of things that are mediocre. That's what happened with Jessica. Not that Sophie is mediocre in any way, but living here would be. It would be filled with ferrets and tractors and apple pies from the resident cougar. Not at all like the life filled with challenge and success and self-accomplishment I want.

I stand up and gather my things from the bedroom and bathroom. It doesn't take long.

Before I leave, I pull out my phone and find my grandfather's number. It rings only once before he picks up.

"Hello?" he says.

"Hey, Pap."

"Holden. What's wrong?"

I chuckle in frustration. "I, um, I just got done talking to Sophie, and we decided it was best if I headed out to Florida right away."

He whistles between his teeth. "Are you sure this is what you want?"

"Yes."

Not really, but what choice do I have? Should I give up everything I knew was right for me before this crazy trip to Tennessee?

"Well, okay. Do you need anything from me?" he asks.

I look around the room one final time. I close my eyes and imagine her lying in bed, waiting on me. The smell of her skin and the warmth of her proximity that fills my core with a comfort I didn't know existed.

When I open them, a chill rips through me.

"Can you check on Sophie tomorrow?" I ask. "Just make sure she's okay?"

Pap sighs. "I don't know what's going on, but I assume it's more complicated than you're letting on."

"Yeah. Kind of."

"I figured." He sighs again—heavier this time. "I'll check on her. Don't worry about that."

"Thank you."

The line grows quiet between us as we both take in the enormity of what I'm saying.

I'm leaving. I'm leaving him *and* Sophie. And as much as I hate for people to need me, I'm torn. I wish Sophie needed me more and Pap needed me less. But I won't make her look like the fool here—like she fell for a man and got dumped within days. She deserves more than that. I'll do whatever it takes.

"I'll call later this week. But don't hesitate to call me if you need me, okay?" I ask.

"Absolutely. I love you, kiddo," he says. "And I know you're going to do great."

"Thanks. I'll talk to you soon."

"Holden!" Pap's voice barrels through the line as if catching me before I hang up might save the planet.

"Yeah?" I ask.

"You are a good man. You deserve good things. And if you get out there in the world and forget that, come home and we'll remind you."

I can't say anything. I can't tell him I appreciate that more than I could ever put into words or that I love him more than I love my father.

All I can do is nod my head and wipe the single tear slipping down my face.

"Goodbye, Holden," Pap says and ends the call.

I hoist my bag over my shoulder and make my way out of the Honey House. Pausing at the front door, I take in the dining room, where Sophie served the delicious chicken dinner, and her office, where Liv teased me with a soot-covered face.

I can hear their laughter echoing down the halls, smell sausage cooking in the kitchen, and feel the excitement of another day here.

Unfortunately for me, there will not be another day.

This is it.

This is where our journey ends.

I step onto the porch and lock the door behind me. My gaze lingers on Liv's house before I climb into my car and head toward Nashville to catch a flight.

☙

SOPHIE

"Why are you doing this to yourself?" Liv asks from somewhere behind me.

I keep my eyes fixed on the road, where, just a few seconds ago, Holden's car sped away. I could barely keep myself from racing out the door and into the street and begging him to stay. If Liv hadn't been here, I might've.

When Chad left, I was irritated. Sad, yes, but more frustrated by his audacity. Then I was angry that he left me in such chaos and ruin. But watching Holden go is different.

My chest is splintered, as if my heart has decided to fray into sharp shards that press into my ribs. It's painful in a way I didn't know existed, and I wonder if this is what they mean when they say "heartbroken."

I'm grateful for the tears that blind me. At least I won't have a clear visual to haunt me in my dreams. I can make up details and pretend he looked back at me or that his taillights flashed as if he had second thoughts.

Because I'm pretty sure he didn't.

I wipe my nose with the back of my hand and ignore Liv's disgust.

"This is the way it was designed to go," I say. "So why does it hurt like this?"

She pulls me against her again as the dam breaks and tears flood my face once more. Her shirt is already damp from the first round of this, so I move my face to get a dry spot. There's no satisfaction in rewetting a damp spot.

It's softer, more cushiony. It reminds me more of Holden.

My body shakes as I cry harder.

I cry for my naivete, for thinking that I could pull this off without getting hurt. I cry, too, because I know I'll never be that naive again. The Sophie who marched into the clinic and asked Holden for antibiotics is gone for good. In her place is this Sophie—a woman who knows what it's like to actually love a man and lose him.

Two things I thought I'd experienced before.

Liv pulls away and takes a quick scan of my face. She then takes my hand and pulls me around the vacuum in the center of the living room floor and into her bedroom. Guiding me onto the edge of her bed, she finds a box of tissues and hands them to me. Finally, she sits beside me.

"This hurts because you love him," she says. Her voice is without judgment, void of any levity at all. I'm glad for it. It makes me feel less vulnerable.

I think about her statement. *You love him.* I was pretty sure I might yesterday. I thought I did this morning. But tonight, I know I do. This is what love is.

If I never have love again, at least I know what it feels like. And I'd take this pain over not knowing.

"This is what men do," I say softly. "They leave. And this is why I should've held to my guns and told him to kick rocks when he asked to stay at the Honey House."

"Cut yourself some slack, sis."

"Why? So I can *not* learn from it? So I can think that it's okay to keep putting myself in positions to get hurt?" I dab at the corners of my eyes with a tissue. "I was right. I'm not cut out for this shit."

"Oh, stop it," she hisses.

"You stop it. You're the one that instigated all this, anyway. You're lucky I don't blame you for this."

She rolls her eyes. "You're lucky I don't get pissed off that you're blaming me for helping you feel love for the first time."

My jaw drops as I look at her. "I would've been just fine thinking I loved Chad. That was so much easier."

We sit on the bed and sway from side to side in a slow, rhythmic pattern. It soothes my raw heart just enough so I don't think I might die.

"You know something?" I ask. "A thought just occurred to me. Chad and Holden both needed me. They both had something to gain from being with me. But neither of them wanted me. Neither of them fought for me."

"He might come back," Liv begins, but I cut her off.

"No. Absolutely not. I'm not even humoring it anymore."

I stand up and kick off my shoes.

"Don't rule him out yet," Liv says.

"He's not coming back. He made it clear from the get-go that this was a momentary thing. He got what he wanted and now he's gone, and I can't be pissed about it. But you know what I can do? Make damn sure the next man that walks into my life wants me as much as he needs me." I look up at her. "Bingo, Liv. That's the golden rule here."

I climb up on her bed and scoot across it. Jerking the blankets back, I slide underneath and get my head cozy on the pillows. Liv watches with amusement.

"What?" I ask.

"What are you doing?"

"I'm sleeping here." I pat the blanket next to me. "Now come lie down, because I'm tired."

She laughs. "Sophie, it's seven o'clock. I'm not going to bed at seven."

"Then get out of here so I can." I watch her eyes grow wide. "What? I'm not going home. I can't go in there and deal with it tonight."

"Fine." She sighs as she gets to her feet. "I'm going to wash my face and grab some snacks. I'll be back in a few."

I snuggle down in the blankets and close my eyes.

Holden's face pops up immediately, his easy smile lighting me up from the inside out. My heart warms, and I wish for a split second that I could've told him I loved him.

It's probably better it ended how it did. It just made it easier to say goodbye. He doesn't need the guilt associated with a woman telling him she loves him as he leaves for better opportunities.

This is his dream. He's fulfilling something his heart set out for way before it met mine. And that's why I couldn't tell him that I love him. It would be unfair.

And it wouldn't change a thing.

CHAPTER TWENTY-NINE

HOLDEN

There have been a number of mornings in my life that have started in pain. The morning after I separated my shoulder in Little League was one. Then there was the time my kitty, Leo, got hit by a car. That hurt. A lot. Of course, the morning I took a right cross to the face in high school didn't feel too good, nor did the sunrise after my first drunken escapade with my buddies in college.

That sucked.

But few of those events hold a candle to this morning.

Today, it's a special kind of discomfort—a malaise that has managed to permeate every part of me. My body hurts from tossing and turning in a Nashville hotel last night, warring with myself as to what to do. I picked up my keys no less than four times to just hightail it back to Honey Creek and rethink this whole situation. My brain hit meltdown mode somewhere on the flight to Orlando. Every mile farther away from Sophie we got, I became more frantic. The Jack and Coke from the stewardess didn't even help. And now, sitting on the patio of a hotel restaurant in Florida, the hot morning sun beaming across my face, it's my soul that hurts the worst.

The worst kinds of pain are bottomless. You can't fix them or repair the wound; you can't stop the bleeding or find a cure. It just sits there, festering, an open sore that screams with every move.

That's what this is.

"Can I get you anything else?" Roxie, the waitress, stands on the other side of the table. She's cute with her pixie cut and bright-pink bubble gum and deserves a medal for putting up with my broody ass for the last hour. "Want me to take that?"

She points at the omelet I've yet to touch. The menu item I forgot I ordered.

I blow out a breath. "You might as well."

She takes the plate and gives me an odd look before disappearing into the expanse of the restaurant behind me.

I pull the chair with my briefcase closer and take out a notepad and pen. Scribbled on the front page is a hodgepodge list of things I need to do. I started it on the plane this morning, hoping that getting something on paper—some kind of game plan—would help ease my mind.

It didn't.

Staring back at me is a list of things to do to get my life started here. I need to call Montgomery's office and formally accept the job. Find somewhere to live. Move my belongings from Arizona. Check on Pap and Sophie.

My temples throb, and I wince as I press them with my fingers. How this went from a best-case scenario to a nightmare is beyond me.

I position the pen between my fingers and scratch another note on the list: check on Dottie.

I miss her this morning too. I wonder if she's looking at the clock, wondering where I am and prepping her "You're late" line to fire my way as soon as I open the door. A smile graces my lips as I realize it's the day Joe will be coming with the floor mats, and I wonder if Dottie will finally pick up on the fact that he has a thing for her.

My pen taps against the notepad over and over.

I wonder if Fidget the ferret has been behaving and what kind of pies Birdie will bring this week. I'm curious, too, if the man with the fishhook on his hat at Tank's is watching for me to come in for a coffee today. It just became a part of my routine. Not because I needed the coffee, but because I liked the ritual of it. It was sort of cool in a very weird kind of way to start to understand the threads of small-town conversation and to maybe be a part of them in some way.

"What do you think about the mayor over there running for reelection?" someone from the round table at Tank's would ask me.

"You ever see a horse that won't eat apples?" they'd ask.

Or they'd point at something in the newspaper and want my opinion.

It never mattered what the topic was, and my opinion surely didn't matter, but it was requested. Valued. As if they were starting to accept me as a potential piece of the fabric of their lives.

And I left.

"They probably won't even notice," I mutter as I doodle a ferret in the top corner of my notepad.

The awning overhead moves in the breeze. The sunlight that filters in shines on my darkened phone screen. As soon as my eyes land on it, my stomach twists until it's raw again.

Just before I booked my flight, my dad sent me a text.

Have you come to your senses?

I didn't respond. Instead, I just turned my phone off and boarded the aircraft. That didn't keep me from thinking about his question over and over.

It's a reasonable question in a way he didn't intend for it to be. It's straightforward. It's thought-provoking.

Have I come to my senses?

The question has slowed me down, and coupled with the flight to Orlando, it's giving me a lot of time to think.

I'm in Florida and about to take a position to lead a company. All the while, I've misled the man who's opened himself up to me as a mentor.

I wrote it off at first—brushed away the first stabs of guilt. But the closer I got to the hotel, and every time I picked up the phone to call Montgomery's secretary to take the job, it got worse.

How did I let myself get like this? How did proving my worth to my father become so damn important that I lowered the values I pride myself on?

"Here's your ticket," Roxie says, placing a bill facedown on the table. "You need anything else? I know I just asked you that, but . . . you seem a little lost, if you don't mind me saying."

I look up at her. Her face is clean and pretty, and it kind of reminds me of Sophie. An honest vulnerability shines in her eyes, and I find my heart shattering all over again.

"I guess I am a little lost," I admit. "I'm new here. Have lots of things to do."

"Where are you from?"

"Arizona. Taking a job at Montgomery Farms."

She nods politely. "Arizona, huh? One hot place to another."

"Coincidentally, yes. Now I need to find a place to live and get my things hauled over here."

"There's an apartment open in my complex. A couple of them, actually. Some of the girls moved out since the boys aren't coming back on time . . ." Her face falls. "If you want the number, I can give it to you."

"Sure. But may I ask, why aren't the boys coming back?"

She grins. "My boyfriend is in the marines. They're overseas right now. They were supposed to be gone a few months, but it got extended. It's sad, you know. Hard for them. But some of the girls move on with their lives. Some of them have to for school or for family support. There are all kinds of reasons."

"Wow. That's rough."

She shrugs as if she's resigned to the situation. "It's just how it works. I mean, I don't like him leaving, but he loves it. So I deal."

"Has he ever thought about doing something else? Because, man, that has to be hard to go without seeing each other like that." I force a swallow. "I just . . . Well, my wife is back at home, where her heart is, and . . . here I am."

My face gets hot, and it's not from the sun.

The truth hanging out there like that cuts deep. It exposes the rawness of the situation and how simple yet complicated it is. But if anyone should understand, it's Roxie.

She looks around the patio. Most of the customers who were here when I arrived have gone, the brunch rush now over. Only a few tables are full, and they seem to be leisurely reading on their phones or having breezy conversations with their tablemates.

Pulling out a chair across from me, she sits.

"Would it be okay if I make a quick observation?" she asks.

"Sure."

"I've watched you since you got here. And not watched you like I've spied on you or something, but more like I've been curious as to what your story is. Everyone has a story. Believe me—I've heard them all. And I make a little game out of it, if I'm being honest. I make up little backstories for people, and it's fun to see if I'm right." She tilts her head to the side. "I was both right and wrong about you."

"Oh really? What did you think my backstory was?"

She grins. "I knew you were heartbroken. That was easy. You kind of wear it on your sleeve."

"I beg to differ," I protest.

She laughs. "About what? That you're heartbroken or that you wear it on your sleeve?"

"I think I hide my misery very well, thank you."

Her face wrinkles up like she's embarrassed for me. It makes me laugh. That feels good.

"So your wife is in Arizona, huh?" she asks.

"No. She's in Tennessee."

"But you said she was back at home. Didn't you say you were from Arizona?"

Her question echoes through my mind as she sits patiently and waits for my response. I gaze into the distance as I replay her words again and again.

"You said she was back at home."

I did say that. She's at the Honey House. Her home. But . . . why does it feel like my home too? Why did I mean it to mean my home when I said it originally?

"She must really love you," Roxie says with a laugh. "That's all I can say."

My head snaps to her. "Why would you say that?"

"Well, for one, don't take this the wrong way, because loyalty is my jam and I'm in a very happy, albeit very distant at this point in time, relationship, but you're super cute. And you seem nice and like you do well for yourself. And if she let you go, she must really love you."

It's like the world stops moving. Everything outside of the table, everything besides me and Roxie blurs as I digest that.

"I mean, I love my man," she continues. "It's the only reason I stay with him. And it's the reason why I don't ask him to leave the forces even though he could."

Holy. Fucking. Shit.

"Wait," I say, sitting. My eyes are wild. I can tell by the way she recoils. "Say that again."

"What?"

I waggle a finger her way. "The thing you just said. About why you don't ask him to stay home."

"It's his passion. He loves it. And although I hate that he's gone and the worry that comes with it, I won't be the reason he doesn't live a fulfilled life. I won't do that to him, and I don't want to carry that guilt around either. I love him too much."

My brain scrambles to process this. *Could it be true? Could this be why Sophie didn't ask me to stay?*

"That's how I knew I loved him. I've lived a pretty wild life—partying and carrying on. I've always said I could not be tamed." She lifts her chin in a hint of defiance. "But then Blake walked into my life, and it was like my world was flipped on its axis. Like it started spinning the opposite way. And I knew who he was and what he did from the beginning, but man, I'd rather build a life with that boy and deal with the inconvenient stuff than to try to have a life with a man that didn't give a shit about me. Because I've tried that. It doesn't work."

She rambles on and I feel guilty not listening, but my head has already checked out of the conversation . . . and is checking into the Honey House.

If Roxie's right, Sophie didn't ask me to stay because she knew I wanted to come here. The exact reason I didn't ask her to come with me.

If we would do that for each other out of respect, then . . .

"The key is respect." Pap's words ring loud through my ears. *"That's good. Always respect her. Prioritize her. She gave you her heart."*

I'm a fucking idiot.

I'm a fucking idiot for not seeing this. I'm a fool for leaving her behind. I'm an idiot for thinking it would be okay to take this job after misrepresenting myself in the first place, and I'll be damned if I follow through with it. I know better. I am better. And I will be better.

Everything is suddenly clear.

My chair screeches against the patio tiles as I propel myself back. Roxie flinches, taken aback by my sudden movement. I shove my notepad in my briefcase and find my wallet. Fishing a hundred-dollar bill out of the cash in the billfold, I hand it to Roxie.

"Will this cover my bill?" I ask hurriedly.

"Yeah. About four times."

"Keep the change," I say, locking up my briefcase.

My heart is pounding in my chest, sweat is dotting my forehead, but it's not the right sun.

"Follow the sun, kiddo. Go where your soul feels warm . . . You'll know what choices you need to make in life if you follow the sun."

Pap's words clang through my mind.

Sophie. She's my sun.

And I bet Pap knew it all along.

I can't help but chuckle. I bet he's watching the dog clock with a stethoscope around its neck to see how long it takes me to figure it out.

I start toward the door but stop. I turn to see Roxie watching me.

"Thank you," I tell her. "You have no idea what you've just done, but thank you."

"Go get her," she says with a grin.

I smile back at her. "I intend to."

CHAPTER THIRTY

SOPHIE

Gravel crunches beneath the tires as I pull into the Honey House's driveway. It's a perfect almost-fall day. The air is warm with a slight chill—a breeze ever so slight that it warrants a hoodie. The leaves on the trees in the yard are tinted with golds and burgundies, and I could sit on the porch swing all day and enjoy the shift in seasons.

I could. But I can't. And not because my painting project can't wait or because a couple from Ohio is coming this afternoon for a long weekend.

I can't because I'm afraid that if I sit too long, I'll start to cry. Again.

Sometime around two in the morning, I woke up and couldn't fall back asleep. The pain from missing him was almost completely overwhelming. If I hadn't been in Liv's bed, I'm not sure how I would've made it. Having her next to me kept me from breaking completely down.

As the night crept along, I found a nugget of peace. It was a small nugget, a tiny sliver of contentment that I'd done the right thing. With it came a little hope. I'm not sure for what, exactly, other than the fact that I didn't feel . . . broken. Splintered, yes. Devastated, absolutely. But not broken.

When I was left before, I was empty. Tangibly, in the sense that he had taken much of my money and some of my belongings. He had also loaded up my self-esteem too. But as I lay in Liv's room last night, I realized how different it is this time.

Holden is gone. But that was a choice I made because it was the best for both of us. And unlike my marriage to Chad, I don't regret marrying Holden. Although it lasted far less time than we expected and maybe wasn't even necessary to start with, seeing it from this side of things, it changed me.

I know now without a doubt that I know what love is. I understand what it's like to be appreciated. For the first time, I stayed up late with a man and just laughed. Someone made me breakfast. Another person cared whether my doors were locked.

Holden gave me more than a zero balance on my taxes or a new last name. He gave me the chance to see myself from a new angle. And it turns out that I like this me.

That's a gift I could never repay him for.

I take out my phone and pull up my photos. I flip between the snaps that Haley sent to me from our wedding day. There's so much excitement in our faces, so much happiness.

I wouldn't give that day back. Not a chance. That day led me to so much that I never would've experienced or learned otherwise.

Everything happens for a reason. I grin sadly.

My phone rings as I climb out of my car. Naturally, my heart leaps in my chest because it's stupid. It hopes it's Holden. As if not to jinx it, I refuse to look at the screen before I answer it.

"Hello," I say, holding my breath.

"Hey, Sophie Girl." Fred's voice is soft and kind, and the sweetness in his usually laughter-filled tone brings tears to my eyes.

"What's up, Fred?"

"How are you? You holding up okay?"

I climb the stairs but don't go inside. When I walked in this morning from Liv's, reality hit me hard. I don't want to be on the phone with Fred if that happens again.

"Well . . ." I choke back a half laugh, half sob. "I'm hanging in there. You?"

"I miss the little shit already."

My laugh breaks free. I wipe a tear from my face. "Yeah, well, me too."

"He called me last night and told me he was taking the job. He said you were staying here."

I look around the yard of the Honey House. It's where I belong. I've known that since I left for college, and I promised myself I'd never leave again.

And I won't. Not even for him.

"I can't leave Honey Creek," I say. "This place is a part of who I am. And I know that sounds crazy and I should probably just reconsider leaving, but—"

"No. You can't do that." He blows out a hasty breath. "Holden left here because he's trying to find meaning in his life. I know he has all of these other reasons for it, but they're all inconsequential."

I lean against a post and listen.

"He was raised in a very interesting way by his parents. His mother, my daughter, was raised with the values my wife and I taught her. Things like family and community were important to us. But his father has a different set of standards. He values things like money and cars and stuff that you can see.

"He's not a bad guy, per se. Just a bit . . . ostentatious," Fred continues. "It's just that a lot of what he values conflicts with the things Becky, my daughter, taught Holden. And then she passed away, and Holden was left as a teenager trying to decide who he was in the midst of all of this. I don't think he's ever really figured that out."

"I know who he is," I say quietly.

"Me too, Sophie Girl. And Holden will figure it out. It just takes boys longer than girls sometimes. We're a little slower on the start."

The first true smile since Holden left slips across my cheeks.

"Thanks, Fred."

"Anytime. If you hear from that grandson of mine, tell him to call his old grandpa. I have a feeling he'll call you way before he remembers to call me."

"I will."

"Take care of yourself," he says.

"You too. Goodbye."

"Bye now."

I slip my phone in my pocket.

Fred's words serve as a balm over the edges of my hurt. He didn't have to call, but I'm glad he did.

And maybe he's right, I think as I enter the house. *Maybe Holden will sort his shit and miss us.*

Miss me.

I pad quietly through the hallway and into the kitchen. I'm trying to figure out how to end my day—with wine that I don't even really like, or with a bubble bath and a book, when I stop dead in my tracks.

A piece of paper sits on the table. A purple goo oozes from under it—a goo that looks an awful lot like grape jelly.

My throat burns as I inch closer to the table. My knees threaten to buckle beneath me as I reach the edge and see Holden's handwriting on the white, lined paper.

Sugar,

I know you will be surprised to learn that I messed up. Turns out that I'm not perfect. Total shocker, right?

I left last night to go to the Sunshine State only to learn that the sun really shines here. I know this thing between us was built to get to an end point. But what if we are the end?

There's no easy way to explain this. I guess I just had to know what would happen if I took the job. What I learned in my few hours in Florida is that I don't want to be anywhere without you.

Is that crazy?

I want a chance to build something real between us. I want to see where this goes. We can take it at whatever speed you want—I'm moving back into the blue room as we speak. But if you'll give it a try, I really think that this marriage of convenience can be a marriage for a lifetime.

Holden

P.S. Lock your damn doors!

My hand shakes as I set the jelly-stained paper back on the table. Blood pours through my veins so fast that I think I might pass out.

I try not to run to the stairs and do my best to take them only two at a time. I pass the yellow room, the green room, and the bedroom with ugly flower wallpaper that people seem to love. Finally, across from the bathroom, I get to the blue room.

The door is open, and if I didn't already know he was in there, I'd know. I can feel his energy spilling out of it.

I get to the doorway and peer in. He's on the floor doing sit-ups. He looks over and sees me and springs to his feet.

"Sit-ups?" I ask, lifting a brow. "Really?"

"Energy to burn."

He eyes me carefully, as if he doesn't know what to do with me. I don't move, either, unsure what to say.

His chest rises and falls as he inhales a deep breath. "Did you get my note?"

I nod.

He waits a few seconds before chuckling. "Damn it, Sophie. Talk."

And, just like that, my uncertainty vanishes.

It's a weird feeling, really, because nothing is certain. He wants to try. That I know. But I don't know if it will work or how it will work or what it really means at the end of the day.

But what I do know is that he's here. He came back. For me. And even if he hadn't, I would've been okay.

It's that last fact that's most important. That's the reason taking this step doesn't worry me. Because it took all this jostling—him leaving— for me to realize that I'm strong on my own. Knowing that, I can give him all of me instead of parts that need putting back together.

My lips tug toward the ceiling. "So if we're going to try this, we need an addendum to our agreement."

Relief washes across his face. His fingers twitch at his sides, but he stays put.

"What are you thinking?" he asks.

I lean against the doorframe and take in his handsome face. "I'm thinking that I'm still not doing your laundry."

His smile is quick and wide. And I'm glad he doesn't know that he could get whatever he wanted from me just by flashing it my way.

"Good. Because you do laundry how often? I'd like clean clothes weekly."

I laugh. "And since I know you can make breakfast, I'm going to need you to flex those muscles routinely."

I must be a sure thing, because he saunters my way. His smirk is back, the one that makes me want to shed my clothes without being asked.

"I'll only agree to that on one condition." He stops in front of me. Peering down, his eyes dark and hungry, he grins. "You have to let me flex certain other muscles whenever I want."

"Maybe not whenever you want," I say, trying to maintain some power. "But often."

He lifts a brow. "Daily?"

His lips are swollen, the bottom sticking out as if he's been biting it all morning. The silky strands of hair on his head are gorgeously messy, and the scent of his cologne hits my bloodstream like a shot of heroin.

I tilt my head toward his. "How about now?"

"I like the way you think, Mrs. McKenzie."

His eyes catch mine before he sweeps me off my feet. My giggle pierces the air as he runs down the hallway and down the steps.

"Where are we going?" I shriek as he takes the corner toward my bedroom so sharp that the tips of my toes brush the doorframe.

He tosses me onto my mattress. The headboard slams against the wall just before he pounces on top of me.

Hovering above me, his face inches from mine, he grins.

His eyes are crystal clear. His face lined only by the smile. It's the happiest I've ever seen him.

And it's the happiest I've ever felt too.

This is the way I've always pictured my life. Maybe even a little better. For the first time ever, each piece that belongs in my heart is snapped into place.

I wouldn't give it up for the world.

I reach up and lace my fingers through his hair. "You aren't going to dangle spit in my face, are you?"

He laughs. "Not what I had planned."

"What do you have planned?"

He presses a kiss to my forehead. "Buying you flowers. Holding your hand. Making you laugh all night so you'll be sleepy the next day and think of me."

I tug on his hair until he falls onto the mattress next to me. His arms cage me in like he thinks I might try to escape.

Silly boy.

He peers down at me with a solemnness that takes my breath away. "My plan, really, is to love you. To be here every day. To learn what's important to you and make that matter to me too."

My lips quiver at his words. "Holden . . ."

"I want you to be proud of me," he says, smoothing his hand over the top of my head. "To call me your husband and mean it. To hear that little thing in your voice that my grandma used to have when she was talking about my grandpa."

I raise up just enough so he can see into my eyes. I want him to hear this even more than I wanted to hear his precious words.

"You are the smartest, sweetest, slightly annoying but sexiest man I know."

He grins.

"And I respect you more than I've ever respected anyone," I say.

His eyes cloud and he pulls me close to him. Over and over, he presses kisses just above my ear.

"I love you," he whispers just loud enough for me to hear.

I'm not sure if he was afraid I wouldn't say it back or afraid it's too soon.

But I don't care.

I pull back, fighting him to get a bit of space between us, and look at him.

"I love you," I say. "It's why I let you go."

"I know." He brushes a strand of hair out of my face. "Promise me you'll never do that again."

"Promise me you'll never leave."

"Oh, sugar. I'm not going anywhere."

Time stands still as a slow smile creeps across his face. I grab his cheeks in my hands and lower his mouth to mine.

As soon as our lips touch, it's game over.

Or maybe it's just the start.

Who knows? All I know is that I'm here for it.

CHAPTER THIRTY-ONE
HOLDEN

Y ou're late." Dottie sets the pen in her hand down and smiles. "Very, very late."

"Am I? Because I didn't think you were expecting me today."

She takes in my fingers that are interlocked with Sophie's. "Yeah, well, you might have gotten me there. But I can't say this doesn't make me happier than apple pie."

Sophie laughs. "Good morning, Dottie."

"Morning, sweetheart."

"Dottie, have you seen my . . ." Pap comes around the corner and stops in his tracks. His forehead wrinkles as if he can't believe what he's seeing. He takes his time assessing the situation before him—Sophie and me standing hand in hand in the middle of his clinic.

Maybe I should've called yesterday. But that would have required paying attention to anything other than my wife. And as much as I love my grandpa, I love Sophie more.

I look at her over my shoulder. Sophie grins like a loon at Pap. My heart swells every time I see her and the happiness on her face.

How on earth did a girl like her fall in love with a guy like me? I couldn't sleep at all last night, worried that I'd wake up and something would've changed. That maybe she'd had enough time on her own to think about it again and her conclusion was different.

Not that me staying awake made a difference. But it sure didn't hurt.

Besides, it let me revel in the life I've lucked into.

"Well, well, well," Pap says, placing the folder in his hands on the counter. "Look what we have here. What's this all about?"

"Turns out that your grandson is, indeed, a little slow to start. But I guess I'm pretty hard to live without." She looks up at me and laughs. "That's what you said, isn't it?"

"Something like that."

Dottie and Pap laugh. The sound fills the room.

This is what I never could've gotten in Florida. It's the one element of life that's hard to pinpoint, almost impossible to describe. It's knowing inherently, on some cellular level, that you're connected to people and a place—that your roots are somehow intertwined with theirs.

My roots are here, in Honey Creek. It's where I matter. It's where I can make a difference and not just as a vet, but as a human being.

It's where I can dance with my wife under the string lights in my backyard because life isn't stressful from morning until night. It's where I want my kids to grow up and play with their cousins. I want to take them to the Lemon Aid and get milkshakes after school. I want to stretch a sheet in the backyard and project a movie like they used to do at the Honey Creek playground in the summertime.

I want to grow here too. Learn to be a better veterinarian, friend, husband, and man.

I called Montgomery this morning and told him I was truly honored by the faith he'd put in me. I also told him I wasn't quite ready, or deserving, of the position and that he should choose someone else. He didn't quite understand but told me I could always call him back. He'd be willing to reconsider me in the future.

Maybe I'll do that.

And maybe I won't.

I glance up at Pap. His chest is all puffed out as he nearly bursts with pride at seeing me in his lobby.

"So," I say, feeling him out even though I know the answer. "You think you have a job opening around here?"

He grins. "I don't know. What do you think, Dottie?"

Dottie pretends to consider my request. Her head cocks to the side as she wraps her hands around her coffee mug. "Maybe, but I have some parameters."

"Shoot them my way," I say.

She smiles. "You have to be on time. Every day. And I'm not calling you 'handsome.'" She looks at my grandfather. "Did you know he wanted me to call him 'handsome' on his first day?"

"I did not," I tell her. "*You* called me 'handsome.'"

"Well, you are pretty handsome," Sophie says, resting her head on my arm.

Pap shakes his head as he sets down a piece of paper. "Well, if there aren't any objections from the boss, Dottie, then I guess you start Monday. Be here when Dottie tells you to. Leave when she tells you to. And don't expect me in for two weeks."

"Wait. What?" I ask, suddenly confused.

Pap just laughs. "Hell, if you're gonna be around, I'm heading back to Florida. The boat is fixed, and the captain assured me there will be beer on board. There are fish out there calling my name."

We laugh, our conversation changing to Grady's dog and pies. And it hits me how strange this all seemed not that long ago, but how it now feels like it's just the way it should be.

I squeeze Sophie's hand again. She has to wonder why I keep doing it, but I like the confirmation that she's there.

I grab a seat on one of the chairs in the lobby and pull my wife onto my lap. We listen to Pap and Dottie tell us a story about a man who brought in a pregnant goat yesterday. Apparently, it had a thing for crayons.

Sophie leans back and rests her head on my shoulder. I keep her as close to me as I can.

We sway back and forth as we listen to my grandfather. My mind ventures off into a time and place that feels like forever ago—the night I told her she'd have to act like she loves me.

Little did I know that would start a fire that neither of us would be able to stop. That it would spark a love story that we'll pass down to our children and grandchildren.

She reaches back and touches my thigh.

And if she doesn't quit, we'll get started on that sooner than later.

EPILOGUE

SOPHIE

One week later

"Talk me down."

Liv storms into the kitchen and plops herself into a chair. Her hair is unruly, her cheeks red, and it's all I can do not to laugh.

But I don't. Because when Liv is this fired up, someone is in trouble. Usually her.

"What happened?" I ask, brushing against Holden as I walk by the stove. He reaches for me, but I leap aside just in time. I was a half of a second from getting caught in his arms. That's a place I find myself often these days. But I'm not complaining.

We've melded easily into each other's lives over the past week. He makes breakfast, and I make dinner. We do our own laundry. Evenings are spent watching a movie or reading out loud from romance novels or taking walks around town. He even has taken an interest in the Honey House and has been helping me pick out the new gazebo design.

I don't know what the future holds for us. That conversation hasn't really come up. I just take it day by day and hope it continues like it's going.

Because this life with him is the life I've always dreamed of.

"I think I hate my new boss already," Liv whines.

Holden looks over his shoulder. "I thought he starts next Monday."

"He does. But I got my first email from him today, and he's a dick."

"Why?" I ask.

She sighs dramatically. "He's so . . . bossy."

Holden snorts. "Well, he *is* your boss."

"Like that matters." Liv shimmies up in her seat. "He could be a little nicer and realize that I'm the one that's kept that office running for the last six years. He's going to come here and screw up all my systems. I know it."

I walk past Holden at the stove. He reaches out and pulls me into him. His hands lock around my middle, and his chin rests on top of my head.

He does this a lot. If we're in the same room, he's touching me in some way every few minutes. It's almost a game at this point: How long can Holden go and not brush against me or reach for me? Thankfully, not long.

"You two were cute at the beginning," Liv says, her nose wrinkled. "But it's annoying now."

I can't help but laugh. "It's just annoying because you're in a bad mood."

She considers this.

"Maybe your new boss man will be great. You can't always read tone in emails, you know," Holden points out.

Liv shrugs. "Maybe."

"Now that that's settled, I have a favor to ask of you, Liv," Holden says as he lets me go.

I turn around to face him. His eyes twinkle as the corners of his lips turn toward the ceiling.

Backing away, I return his grin. "What are you doing?" I ask.

He winks before looking up at my sister. "Can you help me with something?"

"Sure. I guess. Unless it's the freaking chimney. I'm never doing the chimney again."

Holden laughs. "No. I need a wedding planner."

My heart skips a beat as I look at him. "Holden? What are you doing?"

He doesn't look at me. He stays focused on my sister. "Do you think you can find me someone, Liv?"

Liv springs from her seat. Her mood is totally changed. Her hands plant on the counter, and she looks at my husband with wide eyes.

"Why?" she asks. Excitement drips from her voice. "What are you thinking?"

"Well, I'm thinking that I need to remarry my wife."

I turn to mush as I look at his sweet, handsome face. He turns his head toward me, and the twinkle from before has softened. It's now filled with a tenderness that brings tears to my eyes.

"I want to do it the right way," he says. "I want you to have the wedding of your dreams."

Liv squeals from the other side of the room.

I blink back tears and launch myself at Holden. He wraps his arms around me and holds me tight against him.

"Let me plan it," Liv begs. "Please? I'll stay within budget and I'll do whatever you want, but she's been married twice and I've not even gotten to go to one of them and—"

"Liv," I say, moving my face from against Holden's chest. "Stop."

"So, can I?"

Holden pulls away just enough to look me in the eye. His irises are my favorite shade of green—bright and slightly wide and full of love.

"You don't have to do that," I tell him. "We're already married."

"But I want to be married in front of the whole town. In front of Pap and Liv and Jobe. I want you to wear a white dress, and—"

"And I'm maid of honor," Liv says.

I laugh as my entire body fills with a warmth that I've never known before. Like the sun is shining inside me somehow.

"I'm taking your silence as a yes," Liv says. "I'll get started planning right away."

"Wait," I say, turning around in Holden's arms. "We don't have a date or anything. This was just sprung on me."

Liv's face scrunches as she takes her phone from her pocket. "Ugh. I hate this man already." She slides it back into her pocket. "Okay. I'm going to go deal with Mr. Boss Man's email. You two be at my house in an hour. I'll order pizza, and we're going to plan a wedding. Eek!"

Holden and I laugh as Liv nearly skips out the door. As soon as it closes behind her, he twirls me in his arms to face him again.

He studies me closely. "Will this make you happy, Mrs. McKenzie?"

"You make me happy."

He touches the side of my face. "But I want to give you everything— every memory. Every experience. Every expectation. And I really want to start that by promising it to you in front of everyone you know."

Tears pool in my eyes. I try to blink them back, but a lone, solitary drop streams down my cheek. Holden catches it with the pad of his thumb.

"You know something?"

"What's that, sugar?"

"I always thought I wanted all these different things in life. But there's only one thing I've ever *really* wanted." I lace my fingers at the back of his neck and tip his head down toward mine. "I've just wanted someone to look at me like you look at me."

"How is that?"

I grin. "Like you love me."

"I most certainly do."

ACKNOWLEDGMENTS

First and foremost, I'd like to give thanks to my Creator for blessing me beyond measure.

My husband, Saul, is the inspiration behind so many of my heroes. He's much of what's good in Holden's character in *Like You Love Me*. Like Holden and Sophie, our personal love story is built on a foundation of friendship and respect, and I'm reminded again and again of its importance in a relationship. Love runs stronger when rooted so deeply.

Our love created four little boys, who have taken our hearts and lives places I never dreamed possible. Alexander, Aristotle, Achilles, and Ajax are the reason I get up in the morning and why I work so hard. Thank you for being so patient with my deadlines, boys. I love you.

I'm blessed to have the support of my mother, Mandy, and my mother- and father-in-law, Peggy and Rob. Their love and cheerleading pick me up when I need it most.

Thank you to my team at Montlake Publishing. I'm overwhelmed and beyond grateful for the support you give me and my books. Alison Dasho deserves a gold medal for her patience. You are the best. Also, Lindsey Faber's help in polishing this story was instrumental. It is an honor to work with you again. I would also like to give a warm thank-you to Karen for her help in polishing this manuscript.

Tiffany Remy and Kim Cermak are my right and left hands. You both are more to me than I can sum up in words. Thank you for going the extra mile. I see it and appreciate it. I appreciate you.

Kari March, Carleen Riffle, Jen Costa, Susan Rayner, Dana Sulonen, Kaitie Reister, Ebbie Moresco, and Stephanie Gibson are some of the best people I know. Thank you all for adding to my life in your unique, special ways.

Thanks to Marion Archer for always knowing what to say, and to Becca Mysoor for answering all my calls.

I can't remember the day I met Mandi Beck. Little did I know that day that my life would never be the same. She's the most support-ive, selfless, remember-the-details person I know, and my life would be incomplete without her. Every woman needs a best friend like her.

Also, I would like to thank S.L. Scott for her friendship and unwav-ering support. There are days I wouldn't make it without our chats. You are never without an idea and always willing to bounce them back and forth. I'm blessed to have you in my life.

Katie Harris took my call about veterinary medicine. Thank you for answering my questions with so much patience and kindness. You are a true professional.

I am nothing without the bloggers and readers who choose to read my books out of the millions of choices out there. Thank you for sup-porting me and my storytelling. I appreciate it more than you'll ever know.

ABOUT THE AUTHOR

Adriana Locke is a *USA Today* bestselling author who lives and breathes books. After years of slightly obsessive relationships with the flawed bad boys created by other authors, Adriana created her own with such series as Dogwood Lane, The Gibson Boys, and The Landry Family.

She resides in the Midwest with her husband, sons, two dogs, two cats, and a bird. She spends a large amount of time playing with her kids, drinking coffee, and cooking. You can find her outside if the weather's nice, and there's always a piece of candy in her pocket.

Besides cinnamon gummy bears, boxing, and random quotes, her next favorite thing is chatting with readers. She'd love to hear from you! Visit the author at www.adrianalocke.com.